Nora hesitated. Jessica looked exactly like her. She was about to plunge a knife into her own chest, to watch the life drain from her own body. For a moment, Nora wondered if she was killing the right person. Maybe the person in the bed was herself. Maybe she, standing with the knife in her hand, was the imposter.

It's time, the voices told her, rising to a crescendo in her head, like a hurricane-force wind. *Do it!*

In one fluid motion, Nora pressed the pillow against Jessica's open mouth—while with the other hand, she stabbed downward with the knife, at Jessica's Sweet Valley High nightshirt. As she stabbed her victim repeatedly, a faint, sweet scent danced along the edge of Nora's awareness, tantalizing her with tendrils like mist.

Suddenly, she recognized the smell. Magnolia. It was not logical. But somehow, it made sense. It had symmetry.

Nora smiled, understanding. The old Jessica Wakefield was dead. A new Jessica Wakefield was about to be born.

Magna Edition

RETURN OF
THE EVIL TWIN

Written by
Kate William

Created by
FRANCINE PASCAL

BANTAM BOOKS
NEW YORK · TORONTO · LONDON · SYDNEY · AUCKLAND

RL 6, age 12 and up

RETURN OF THE EVIL TWIN
A Bantam Book / December 1995

Sweet Valley High® is a registered trademark of Francine Pascal
Conceived by Francine Pascal
Produced by Daniel Weiss Associates, Inc.
33 West 17th Street
New York, NY 10011
Cover art by Bruce Emmett

ISBN: 0-553-57002-1

Published simultaneously in the United States and Canada

Bantam Books are published by Bantam Books, a division of Bantam
Doubleday Dell Publishing Group, Inc. Its trademark, consisting of the
words "Bantam Books" and the portrayal of a rooster, is Registered in
U.S. Patent and Trademark Office and in other countries. Marca
Registrada. Bantam Books, 1540 Broadway, New York, New York 10036.

PRINTED IN THE UNITED STATES OF AMERICA

OPM   0 9 8 7 6 5 4 3 2

155479

To Briana Ferris Adler

Prologue

Light spilled from the Palladian windows of the mansion at Fowler Crest, illuminating the wet, gray dawn. Two teenage girls stumbled along the flagstone path from the pool house. Their arms were around each other's waists; a single blanket was draped over their shoulders so that they seemed to move as one. The illusion was heightened by the girls' identical blond heads and heart-shaped faces, which glowed intermittently in the strobe lights of three police cars and an ambulance.

The storm had quieted to a drizzle. As the twins watched, uniformed attendants lifted a stretcher into the ambulance. A blood-spotted sheet covered the prostrate form. From one end dangled the fuchsia hem of a full-skirted party dress; from the other hung a few long locks of golden-blond hair. One twin shuddered and turned away, her own fuchsia dress slapping, wet, against her knees. It could have just as easily been her own body on that stretcher. It practically *was* her own body. Only her sister's arrival had saved her.

The other girl, in cobalt blue, tightened her grip on her twin's waist and murmured into her ear. "I don't know if I'll ever understand it," she said, gesturing back toward the covered body on the stretcher. "She came all the way from Ohio to California to find you—to kill you. To *be* you?"

The rain stopped. Behind Fowler Crest the sky brightened into pink to herald a new day—the first day of the New Year.

The twins paused to gaze at the whispered promise of the sunrise. Then the girl in blue led her sister off the path toward a group of people huddled on the lawn in bedraggled party clothes. A man and a woman were running around the side of the house. They could only be the girls' parents; the golden-haired woman with tears streaming down her face looked exactly like an older version of the twins.

The ambulance pulled onto the long driveway and headed toward Country Club Drive. By the time it reached the road, the group was crowding around the twins, hugging them tear-

2

fully. Nobody noticed when the ambulance halted abruptly just after it turned off the driveway, its red and white lights flashing streaky reflections in the rain-soaked pavement. And nobody noticed when it jerked into motion again and raced off down the road, speeding and swerving.

Chapter 1

Jessica Wakefield bounded into her family's sunny Spanish-tiled kitchen on Thursday morning, her long blond hair flying out behind her. She plucked a slice of orange from her twin sister's breakfast plate. "Have you and Todd decided what you're going to do for New Year's Eve?" she asked. In Jessica's opinion, Elizabeth's boyfriend, Todd Wilkins, was gorgeous but hopelessly uptight.

Elizabeth shrugged as she leafed through the morning edition of the *Sweet Valley News*. Jessica drummed her fingers while Elizabeth handed the business section to their mother, who was sitting across the butcher-block table.

"Maybe we'll just stay home," Elizabeth said finally, "and watch a movie on the VCR."

"Sit home and watch a movie? On New

Year's Eve?" Jessica shrieked. "Are you crazy?"

The twins' father turned toward them from the counter, where he was pulling a bagel from the toaster oven. "I think staying home for New Year's Eve sounds like a wonderful idea," he said. "It would be a lot easier on my nerves— and your mother's."

Mrs. Wakefield nodded tensely. "You girls had enough excitement last New Year's Eve to tide you over for the rest of the decade."

"Last year is ancient history!" Jessica declared, secretly fighting back the panic that engulfed her whenever she reflected on the horror of the previous New Year's Eve. She still shivered at the thought of that rainy evening on the grounds of Fowler Crest—and the mysterious teenage girl in a fuchsia dress just like Elizabeth's.

Jessica saw a flicker of fear in her sister's blue-green eyes, as well. Surely, the memory of last year's New Year's Eve party still haunted Elizabeth as much as it did Jessica—more, probably. After all, it was Elizabeth who'd been targeted for murder.

The twins exchanged a sober glance. They were absolutely identical in appearance, with the same wholesome looks, golden-blond hair, and heart-shaped faces. Both twins were five foot six and had willowy athletic figures. Each had a dimple in her left cheek.

Of course, people who had known the girls for even a short time seldom mistook fun-loving, irrepressible Jessica for her more serious, studious twin. Jessica wore her hair in loose, sexy waves; practical Elizabeth pulled hers back in a ponytail or barrettes. Jessica preferred the latest fashions, while Elizabeth's taste was more classic. But the differences between the twins ran much deeper than their clothes and hairstyles. Both girls were among the most popular students in their class at Sweet Valley High, but they were popular for different reasons.

Jessica adored being surrounded by people, and in the spotlight. She loved starring in school plays, dancing at the Beach Disco to the latest bands, and leading cheers at football games—especially when her boyfriend, quarterback Ken Matthews, was on the field.

Dependable, well-organized Elizabeth preferred quieter pursuits—like writing and editing articles for the school newspaper, spending time alone with Todd or her best friend, Enid Rollins, or organizing fund-raisers for local charities.

Despite their contrasting personalities and interests, the sisters were each other's closest friends. They could often read each other's thoughts and convey messages with only a glance. Now Jessica nodded at her sister, almost imperceptibly. They silently agreed to put last year's terrifying New Year's Eve out of their minds—as much as that was possible.

Elizabeth steered the conversation back to safe ground. "So what did *you* have in mind for this year?" she asked.

"I don't know," Jessica replied. "I can't believe nobody in this whole town is throwing a party!"

Mrs. Wakefield poured Jessica a glass of cranberry juice. "Oh, I wouldn't say that nobody is throwing a party," she objected. "Cindy and Peter Santelli have invited your father and me to a bash at their house."

"Grown-up parties don't count," Jessica said. "Too dull."

"What about Lila?" her father asked. "I thought New Year's Eve parties were her specialty."

"They are," Jessica said in a grumpy voice as she eased her slender body into a chair. Her friend Lila Fowler was known for throwing the most lavish parties in town. "But Lila can't this year. Her father is having a whole bunch of business associates over that night for some black-tie thing. Boring!"

Elizabeth grinned. "You and Ken are welcome to join me and Todd. I can always make more popcorn!"

Jessica narrowed her eyes at her twin. Elizabeth was entirely too amused at the thought of party-loving Jessica spending New Year's Eve at home.

"If you want," Elizabeth promised, eyes sparkling, "we can even turn on the TV at midnight and watch them lower that electric ball in Times Square."

"Oh, do you really mean it?" Jessica asked, clapping her hands together in pretend delight. "Give me a break, Liz. I'd rather die than watch that stupid ball drop on New Year's Eve."

Elizabeth shrugged. "Well, if watching Times Square gets too dull, we can work on coming up with some ideas for that fund-raising event we're supposed to be planning for the school's service project. I convinced Todd to join the committee you and I are chairing."

"You've got to be kidding!" Jessica protested. "You want to spend New Year's Eve in a meeting with the Hospital Children's Wing Committee?"

"Isn't it a little late to be coming up with ideas for raising that money?" Mrs. Wakefield asked. "Some sort of event has to take place by mid-January if the new children's wing of Fowler Memorial is to open on time. It's way behind schedule."

Elizabeth nodded. "It really is kind of an emergency," she agreed. "When Chro—" She stopped, with a glance at her parents. Then she continued, omitting the high-school principal's

9

nickname, Chrome Dome. "When *Mr. Cooper* asked Jess and me to head up the student committee, he said we'd have to work on it at school next week, and then over the holiday break, as well."

"I don't mind holding committee meetings during break," Jessica said. "But I draw the line at spending New Year's Eve with you and Todd, thinking up ways to raise money for a hospital. That's perverse!" She grabbed the spoon from Elizabeth's cup of tea and held it like a microphone. "We interrupt this breakfast to bring you a special news bulletin," she announced into the spoon. "Two local teenagers, Elizabeth Wakefield and Todd Wilkins, just bored the rest of the world to tears. Film at eleven."

"OK, OK!" Elizabeth admitted. "I'm open for suggestions, if you have any better ideas."

"Let's have a party here!" Jessica exclaimed, jumping to her feet. "We can—"

"Don't even think about it," her father warned, cutting her off. "I'm still picking M&M's out of the sofa cushions from your last party."

Jessica sighed dramatically. "Nobody ever lets me have any fun."

"Jessica, you have more fun than any human being alive," Elizabeth said, turning back to her newspaper.

"Yes, I do, don't I?" Jessica said with a grin.

She swiped another orange slice from her sister's plate and popped it into her mouth. "Well, I can't ruin my reputation now. Come on, Liz. You're supposed to be the smart twin. Help me think up the world's most amazing idea for having an awesome New Year's Eve!"

Elizabeth poked at an advertisement in the newspaper. "This sounds like fun," she began. "A carnival's coming to the Ramsbury fairgrounds, in two weeks. How's that for an unusual New Year's Eve outing?"

"Let me get this straight," Jessica said, pointing a finger at her sister. "You want to go to a *carnival*? For New Year's Eve? Weird city!"

"Why not?" Elizabeth asked. "A carnival isn't much different from the Beach Disco, when you come to think of it. Or Times Square. There are crowds of people, loud music, bright lights, excitement—"

Jessica grunted. "And hundreds of little kids with cotton candy in their hair. Very festive."

"Actually, I had a meeting with the carnival owners this afternoon," the twins' father said. "The carnival is a family business—a Mr. and Mrs. Morgini own it. They're originally from Sweet Valley, it turns out."

Jessica raised her eyebrows. "Why were *you* meeting with them, Dad?" she asked. "Are you and Mom planning to run away from home to join the carnival? You'd look really cute dressed like one of those big cartoon characters."

"They hired my firm to help them secure some local permits," he explained. "As for New Year's Eve, I think the Morginis would be thrilled to have the business. They're worried about a lousy turnout that night. In fact, they were wondering if they should open on New Year's Eve at all."

"That's it!" Jessica screamed, jumping to her feet.

"That's what?" her father asked.

"Don't you see, Liz?" Jessica asked. "The fund-raiser! We rent the whole carnival for the night!"

Elizabeth looked up, interested. "What do you mean?"

"We sell tickets," Jessica explained, "and we get everyone from school to come! Then we split the profits—half for the Morginis, and half for the children's wing!"

Elizabeth drank a sip of tea, a thoughtful look on her face. "That's not a bad idea, Jess," she said finally. "Maybe the Morginis can convince their employees to donate their time that night, since it's for such a good cause. That would increase the profits."

"You girls might be onto something," her father agreed. "Mr. and Mrs. Morgini would probably love to help the hospital."

"This is going to be a blast!" Jessica exclaimed. "We'll have the carnival all to ourselves. The Ferris wheel, the House of Mirrors, *the Tunnel of Love* . . ." She closed her eyes, imagining Ken's sandy hair and chiseled features.

"And rides, and games, and candied apples!" Elizabeth added. "And popcorn!"

"And we can sell tickets for dancing in the big tent!"

Elizabeth nodded, grinning. "I bet every student from Sweet Valley High will come! And we can market it to the kids at Big Mesa, Palisades, and some of the other high schools in the area."

"It would be a load off their parents' minds, knowing they're somewhere safe," Mr. Wakefield pointed out. "Especially the parents whose kids were at Fowler Crest last year," he added darkly.

"I hate to be a spoilsport," the twins' mother said. "But New Year's Eve is almost three weeks from today, and this would require an enormous amount of planning. . . ."

"Planning, schmanning!" Jessica said, waving a hand. "It's not a problem! Especially for Elizabeth *Planning-Is-My-Middle-Name* Wakefield."

"Wait a minute!" Elizabeth protested. "I thought we were cochairs of this fund-raiser! You're supposed to do as much of the work as I do!"

Jessica shrugged. "I already did! I thought of the idea. Now it's your turn."

Mr. Wakefield laughed. "Well, your mother's right about one thing. You'll *both* need to get on this right away, if you're going to pull it off. I can arrange the meeting with the Morginis as soon as you'd like."

Jessica sat down, leaning backward until the back of the chair rested against the wall and the front legs dangled in the air. Her mother opened her mouth to protest, but Jessica spoke before she had the chance.

"The dream team of Wakefield and Wakefield has done it again," Jessica announced. "This is going to be the most exciting New Year's Eve ever!"

It was Thursday afternoon, a week later, and the scent of magnolia hung in the air, so heavy that Nora Chapelle could close her eyes and imagine that it looked like smoke. She could practically see creamy white billows and tendrils floating around the stuffy parlor of her stepmother Blanche's Savannah mansion. In her mind's eye the magnolia smoke trailed sticky nectar onto the lace curtains. It filled the mouths of Blanche's silk-suited relatives until they gagged and choked on it. Nora rubbed at the skin on her arms, as if the flowery scent had left a residue.

14

As she watched, a puff of magnolia smoke leaped into the air, mocking her, and bounced off the rim of the open coffin in the center of the parlor.

Nora gazed at her father's still face. "I am an orphan now," she whispered to him, stepping closer. For a moment her eyes held sorrow, but then she narrowed them. In many ways she had felt like an orphan for most of her life.

Grief and rage tore through Nora's body like a bolt of lightning. On the inside she was screaming, sobbing, and clawing at her hair and clothes. But to the other mourners gathered in the room, she knew she appeared poised and aloof. Years ago Nora had perfected the art of hiding within herself.

Why, Daddy? Why? she screamed silently.

Why had he allowed her mother—her real mother—to die when Nora was a baby in New England? A blurry, faded photograph was all Nora had left of her mother, except for a hazy memory of dark hair, a soft voice, and a warm feeling of security.

Like Blanche, Emmeline Carter Chapelle had come from Savannah, Georgia. She had been beautiful, with long raven hair like her daughter's. And like Nora's, her face in the blurred photograph looked sad.

"Your mother was sick," her father had told

Nora. *"There was nothing anyone could do to save her."*

I would have saved her, Nora thought. *You didn't try hard enough, Daddy!* she silently accused her dead father, somehow certain that he could hear. *Why didn't you try harder?*

Dan Chapelle had moved the family from New Hampshire to Georgia so that his first wife could be near her parents in the final months of her illness. Soon after her death he had married Blanche, a beautiful, spoiled debutante who hated two-year-old Nora from the start. Now Nora was sixteen, and the hatred was mutual. *Why did you have to marry her?* Nora asked her now silent father, for the hundredth time.

This time the only answer was the memory of his voice: *"I did it for you, honey. I know you'll grow to love Blanche. And her family is important in Georgia. With Blanche as your stepmother, you'll have everything you could ever want. You'll be accepted by Savannah society—by the right kind of people."*

He had spoken it proudly, as if he'd been bestowing a gift. But his smile was a facade. Even as a small child, Nora had seen an unnamed sorrow in his eyes.

A tear spilled from Nora's eye and slid down her face, disgusting her. She despised weakness. And crying was weak. She peered out from behind her veil of hair, hoping that nobody had noticed. She closed her eyes and pursed her lips. Crying was sloppy. She would not cry.

Suddenly Nora realized that she no longer felt like crying. She felt like screaming—no, *roaring*. Anything to dislodge the magnolia smell that filled her mouth and nose. She wanted to tear off her black linen suit and race around the room, upsetting chairs, spilling people's drinks, and shaking her father's coffin until he woke.

Why did you have to die? she screamed at him in silent fury. *Why did you have to leave me alone with Blanche?*

"She's so composed," came a cultured murmur that wasn't meant for Nora's ears. Two of Blanche's cousins—with the ridiculous names of Junebug and Cater Lee—were holding a whispered conversation nearby. Nora watched from behind her hair as the middle-aged sisters gestured with their drinks.

"You'd think the child hadn't loved her father at all," Cater Lee replied.

Junebug sniffed. "She always was a cold little thing, even when she was no bigger than a tadpole!"

"It's no surprise," Cater Lee drawled. She moved her finger in a circle near the side of her head and gave a knowing nod. "You know what folks say about that mama of hers, Emmeline Carter."

"It's bad enough to marry trash like the Carters," Junebug said, "not that the Chapelles ever had much to brag about, when it comes to family. I mean, nobody's going to be asking any Chapelles to join the Daughters of the Confederacy. But with insanity in that woman's family, to boot . . ."

Cater Lee sipped her bourbon. "It's like our dear mama used to say—the peach doesn't fall far from the tree. Of course, Dan Chapelle was a handsome man," she admitted. "And he doted on Blanche. But I never will understand why Blanche insisted on marrying beneath herself that way."

On the inside, Nora screamed again. Outwardly, she only gripped the edge of the coffin until the skin on her knuckles grew as white as her father's lifeless hands. As white as the magnolia smell that was choking her.

She yanked her fingers away from the edge of the coffin, as if she'd been burned. She yearned to wash her hands. But she couldn't leave her father with *them*. Not yet. Instead, she wrung her hands together as if she could peel the skin off.

For a moment Nora imagined herself lying in the rectangular box, at peace. She

18

wore a tailored suit of spotless white linen. Her shiny black hair was combed, and her face was clear and calm. Her hands lay across her chest, perfectly clean and bone white.

Chapter 2

"Ouch!" Jessica yelled above the din of the crowded hallway after school on Friday before holiday break. "I broke a fingernail on my locker door! What a rotten way to start the vacation."

Elizabeth laughed and slammed her own locker shut. To Jessica, breaking a nail was as serious as failing an exam or coming down with the flu. "I think you'll live."

"Some twin you are," Jessica said, hurling a stack of notebooks into her locker. "You're supposed to be sympathetic when tragedy strikes."

"Do you want me to kiss it and make it better?"

"If there's any kissing to do—," blond-haired Ken Matthews said, coming up behind the twins. He placed his hands on Jessica's

21

shoulders and leaned in to nuzzle the side of her neck.

"What's all this talk about kissing?" said another voice. "How does a guy get in on this deal?"

As usual, Elizabeth felt warm all over when she saw Todd grinning at her from Ken's side. He was definitely the best-looking guy at Sweet Valley High, she decided again. In fact—with his tall, lean body and dark, wavy hair—Todd was probably the best-looking guy in all of southern California. And the sweetest. Sometimes she just couldn't believe her luck. She gave him a quick kiss on the cheek.

"I heard Chrome Dome's announcement this afternoon about the New Year's Eve party at the carnival," Todd said. "Good job, Liz! I guess that means your final meeting with the carnival people was a success today."

"And not a moment too soon," Elizabeth said. "New Year's Eve is exactly two weeks away."

"I thought you already had the place locked in," Ken said, finally coming up for air. "I mean, I bought tickets for me and my family yesterday."

"The meeting today was just to firm up the details," Elizabeth explained. "We had to make some final decisions about splitting up the profits."

"I take it the Morginis were bowled over by the Wakefield offense?" Ken asked.

"Of course," Jessica said. "Nobody can resist *both* of us."

Ken grinned. "No argument here."

"It didn't take much convincing," Elizabeth admitted. "Dad was right about the Morginis. They were happy to be able to help raise money for the hospital." Her smile spread mysteriously. "And, man, are we going to raise a ton!"

"Oh?" Todd asked. "What's the big secret? Did you work out a special deal? Did you get them to give the hospital more than half the profits?"

Jessica flung out her arms. *"Half? Ha!"* she cried. "After they cover their expenses, the Morginis are donating *all* the profits from that night! Are we good, or what?"

"We?" Elizabeth asked. *"I* was the crackerjack negotiator, if I remember correctly."

"And you cracked them very well," Jessica admitted, "while *I* smiled encouragingly and won them over by sheer force of will—not to mention amazingly good looks."

"And modesty," Todd added.

"That, too," said Jessica, nodding.

"How about driving to the mall for a celebratory sundae at Casey's?" Elizabeth asked as the four began threading their way down the crowded hallway. She glanced at her watch. "We'll still have time to get home and change before Enid's caroling party tonight."

Todd checked his own watch. "All right, but I'd better make it a quick one. I promised my parents I'd run some errands for them later. Do you mind if I meet you at Secca Lake for the party, instead of going over together?"

"No problem," Elizabeth said. "In fact, Enid wants me to ride with her and help set up before everyone else arrives."

Jessica ran her fingers up and down Ken's arm. "Are you sure you can't come tonight, Ken?" she wheedled. "It just won't be the same without you to keep me warm."

"I wish I could," Ken said, squeezing her shoulder. "But you know it's my grandfather's birthday. I promised my parents I'd be there."

Jessica shook her head regretfully. "You'll have to miss hearing me sing Christmas carols."

"See?" Ken said mischievously. "Every cloud has a silver lining!"

Elizabeth laughed. Neither she nor Jessica had the best singing voice in the world. Ken jumped out of the way as Jessica swatted him on the backside.

"Come on, guys!" Elizabeth urged. "There's a hot-fudge sundae waiting at Casey's, and it has my name all over it!"

"Ken and I will go in the Jeep," Jes.
said, referring to the black Jeep Wrangler sh.
and Elizabeth shared. "We want to be alone
for a few minutes, to make up for all the time
we won't spend together tonight. You two
take Todd's car, and we'll meet you at the
mall."

"Actually, I don't have the Beemer today,"
Todd said. "I've got to get the oil changed in
my Dad's old T-bird, so I'm driving that."

Jessica rolled her eyes. "You mean that big
old green boat that's held together entirely by
rust spots? Better you than me! I sure wouldn't
want to be seen in that thing!"

"But, Jessica, that car is a classic!" Ken said,
laughing.

"A classic eyesore," Jessica said.

"You're heartless, Jessica," Todd said, his
brown eyes warm with laughter. "I can't believe
you would make fun of a prized family heir-
loom!"

"Personally, I don't care if we go by mule
train," Elizabeth said. "But if I don't have that
ice cream in front of me in half an hour, I may
fall into some kind of coma. It won't be pretty, I
promise you."

It was Friday afternoon, and the funeral
was over. Nora had watched, dry-eyed, as her
father's casket was lowered into the red clay.

Now she was at her house. Blanche's relatives were gathering at the mansion again. And the smells of so many bodies—of their perfume and their breath and their mothball-stored funeral clothes—mingled with the magnolia scent that still filled the air. Nora's stomach churned.

A hand tightened on her shoulder. "Come with me into the library, Nora," Blanche commanded.

Her stepmother's perfume reminded Nora of enormous, obscene roses—the kind as big as cabbages. And mixed with the magnolia scent that clung to everything in the room, it turned the thick white smoke that only Nora could see to a putrid pink. Blanche was five foot two, with a lush hourglass figure. Her curly blond hair and bow-shaped mouth gave her a sweet, innocuous look. But Nora knew that her stepmother was as tenacious as a crawdad and twice as mean. Nora gritted her teeth and followed her into the room that the family had always called the library—somewhat loftily, in Nora's opinion.

Blanche still oozed roses as she settled herself behind her gleaming mahogany desk. She ignored Nora for several minutes while she shuffled through some papers. It was December, but the library was stuffy. Nora felt as if the heavy velvet curtains would suffocate her.

"Sit down, Nora," Blanche commanded finally, pointing to a chair with slippery-looking upholstery. Nora perched on the seat, pushing against the floor with her feet to keep from sliding off. Briefly, she considered pulling over a more comfortable chair. But no. Blanche had orchestrated the seating arrangements to make her feel off balance. And Nora refused to give her stepmother the satisfaction of knowing that she had succeeded.

Blanche sighed heavily. "I declare, Nora, you were a disappointment to me from the start. Lord knows I tried. I gave you everything a girl could want. But you never were grateful to your betters."

Nora narrowed her eyes, but Blanche didn't notice.

"I suppose you couldn't help it," Blanche continued. "It's all that bad blood from your poor mother's side."

Nora jumped from her chair, her eyes blazing. "Leave my mother out of this!"

Blanche rose with a haughty glare. "It is exactly this kind of wretched behavior to which I am referring!" Her voice filled the room like an evil scent, making it hard for Nora to breathe. "And on the day of your dear father's funeral, too. . . . I declare, Nora, I have had enough of your ingratitude and your atrocious manners!"

"And I've had enough of you," Nora said coldly.

Blanche blanched. "That is it. I tolerated your unsociable behavior when your sainted father was alive. But I will not tolerate it one second longer!"

"Does that mean you're sending me off to another boarding school?" Nora asked, crossing her arms in front of her.

"With your shocking grades and your attitude, young lady, there isn't a decent boarding school left in the South that would have you!" Then she wrenched open a desk drawer and pulled out what looked like a signed check. She slid the slip of paper across the desktop.

"What is it?" Nora asked, suspicious.

"That is a check for $50,000, made out in your name," Blanche said. "I believe it's quite generous, under the circumstances. The money is yours, free and clear—but only if you agree to leave my house tonight and never set foot in this town again."

Nora looked at her stepmother suspiciously. "Why the money?" she asked. "Why not just throw me out?"

"Don't be a fool, Nora. There's nothing I would like better than to cut you off without a cent. But it should be obvious why I cannot."

"Enlighten me," Nora challenged, placing

her hands on her hips so that Blanche wouldn't notice their trembling.

Blanche glared. "You despise me as much as I despise you. And you have a mean streak as wide as the Savannah River. I know you would love to bring me down by telling the authorities that I've abandoned a helpless, orphaned minor—though you're about as helpless as a cottonmouth. Well, be that as it may, I don't need that kind of publicity."

Nora stared at the check that still lay on the desk. "So you're paying me off to disappear."

"I have found that money can buy just about anything," Blanche responded smugly. "Or anyone. I'm offering you the chance to make a clean break—and I'm providing the means to make that possible. And if you give me further trouble, I'll gladly have you thrown into the state institution for the insane—before you can say Emmeline Carter Chapelle!"

"Stop talking about my mother that way!" Nora screamed. "There was nothing wrong with my mother! She was beautiful and kind and . . ." Nora's voice trailed off when she noticed the mocking tilt of Blanche's perfectly made-up pink mouth.

"Your mother was as crazy as you are," Blanche said. "So was your sister!"

Nora's back prickled as she looked at her stepmother. "What are you talking about? I don't have a sister."

Blanche perched on the edge of the desk, smiling at Nora's discomfort. "Honestly, child!" she exclaimed. "You are so naive! Anybody else would have guessed the truth years ago. Your father wanted to tell you, of course. But I convinced him that you weren't mature enough to handle it."

Nora froze. "What truth?" she asked in a whisper.

Blanche laughed—a loud, evil laugh. "I suppose there's no reason to keep it from you any longer," Blanche said after a moment, shrugging. "The truth of the matter is that you once had a twin sister."

Nora sat down limply. "A twin sister?" she asked, astonished. "What do you mean? Why don't I remember her? Where is she?"

"Heavens, I haven't the slightest idea where she is," Blanche said, waving her hand dismissively. "We put the wretched child up for adoption years ago."

Nora was almost too stunned to respond. "Why?" she finally managed. "What happened?"

Blanche seemed to feed on the pain in her voice. "You and Margo were not even two years old when I married your father," she explained, her eyes brightening. "You were as much alike as two bolls of cotton—you both had that jet-black hair and those stormy gray eyes."

As if she were watching a home movie, Nora could see herself and her identical twin as toddlers, somewhere in New Hampshire. They were dressed exactly alike, and they smiled at the camera with happy gray eyes as they swung in perfect time on a perfectly symmetrical swing set—like reflections of each other. The air was faintly scented with clean, fresh pine and a touch of talcum powder.

"You both were dreadful children," Blanche continued. "You, Nora, were a moody little thing, even then. And Margo was worse."

A wave of suspense overpowered Nora, so that she could hardly breathe. She had to know everything there was to know about her twin sister. "Tell me about Margo!" she urged.

"Your sister was as mean as a nest of hornets," Blanche said, smiling coldly. "I once caught her pulling clumps of fur from my cousin Junebug's kitten. Margo said she was punishing the creature for talking back to her."

Suddenly, in a strange way, Nora felt Margo's presence—the way an amputee feels pain in a limb that is no longer there. The presence Nora felt was calm and familiar. It brought a sense of peace and order into the dark, cluttered, floral-and-decay-scented room.

Margo would never smell like cabbage roses.

"All the other children were terrified of Margo," Blanche continued, her eyes glittering. "We couldn't leave her alone with them. She would bite and kick and pull their hair, like a wild animal."

"But she would never hurt *me*!" Nora blurted out, somehow certain that Margo would have protected her.

Blanche's eyes widened. "That's right," she said, surprised. "She never harmed a single hair on your unruly little head. In fact, Margo had a fierce devotion to you—like a mother bear with a cub."

"Why did you send her away?" Nora asked again. "I can't believe that my father wanted that!"

"He most certainly didn't, at first," Blanche bragged. "But your father was a weak man— though I've always thought that phrase to be redundant."

"Why send Margo away? Why not me?"

"Actually, I wanted to put the pair of you up for adoption as soon as I married your father," Blanche told her. "You both looked so much like that crazy mother of yours. I knew that all of Savannah society would see you two little fools with your black hair and heart-shaped faces and would remember your daddy's first wife. I didn't need that cloud hanging over my marriage."

"So why didn't you get rid of us both? Why keep me around when you hated me, too?"

Blanche sighed. "Your father was much too sentimental for his own good. I was unable to persuade him to put both of you up for adoption. So we compromised. I got rid of Margo, and he got to keep *you*." She made a face.

Nora let it slide. "Who adopted her? Where did she go?"

Blanche laughed—another inhuman laugh that set Nora's nerves even more on edge. "I told your father I arranged for a private adoption through my attorney," she explained, her eyes lighting up. "I told him we'd found Margo an excellent home with a fine, upstanding family."

A sick realization clutched at Nora's heart. "You lied to him!"

"There was little point in wasting time on such a futile effort," Blanche said. "With Margo's antisocial behavior, even at that tender age—and with the history of instability in your family—well, I knew we'd never find her a respectable home."

"So what did you do?"

Blanche shrugged. "Junebug called some people she knew up north, and we arranged to have Margo placed in an institution for abandoned children. Your sister became a ward of the state of New York."

"But that's illegal!" Nora protested. "You'd need my father—"

"Believe me," Blanche said, smiling smugly. "I had the power to make that creature disappear into the system—with or without your daddy's permission."

"So you have no idea where Margo is?" Nora asked.

Blanche shrugged. "I didn't care where she went, as long as it was out of my sight."

Nora imagined Margo at sixteen, living in a small but immaculate hovel, near a railroad track somewhere. Her clothes were patched, but clean. And she bravely and cheerfully helped her poor, struggling foster parents to make ends meet. Nora would join her there, near the railroad tracks, and use the fifty thousand dollars to buy them a nicer place to live. The twins would be together at last, and Nora would be part of a real family.

"If you must know," Blanche continued, "I believe that Junebug's contact in New York kept records. He said it was in case we should ever change our minds about wanting to contact the little she-devil."

"I'm going to find my sister," Nora said in a quiet, determined voice, her eyes blazing.

Blanche laughed. "You have all of Emmeline's stability, combined with your father's misplaced devotion to people who aren't worth the red clay it would take to bury them."

"I mean it!" Nora insisted, rising to her feet again. Fury and purpose rose like a tide within her. Nothing in her life had ever made sense—until now. Now she had a goal. "I'm going to find Margo, wherever she is!" she vowed, screaming. "Don't you dare try to stop me!"

Her stepmother stared into Nora's eyes. "I don't care if you spend your entire miserable life searching for that no-count sister of yours," Blanche said in a stage whisper. "And I wouldn't dream of trying to stop you—because frankly, my dear, I don't give a damn about where you go or what you do."

"Fine!" Nora yelled, grabbing the check from the desk. "I don't give a damn about you either! Only your fifty thousand dollars!"

"If it removes your vexing presence from my life, it's the most auspicious investment I ever did make," Blanche declared. "Take the money, remove yourself from my house, and don't ever show your face in Savannah again!"

Elizabeth held her hands out toward the roaring bonfire, but she couldn't get warm. Around her, orange firelight flickered on the faces of her friends.

The flames picked out coppery highlights in Enid's curly brown hair as she passed a bag of jumbo marshmallows to Winston Egbert, who

35

grabbed three of them and began to juggle. Bruce Patman sat beside Winston, drinking a mug of hot chocolate. And Lila looked like a skiwear model in a chic aqua parka with rabbit-fur trim—in stark contrast to Dana Larson, lead singer for The Droids, who wore leggings and the oversize top to a Santa Claus costume, trimmed in white fake fur and belted in black patent leather.

In fact, almost everyone Elizabeth knew from school was on the shores of Secca Lake that night to kick off Enid's caroling party. Everyone except the two people she most wanted to see.

Enid nudged her arm. "It's after eight," Enid reminded her. "I know you want to wait for Jess and Todd, but everyone's getting antsy. We should get going pretty soon."

"Can we just wait a few more minutes?" Elizabeth asked. "Maybe Todd had a flat or something. It's not like him to be late."

Enid laughed. "No, but it's exactly like Jessica to be late. Who knows when she might show up?"

"You're right," Elizabeth admitted, forcing a smile. "She's probably standing in my closet right now, trying to decide what outfit to borrow without asking."

Enid's brow wrinkled with concern. "You really do seem spooked, Liz. Come on—

Jessica's never been on time for anything in her life. Why should tonight be any different?"

"You're right," Elizabeth said. "But I'm still worried."

"Twin's intuition?" Enid asked suddenly, her face tense.

For no rational reason, Elizabeth could sometimes sense when Jessica was in trouble, and vice versa. Enid had been best friends with Elizabeth long enough to take the Wakefield twins' gut feelings about each other seriously.

"No," Elizabeth said, slowly shaking her head. "It's not exactly that." She smiled gratefully at Enid's understanding. "I'm not getting the screaming meemies about Jessica's being in terrible danger, or anything like that. I guess I'm just plain worried—about her, and especially about Todd."

"I'm sure they both just got held up somewhere," Enid reassured her. "Besides, they know our caroling route. If they don't meet us here in time, I'm sure they'll catch up with us along the way."

Dana tapped Enid on the shoulder. "OK, mistress of ceremonies," she said, holding out a pile of sheet music. "I've organized all the songs for everyone. We'll start with 'Jingle Bells,' 'The Little Drummer Boy,' 'Grandma Got Run Over by a Reindeer,' and 'Silent Night.'"

Winston pelted Dana with a marshmallow. "It doesn't sound like a very silent night to me—what with all those jingling bells and drumming drums and hit-and-run accidents involving venison." He turned to Elizabeth. "On second thought, it is more silent than usual. We seem to be missing your less-silent half. Where's Jessica?"

"She's probably at home agonizing over what to wear," Enid speculated with a reassuring smile at Elizabeth.

"You know Jessica," Lila said, rolling her eyes. "If she can't be fashionable, she'll settle for being fashionably late."

Jessica gazed into the full-length mirror in Elizabeth's bedroom, wondering if she could send a telepathic message to her identical twin by staring at her own image. It might help, she reasoned, that she was wearing Elizabeth's new candy-striped sweater and white stirrup pants.

"Don't leave without me, Liz!" she begged, running a brush through her static-filled hair. "Darn—bad hair day!"

She stared at her reflection, exasperated. "I can't miss the caroling party," she wailed. "They'll wait at the lake for me! They just have to!"

Jessica rushed into the bathroom for some hair spray and nearly tripped over Prince

Albert, the Wakefield family's golden retriever. The dog barked a cheerful greeting as Jessica sprayed her hair into submission.

"No, you can't come along to the caroling party and sing that barking-dogs version of 'Jingle Bells,'" Jessica told Prince Albert a minute later, frantically rummaging through a drawer in her bedroom for her earrings that looked like little Christmas-tree ornaments. "This caroling party is for people only. And you're just a dog."

Prince Albert rested his chin on his furry paws and looked up at her with pleading eyes.

"Sorry, pup," Jessica said as she located the earrings and threaded them through her ears. "But you're on your own tonight. I know— Mom and Dad went to the movies, and you're lonely. But I'm late enough as it is. I don't have time to play with you!"

Jessica grabbed her purse and skipped into the hallway. She was at the bottom of the stairs before she realized she was wearing only one shoe.

"Rats!" she screamed, racing back up the steps, two at a time. "Where is that other shoe? And where are the keys to the Jeep?"

Prince Albert met her at the door of her bedroom, the missing pump grasped in his mouth.

"That's gross, Albert! You're getting dog

slobber on my shoe!" Jessica chastised him. "Or Elizabeth's shoe, anyway. But thanks." She patted his nose, grabbed the pump, and ran back downstairs to find her car keys, shoe in hand.

Todd swung his father's Thunderbird in a wide arc onto the winding mountain road that led to Secca Lake. "Why can't they put streetlights on these back roads?" he asked aloud. He couldn't remember a night so dark. Off to his left, the lights of Sweet Valley glittered like Christmas bulbs in the canyon below.

Secca Lake and the caroling party were only a few miles ahead. He glanced at his watch and swore under his breath. It was already eight thirty. Enid and Elizabeth had planned to have the carolers leave the lake by eight o'clock to go into town and start singing door to door. "Maybe they're waiting for me," he hoped out loud.

Todd stepped harder on the accelerator. Elizabeth had been looking forward to this evening for weeks; he hated to let her down.

His errands had taken longer than he'd expected. He'd brought the T-bird to the service station for an oil change, only to find that the automatic transmission needed servicing, as well. The brakes on the old car were pretty shot, too, but there wasn't time to fix them that night; he'd have to bring the car back another day. Then the dry cleaner had misplaced his mother's shirts, the pharmacy was all out of his father's medication, and the garden center had tried to sell him an orange tree instead of the lemon tree his mother had ordered.

Now Todd knew he was driving faster than he should on the dark, twisting road cut into the mountain overlooking town. But he just had to arrive at the lake before everyone left. He had promised Elizabeth.

Suddenly a shadowy shape loomed ahead of him in the road. Todd slammed his foot against the brake pedal. But the pavement was slick with oil, and the back wheels of the Thunderbird swung wildly to one side. Todd wrenched the steering wheel into the skid.

The world spun and tilted around him, a kaleidoscope of trees, lights, and gleaming black pavement. Todd pumped the brakes again, but they had given out entirely, and the car only whipped around as if it had been hurled from a giant slingshot. Dark trees and the lights of the valley below swung crazily by. Then the Thunderbird slammed through the guardrail and came to a lurching halt. Time seemed to slow, and he felt the front of the car telescoping around him. The seat moved forward, and he realized that his seat belt was useless. His body was being thrown against the windshield and he was powerless to stop the momentum.

I'm going to die, he thought calmly, as if in slow motion. For an instant Elizabeth's face hovered in front of him. He knew that he had promised her something, but he couldn't remember what.

Then everything went black.

Chapter 3

Normally, Jessica loved driving on twisty mountain roads at night. There was something exciting and almost dangerous about flying around dark corners in the Jeep while the lights of the valley twinkled beneath her and music blared from the radio. The road here was particularly narrow; only a thin guardrail separated the pavement from a sheer drop-off to the canyon below.

Most nights, racing above the steep mountainside would have made Jessica feel adventurous. Tonight she felt only impatient. The cookout had started at six thirty and was supposed to last only until eight. As usual, Jessica wasn't wearing a watch, so she didn't know exactly how late she was. But surely eight o'clock had come and gone.

"Come on, Liz and Lila," she entreated her sister and her best friend aloud. "Make them wait for me! I'm almost there!"

She rounded a bend. For an instant, she stared at a complex dance of black skid marks on the roadway, illuminated by her headlights. Then her mouth dropped open. She slammed on the brakes. Just ahead a car dangled precariously over the side of the mountain, far above the lights of Sweet Valley.

Jessica froze as memories of another accident scene, months earlier, flooded her mind. That night had been as dark as this one. She'd run toward the twisted, dented Jeep, horrified to see blood on the asphalt. Elizabeth had survived that accident; Jessica's boyfriend, Sam Woodruff, had not. Tears blurred her vision. She couldn't go through another night like that one. She just couldn't.

A stray breeze caught the sedan's bumper, and the vehicle rocked forward with a grinding noise. Jessica screamed. She held her breath as the car righted itself, and she trained her headlights on the wreck. It was a rusty old green Thunderbird, and it was slowly slipping forward, over the cliff. Jessica gasped in horror. Somebody was inside the car, slumped over the steering wheel.

"Todd!" she screamed.

Jessica jumped from the Jeep and scrambled toward the Thunderbird. She gulped when she saw and smelled gasoline leaking from the tank and spreading slowly in a phosphorescent pool.

Jessica cupped her hands to peer into the window. In the Jeep's headlights she could see Todd was unconscious, and there was blood on his face. She yanked at the door handle. But the smashed-in door was jammed shut.

"Todd!" she screamed again, pounding on the cracked window. "Todd! Wake up and open the door!"

Another gust of wind took hold of the car, and it lunged forward with a sickening rip of metal. For a moment Jessica thought she would be carried over the side of the mountain with Todd and the car. Then the forward movement stopped. Jessica stared around wildly. The passenger door was already hanging off the edge of the mountain; she'd never get him out from that side. The driver's-side window was her only hope, even though she would have to risk cutting Todd when she broke the glass.

Tears streamed down her face, cold in the wind, as she searched for something to smash the window with. A piece of metal glinted on the ground nearby. It looked like part of the car's exhaust pipe. She swung it as hard as she could and smashed the window. Then she cleared away the glass with her hands, only vaguely aware of the blood on her fingers.

The car lurched again.

"Todd, can you hear me?" Jessica called to the motionless form that lay over the steering wheel. She stuck her head and shoulders in through the broken window. The seat had been shoved forward, and there wasn't much room to maneuver between Todd and the dashboard. But Jessica managed to reach across his body, awkwardly, to unhook his seat belt. Then she grabbed her sister's boyfriend under the arms. Putting one foot against the door for leverage, she tugged with all her strength until she'd dragged him from the car. Todd's feet cleared the window, and Jessica collapsed onto the ground, with her sister's boyfriend, still unconscious, sprawled on top of her.

At the same moment the Thunderbird lurched forward with a horrible screech—and plummeted over the side of the mountain.

Suddenly an explosion boomed against the sides of the canyon. Through her tears Jessica saw a ball of orange fire that shot upward from the valley and hung suspended overhead as the echoes of the deafening blast ricocheted around her.

"Todd?" she whimpered, rolling him onto his back. Sam's face shimmered in her mind, and Jessica began to sob. "Are you alive, Todd? Please be alive!"

Elizabeth stood near the blazing bonfire while her friends' conversation swirled around her. She couldn't remember the last time she'd felt so tense. She could hardly keep her mind on what people were saying.

Lila caught her attention by pulling a set of car keys from her Chanel bag. "I don't know about the rest of you," Lila remarked, tossing back her long light brown hair, "but I'm sick and tired of waiting for Jessica and Todd to show up. It's eight thirty. Let's get this caroling show on the road."

Elizabeth looked up in dismay. "I'm sure they'll both be here soon," she said, fighting back fear. "Can't we wait just another fifteen minutes?"

"As much as I hate to admit it," Enid said with a frown, "Lila is right. We should leave now. They can meet us in town." Enid gestured toward the road that led down the mountain to Sweet Valley.

Elizabeth turned to follow her gaze and gasped. In the distance a ball of orange fire rose above the trees.

For an instant Elizabeth was paralyzed by shock and dread. Then she ran toward Lila, who was gesturing with her car keys as she told

Bruce and Pamela about her latest trip to France. As Lila swept her hand in a graceful arc, Elizabeth snatched the keys from her fingers.

"Hey!" Lila said. "What are you—"

"I'm borrowing the Triumph," Elizabeth said as she ran by her. "It's an emergency!"

"Why, you—"

"Liz!" Enid called. "Wait up!"

Elizabeth barely heard them. Her friends watched, openmouthed, as she raced to the parking area, jumped into Lila's classic lime green sports car, and gunned the engine. The fireball no longer hung in the air above the trees, but in Elizabeth's mind it still blazed in the distance, like a warning. She grabbed Lila's cellular phone and dialed 911 as she sped toward the site of the explosion.

Nora gripped the telephone receiver through a clean handkerchief, to protect her hand. You never knew what sort of germs might be lurking on a hotel-room phone—even when the place was a regal old Savannah landmark, and the room a luxurious suite.

"Look, *Junebug*," Nora said, stressing the idiotic name. "The quicker I figure out where to look for Margo, the quicker I'll be away from Savannah and out of your hair forever."

"Well, I suppose there's some comfort in

48

that," Junebug said, and Nora imagined that the smell of mothballs the woman always emanated was snaking through the phone line. "But I'm not sure how much help I can be. Fourteen years is a long time."

Nora's mind raced. Junebug had always hated her as much as Blanche had. How could she get the woman to help her? Suddenly she knew. Junebug's ego was even bigger than Blanche's. Flattery was the way to go.

"You know, Junebug," Nora began carefully, "Blanche couldn't stop raving about how much help you were to her fourteen years ago. She said she'd never have been able to pull it off without all of *your* connections."

"That is true," Junebug admitted, "if I do say so myself."

"She said you knew more people in high places than practically anyone in the family. I bet it was somebody really important who helped you place Margo."

"It certainly was," Junebug bragged. "The most useful person in this particular case was a former beau of mine—Tucker Nathaniel Bedford the Third, of the Atlanta Bedfords, you know."

"Tucker Bedford?" Nora asked, wary of the note of rambling nostalgia she sensed in Junebug's drawl.

"Tucker was a handsome young man, and

smart as a whip. University of Virginia law school, you know," Junebug confided. "And he was deeply in love with me. When Tucker moved up North, he simply begged me to accompany him. But I could never live among Yankees."

Lucky for the Yankees, Nora wanted to say. Instead she asked politely, "What does Tucker Bedford have to do with Margo?"

"Tucker has been retired for going on two years," Junebug said, with an air of *Don't interrupt me again.* "But fourteen years ago he was a judge in the family court system, state of New York. As a personal favor to me, Tucker consented to make Margo a ward of the court."

"What happened to her next?" Nora asked.

"I have no earthly idea, child," replied Junebug. "I assume the little scalawag lived in some sort of juvenile home for a while, until she could be placed with an unfortunate foster family."

"Who would I contact to find out for sure?"

Junebug sighed. "If it will remove your loathsome presence from the state of Georgia, I will personally call Tucker and make you an appointment to see him on Long Island."

"I'll leave for New York on the first plane out," Nora promised.

Elizabeth floored the gas pedal of Lila's car.

Sirens wailed from the direction of town, coming closer. She wheeled along the dark, winding road, toward their shrieks. She had no logical reason to believe that Todd or Jessica was in trouble. But every instinct in her body screamed at her to hurry.

"Please be OK!" she begged aloud. "Please be OK!"

She estimated that the place where she'd seen the explosion was less than a mile ahead. She prayed she wouldn't be too late.

The sirens screamed closer, and then stopped.

Nora hung up the phone in her hotel suite. She jumped backward as a brownish cloud of Junebug's mothball stench emerged from the tiny holes in the receiver's earpiece. As a small child, Nora had learned that other people couldn't see smells the way she could. They didn't believe her when she told them. They said she had too much imagination for her own good. So she had stopped saying anything about her special power—it was her secret.

Nora smiled in anticipation. She would be able to tell Margo. Her twin sister would never laugh at her.

Nora scampered to the bathroom and scrubbed at her hands and face until they shone red and raw. Finally the mothball stink dissipated. Then she ran to the dressing room. She stood solemnly in front of the full-length mirror, staring at her reflection. Blanche said that she and Margo had been identical as babies. Did Margo still look exactly like her?

She took a step closer to the mirror, and her reflection stepped forward, too. The girl in the mirror had a slender build, with shapely legs beneath her cotton nightgown. Her onyx hair was long and silky, and her face was heart-shaped, with a dimple that punctuated her left cheek on those rare occasions when she found a reason to smile.

As Nora watched her mirror image, her eyes blurred and then refocused. Suddenly the hairs rose on the back of her neck. The girl in the mirror was no longer herself. It was Margo, and she was as alive as Nora was. And the two girls looked absolutely identical, in every way.

Help me, Nora, Margo entreated silently, mouthing the words from inside the mirror. *I need you.*

"I'm coming, Margo!" Nora promised. "I'm coming!"

Tears streamed down Nora's face. But the girl in the mirror was smiling.

The lights of the ambulance flashed red, reflected and multiplied by the oily black surface of the road. Elizabeth's mind raced back to the previous New Year's Eve. For an instant it was as if that night had never ended. The shining pavement, the strobe lights of emergency vehicles, and the blare of police radios were exactly the same as they had been that night at Fowler Crest.

Yellow tape marked POLICE LINE roped off a section of the pavement. Elizabeth screeched the Triumph to a halt outside the police line and leaped from the car. She gasped when she saw the Jeep inside the line, close to the edge of the road. Just beyond it, a broken, twisted section of guardrail gleamed in the harsh headlights of three police cars and a hook-and-ladder truck. The air stank of smoke and oil.

"Jessica!" Elizabeth yelled, staring wildly around her for her sister. But her voice was lost in the cacophony of emergency radios and terse orders. She tried to duck under the yellow tape, but a young, dark-haired police officer grabbed her arm.

"I'm sorry, miss," the woman told her. "Nobody's allowed near the scene of the accident."

"But that's my Jeep!" Elizabeth cried frantically. "What happened? Where's my sister?"

The woman had already turned to speak to the fire chief and didn't respond.

Elizabeth blinked back tears of frustration

as she craned her neck to see around the police officer. A half-dozen police and firefighters stood between her and the Jeep, and she could hardly make out anything.

Elizabeth bit her lip, unable to control her tears as she feared the worst. Paramedics moved into view as they loaded a stretcher onto the ambulance. And a teenage boy lay on the stretcher, with blood on his face.

"Todd!" Elizabeth screamed.

A blond-haired girl climbed into the ambulance beside the stretcher, leaning over Todd as if she were whispering in his ear. For a moment Elizabeth felt a strange sense of unreality. It was as if she were kneeling beside Todd, comforting him. Then her eyes opened wide. The girl with Todd was Jessica, of course. And her clothes were covered with blood.

Elizabeth broke free of the officer's restraining arm and shot underneath the police line. She reached the ambulance just as the door slammed shut in her face.

A hand tightened on her shoulder. "I thought I told you to stay on the other side of the police line!" the dark-haired officer said with a scowl.

"That was my sister! And my boyfriend!" Elizabeth cried. "What happened? Will they be all right?"

The officer's face softened. "I don't know,"

she admitted. "They're taking them both to Fowler Memorial. I'm sure you can learn more there. Would you like—"

Before the woman had finished speaking, Elizabeth was sprinting back to Lila's sports car, which shone a lurid green in the flashing lights of the speeding ambulance.

It was cold, and Todd had no idea where he was. The noise was deafening. He wanted to tell somebody to make the noise stop, but he couldn't find the words. His head throbbed, and his eyes refused to open. He was sore all over, and his left hand wouldn't move.

"I think he's coming to," said a man's voice. "Steady, son. You're going to be just fine."

Finally Todd wrenched his eyelids open. A dark-colored form blurred and waved in front of him, like a mirage. Todd blinked his eyes and tried to pay attention, but he was having trouble making sense of words and images.

"Can you hear me, Todd?" the man asked as his face came into focus. It was a young, kind face, the color of mahogany. "He's in shock," Todd heard vaguely, "but he's going to be OK." The man was speaking to somebody else who was hovering close by, like a golden haze.

"Todd?" the man's voice asked, slightly louder. "Stay with me, son. I'm a paramedic, and you're in an ambulance heading to the hospital."

An ambulance. That explained the noise.

"What happened?" Todd croaked out. He could hardly hear his own voice over the sound of the sirens.

"You were in an accident," said the paramedic. "That old T-bird went over the edge of the cliff. You'd have gone with it, too—if it hadn't been for this young lady."

Todd turned his head, and a sharp pain shot through it. He closed his eyes. A moment later he realized, embarrassed, that he had cried out.

"Todd?" asked a girl's voice. "Todd, are you all right?"

Blond hair shimmered in front of him. Then his eyes focused again, and he was looking at the familiar, heart-shaped face of an angel. Big blue-green eyes stared down at him, full of concern. He reached out feebly, took her fingers in his right hand, and held her hand to his heart. He winced at the effort.

"Thank you," he whispered.

Jessica could barely speak as she gazed at Todd's ashen face in the back of the ambulance. Tears streamed down her cheeks; she couldn't control her quiet sobs. It had been horrible, watching Todd come so close to death. And she hated to see him in so much pain. At the same time, she'd never felt such a rush of adrenaline as when she'd sprung into action to pull him from the car. She'd never felt so alive.

I saved Todd's life, she kept repeating silently to herself, feeling flushed with pride. *I did it*. In a way, Jessica blamed herself for Sam's death. Now she had rescued a boy from a terrible crash. Of course, nothing could bring Sam back. But this almost made up for her part in that awful night. It almost eased the guilt she still carried, deep inside.

Todd still held Jessica's hand against his heart. He squeezed her fingers, weakly, and stared up at her, his beautiful brown eyes full of emotion.

Jessica tried to smile through her tears. She had never felt so close to anyone. From the look in his eyes she would have guessed that Todd felt the same—except that Jessica knew Todd would never be looking at her like that if he knew it was she. *He must think I'm Elizabeth*. She considered letting him continue to believe it, if it made him feel better to think that Elizabeth was by his side. But that didn't seem right.

"Todd, it's me, Jess," she admitted, trying to keep the emotion out of her voice.

Todd squeezed her hand again. Jessica's mouth dropped open at his next words.

"I know," he said.

＊　　＊　　＊

Todd gritted his teeth and tried not to cry out as Dr. Morales fit a cast onto his left wrist in the emergency room at Fowler Memorial that night.

"The break is a clean one," said the lanky, red-haired emergency room chief. "In a few weeks your wrist will feel fine. But you won't be slam-dunking any basketballs with that hand for a while."

Todd attempted to smile through his dizziness. "I score better with my right hand anyway," he said.

Dr. Morales rubbed his beard thoughtfully. "Actually, your wrist isn't the only thing that's going to make any kind of exercise pretty painful. You've got two broken ribs, as well. And a lot more bumps and bruises."

"What about his head injury?" Jessica asked. "How bad is it?"

"I won't be able to tell for sure until the X rays come down from radiology. But it looks like it's only a mild concussion. It could have been a lot worse."

"Is he still in shock?" Jessica asked.

Todd wondered, distractedly, why they were talking about him as if he weren't in the room. He could speak for himself. He opened his mouth to answer, but as he shook his head, a wave of pain and nausea hit him. He closed his eyes.

"No," he heard the doctor saying, his voice sounding as if it were coming from very far away. "He's not in shock any longer. The paramedics got him stabilized in the ambulance. But he's still in quite a bit of pain. I can't give him anything for it until I know more about his head injury. And he's probably feeling a little sick to his stomach, as well."

Todd nodded, and his head bobbed forward as if it weighed fifty pounds.

Dr. Morales smiled kindly. "It may be hard for you to believe it right now," he said, "but all in all, you're a very lucky young man."

Todd looked up into Jessica's concerned face and knew it was true.

"And your girlfriend here is a brave young woman," the doctor continued. "She saved your life."

Todd's eyes met Jessica's. He knew he looked as startled as she did at the words "your girlfriend." Jessica turned away. Neither of them corrected the doctor's error.

Nora tapped her foot against the leg of the desk in her hotel suite. She stared at the handkerchief-covered telephone receiver, willing the airline-reservation agent to come back on the line. Nora loathed being on hold. Finally the reservation agent's voice crackled through the phone again.

"Sorry for the delay, ma'am," the man said. "I've got you booked now on a red-eye flight into LaGuardia airport."

Nora went over the details of the trip with the agent. Then she hung up the phone and ran into the bathroom to wash her hands. You could never be too careful about germs. As she scrubbed her soapy hands in the marble sink, her eyes fell on the small tattoo on the inside of her left elbow. Her mouth dropped open. She'd had her astrological sign tattooed on her arm a couple of years earlier—mostly because she knew it would tick Blanche off. Now she realized that the tattoo meant a lot more. Gemini. The sign of the twins.

Nora stared into the bathroom mirror as the realization washed over her. Once again her eyes blurred and refocused, and Margo stared back at her from the mirror.

"Subconsciously, I think I always knew I was a twin," Nora told her sister. "We were soul mates. We were supposed to be together, but they separated us!" she complained as tears started to slide down her cheeks. "How could they do that to us?" she sobbed. "What gave them the right?"

Margo wasn't crying. Her face in the mirror was sympathetic, but determined. In her head Nora heard her twin sister's voice. *We'll be together soon,* Margo told her silently. *Then we'll get our revenge. Somebody will pay for what they did to us.*

Chapter 4

Elizabeth pushed open the door of the hospital room at ten fifteen Friday night. Todd's eyes were closed, and his face was nearly as pale as the snowy bedsheets. A bandage as big as a wallet covered his temple and one side of his forehead, and a small purplish bruise on his chin was dark against the pallor of his face. There were lines of dried blood on his upper left arm, from a series of minor scratches. And the forearm and wrist were in a cast.

"Oh, Todd," she whimpered, tears streaming down her face.

His eyes opened slowly, and she smiled through her tears. His eyes were full of pain, but they were still the same gorgeous shade of deep brown as ever. It seemed to take a second for him to focus on her. Then he smiled in recognition.

"Jessica," he whispered.

Elizabeth's eyes opened wide. Then she took his good hand in hers. Of course he would think it was Jessica. He was still in a daze and was probably on painkillers. And Jessica had ridden in the ambulance with him. "No," she replied, squeezing his hand. "It's Elizabeth."

Todd smiled again and tightened his hand on hers with a limp pressure that she knew was supposed to reassure her. "I'm glad you're here," he said, his voice as weak as his grip. "I guess I screwed up the caroling party."

"Don't worry about that now," Elizabeth admonished. "I've been trying to get in here to see you for twenty minutes, but the nurses wouldn't let me. They said only family members are allowed."

"I guess you convinced them that you're my long-lost sister," Todd whispered.

"Actually, I sneaked past when nobody was looking," Elizabeth said with a conspiratorial grin. "Speaking of family, I tracked down your parents at your dad's office party. They're on their way here. I told them the nurses said you were going to be OK." She frowned. "But you don't look like you're feeling OK. Can I get you anything?"

"Thanks, sis," Todd said, smiling weakly. "And yes, I'm fine—just a little bruised and battered."

"Enid and Winston wanted me to send their love," Elizabeth told him. "They were here, but the doctor sent them home."

"He thinks I'll be out of here sometime tomorrow," Todd said, referring to Dr. Morales. "Then I can make it up to you for wrecking your evening."

Elizabeth kissed him on the cheek. "I'm looking forward to it," she said, trying not to cry.

The door swung open and Jessica appeared, holding a steaming cup of hot chocolate.

Jessica's eyebrows shot up when she saw her sister. "Hi, Liz!" she said brightly, not quite covering her surprise. "Hello again, Todd," she said, flashing him a warm smile. "It's good to see you awake. Are you feeling any better?"

Todd gazed up at Jessica with a look that Elizabeth knew well—a look he usually reserved for Elizabeth. "I'm feeling a lot better than I have a right to expect," he said softly. "Thanks to you, Jessica."

Elizabeth pressed her lips together tightly, watching her sister and her boyfriend gaze at each other across Jessica's hot chocolate. *This shouldn't make me feel funny*, she told herself. The police officer at the scene had told her that Jessica had saved Todd's life. Of course he would be grateful to her.

"Elizabeth," Todd began uncertainly, "I

need to talk to Jessica alone for a few minutes. Would you mind?"

Elizabeth felt a twisting sensation in her gut. "No, of course I wouldn't mind," she said in as normal a voice as she could manage. "I'll just go get myself some of that hot chocolate."

As she reached the door, Elizabeth looked back. Jessica perched comfortably on the edge of Todd's bed, holding his hand just as Elizabeth had held it a few minutes earlier. Jessica's head was bent low over Todd's, and they murmured to each other in muffled, familiar tones. Neither noticed the pain and confusion in Elizabeth's eyes as the door swung shut behind her.

Jessica bent her head close to Todd's to hear his weakening voice.

"Jessica, I know that you and I haven't always been the best of friends," he began haltingly. His face was looking paler by the minute.

She squeezed his good hand. "You're tiring yourself out," she protested softly. "Why don't you rest? We can talk in the morning."

"No!" he objected. "Jess, I have to say this. You have to hear it." Tears blossomed in his eyes and drifted down his face, but he made no move to release her hand to brush them away. "You saved my life tonight," he continued. "And I'll be grateful to you forever for that."

"Todd, you don't have to—"

"Yes, I do!" he insisted, raising his head as if to sit up. He winced, eyes filled with pain, and Jessica felt tears sliding down her own face as she helped ease his head back to the pillow. "The police and the paramedics said you risked your life to save me," Todd continued, almost in a whisper. "You were a real hero tonight."

"It wasn't like that," Jessica objected, trying to sound modest. "I wasn't a hero—well, not exactly. I didn't even think about what I was doing. The T-bird was hanging off the cliff, and I kind of went into automatic pilot and dragged you out of it. You would have done the same thing if it had been me stuck in the car unconscious."

Todd shook his head. "I don't know. All I know is that I owe you my life." His voice was fading, and Jessica leaned in closer to catch his words, until the ends of her hair touched his shoulder.

"Todd," she began, "you really don't have to feel that way. You don't owe me anything."

Jessica stopped, unsure of what else she wanted to say. On one hand, it felt pretty good to be a hero. She really had saved his life. The knowledge gave her a rush that was better than shopping for bathing suits or listening to people applaud for her in a darkened theater during a school play. And it was always a thrill to hear a good-looking hunk tell her he would make her happy—even if it was only her sister's boyfriend, boring-but-dependable Todd Wilkins. On the other hand, Todd didn't seem so boring tonight. In fact, she'd felt a strong bond with him ever since she'd pulled him from the wreckage—stronger than any bond she'd ever felt with anyone. Except Elizabeth.

"I owe you everything," Todd insisted.

"Well, maybe not *everything*," Jessica replied, grinning, and Todd smiled back warmly.

Jessica gazed into Todd's eyes and realized that she'd never noticed how warm and friendly they were. *Elizabeth's right*, she thought. *He does have great eyes.*

Suddenly a warning bell went off in Jessica's mind.

"Maybe all this gratitude isn't such a great idea," she murmured under her breath, thinking of her sister.

"What did you say?" Todd whispered, gazing up at her with those big, beautiful brown eyes.

Jessica felt her face growing warm. "Nothing," she said, gazing back at him. "Nothing at all."

"After tonight, Jessica," Todd said, "I'll never look at you the same way again."

"Excuse me!" called a voice, sounding startlingly loud in the quiet room. "My name is Jim Goldstein," said a plump, dark-haired man at the door. "I'm a photographer for the *Sweet Valley News*," he explained.

"What can we do for you?" Jessica asked, eyeing the camera around his neck. *Oh boy*, she thought. *I'm going to be famous!* Being a hero had its advantages.

"I heard about what happened out near Secca Lake this evening," the photographer said. "And I'd like to get a photograph of the two of you for the front page of the morning paper."

Todd smiled weakly. "I don't think I'm co-herent enough for an interview," he apologized.

"Don't worry about that. Your doctor made me promise not to bother you with any questions tonight. Besides, it's too late to fit more than a photograph in tomorrow's edition. And the police told me everything I need to know. All I need from the two of you is a smile."

Jessica beamed at him, still holding Todd's hand in hers.

"Beautiful," the photographer said. "Hold that pose—" The flashbulb flashed, and Jessica saw greenish spots for a few seconds. "Let me get just a few more," Mr. Goldstein said. "That's perfect! You know, you two kids make a very handsome couple."

Elizabeth stared at the dark streets of Sweet Valley through the window of the Jeep. It was well after midnight, Todd would sleep until morning, and the twins were on their way home to Calico Drive.

"You never told me how the Jeep got to the hospital," Jessica said as she pulled the vehicle to a stop at a streetlight. "When I left it, it was sitting on the side of the road with the head-lights trained on the spot where Todd's car . . ." Her voice trailed off.

Elizabeth closed her eyes, but she couldn't block out the memory of the huge orange fire-ball that had hung over the trees, marking the spot where the Thunderbird had burst into flames. "You saved Todd's life," she said softly, turning to Jessica. For a moment she felt an enormous sense of gratitude—and awe, al-most—toward her sister. Then the image of the explosion dissipated in her mind, to be re-placed with a picture of Jessica leaning over Todd's hospital bed while he gazed up at her fondly. Elizabeth turned back to the window.

"It wasn't really any big deal," Jessica said with practiced modesty. "It's not like I was *try-ing* to be a hero or anything. I just got to the accident before anyone else, that's all."

"It's a good thing you did," Elizabeth forced herself to say. She tried desperately to regain the feeling of relief and gratitude that had welled up in her only a few minutes ear-lier. But all she felt now was jealousy, and it

68

embarrassed her. *What kind of a girlfriend am I?* she wondered. She knew she should be thinking of Todd's recovery. But instead, all she could focus on was the memory of Todd's face, filled with adoration, as Jessica had stepped up to his bedside.

It's only natural that he'd look at her like that, she said to herself. *She just saved his life. He's grateful to her—like I should be.*

"So what about the Jeep?" Jessica asked. "You said you drove Lila's car to the hospital. Who brought the Jeep? And how did Lila get home?"

"Oh, sorry," Elizabeth said. "I guess I'm a little distracted. Enid or Bruce or somebody must have brought Lila over to pick up the Triumph. And I think one of the police officers drove the Jeep back to the hospital for you. They were all saying what a heroic thing you did."

Jessica shrugged. "I'm sure you would have done the same thing, if it had been you there instead of me."

Elizabeth bit her lip. "I wish it had been me," she said fervently. "I mean, I wish I had been there in time to help."

Jessica glanced at her. Then she laughed, a little too loudly. "Todd pledged his undying gratitude," she said. "It was really kind of cute."

Elizabeth felt as if she'd been punched in

the stomach. "He what?" she choked out.

Jessica's eyes widened with chagrin. "Oh, don't worry about it, Liz," she said in a casual voice. "I mean, it was just talk. And he was heavily sedated at the time. He probably won't remember a word of it in the morning."

Of course Todd will remember, Elizabeth wanted to tell her sister. *And you deserve all his gratitude and everyone's praise for saving his life.*

But she couldn't choke out the words. Instead, she heard Todd's weak, tired voice asking if she minded leaving him alone with Jessica. "Yes, I mind!" she whispered to the window as the Jeep turned onto Calico Drive.

Jessica wheeled the Jeep down the street, noticing that almost every house was completely dark. Even on her craziest nights of partying, she seldom arrived home so late. She glanced at her sister, who sat way over on the window side of her seat, as if trying to get as far away from Jessica as physically possible.

Jessica sighed. The silence in the Jeep was an uncomfortable one. Elizabeth seemed to resent the fact that it was she, and not Elizabeth, who had saved Todd's life. *Well, excuse me,* Jessica felt like saying. *But you weren't there, and I was. What did you expect me to do?*

The tension between the twins reminded

Jessica of another night, a night that had been invading her thoughts all evening—since her first sight of the wreckage of Todd's car. It was the night of the Jungle Prom at Sweet Valley High, more than a year earlier. Tension between the twins that night had been more than uncomfortable; it had been poisonous. Jessica and Elizabeth were vying for the title of prom queen, and both were determined to have it at any cost.

Jessica had won the crown, but she had never imagined how high the cost could be. Her boyfriend, Sam, was killed that night, with Elizabeth at the wheel of the Jeep. It was true that the collision was caused by another driver. But it was also true that Jessica had spiked her sister's drink, not ever imagining that it would lead Elizabeth to get behind the wheel of a car. Well, it had, and Sam had died. And a chain of events was set in motion that had culminated in the attempt on Elizabeth's life at Lila's New Year's Eve party, a few weeks later.

Jessica shoved aside the memories of that horrible time. This was nothing like that, she told herself. In fact, this wasn't a big deal at all. She and Elizabeth were just feeling a little weird about the bond Jessica and Todd now shared.

Jessica looked over at her sister, but Elizabeth was still staring at the darkened houses, looking angry and forlorn at the same time. Watching her twin, Jessica felt her own ire rising. Elizabeth had no right to be mad. In fact, Elizabeth should be falling all over herself to thank Jessica for risking her own life in order to save Elizabeth's boyfriend.

It wasn't Jessica's fault that Todd happened to be a gorgeous hunk with big brown eyes. And it wasn't Jessica's fault that Todd wanted to show his gratitude to her.

Jessica sighed again. Being a hero was hard work.

Elizabeth stood on the shores of Secca Lake, wondering why it was so quiet. It wasn't just the usual peacefulness of one of her favorite spots. It was an utter, eerie silence. The water was perfectly still, without the slightest ripple or current. There was no breeze to stir the leaves in the treetops. She heard no birds singing and no children playing in the distance. All she could hear was a vibration in her ears, a faint humming.

She shaded her eyes against the brightness that glinted off the lake's surface. The day was sunny, but the sky glared down at her like stainless steel, and the air was cold.

Elizabeth thought she was alone. Then she sighed with relief. A girl stood a few hundred yards away, staring at the water's sapphire surface. It was Jessica. Elizabeth's hair streamed behind her as she ran down the beach to meet her twin. They were dressed identically, in jeans and leather jackets. But Jessica's hair was tucked under a knit hat of the same blue-green color as their eyes.

The girls turned toward each other, and Elizabeth stared, suddenly frightened. Jessica's eyes were not warm and sparkling with life. They were cold and hard, and as lifeless as the ominously still water of Secca Lake.

"Jessica?" Elizabeth asked uncertainly. But this girl was not her twin sister. That icy gaze could not be Jessica's. And then suddenly the girl began gliding toward her, with her right hand behind her back. The humming in Elizabeth's ears grew louder. But the only movements to be seen were fluid movements of the girl who looked just like Jessica but was not. Elizabeth's limbs were frozen. She could only watch while the girl advanced.

The girl flashed a chilling smile. Then she raised her left hand and whipped off the knit hat. Elizabeth gasped. Her hair was long and midnight black. Her right hand lunged at Elizabeth, and the cold sunlight glittered off a long, sharp knife. Elizabeth was powerless to help herself as the gleaming blade swung toward her heart. She opened her mouth and screamed. . . .

Chapter 5

Elizabeth sat up in bed, gasping. Her pulse was racing, and tears spilled from her eyes. She groped for her bedside lamp, and its glow created a golden cocoon in the dark room.

"It was only a nightmare," she whispered fervently. "There's nothing to be afraid of." She clenched the edge of the blanket until her knuckles turned white, but she couldn't keep her hands from shaking.

The dream was a familiar one. It had begun last year, just after the night of the Jungle Prom and the accident. She'd had the same terrible nightmare again and again. Once Jessica had even dreamed the same dream. Then the nightmare had come true during the New Year's Eve party at Fowler Crest.

Elizabeth shuddered. It had been almost a

year since she'd awakened in a cold sweat, her mind filled with the image of the dark-haired girl with the butcher knife. There was no reason for her to have the dream now. Margo was dead. The sick girl from Long Island had died after falling through a window to the cold tile patio below the pool house at Fowler Crest. "Margo can't hurt me anymore," Elizabeth reminded herself aloud.

But she couldn't stop the trembling of her hands.

Nora fidgeted in the well-appointed study of Tucker Bedford's beachfront estate in the Hamptons early Saturday morning as the retired judge shuffled through file-cabinet drawers. He ran a hand through his thick, snowy hair. "I do apologize for the disarray of my personal papers," he said in a courtly voice. "I just can't seem to locate anything at all under Chapelle—although, of course, I do remember making some arrangements in the matter."

Nora slumped in her chair. At this rate she would never find her sister.

"Wait just a minute!" Judge Bedford cried suddenly, interrupting her thoughts. "I know why I have no records under Chapelle. Fourteen years ago I decided it would be prudent to call your sister by a different name."

Nora just stared, confused.

Judge Bedford shrugged. "It was a matter of expediency. The name Chapelle might have been traced back to your father and Blanche."

"So what name did you give her?" Nora asked.

He thought for a moment. "I didn't know what to call the child," he remembered. "Finally I entered your sister into the system as Margo Black, because of the color of her hair."

Without thinking, Nora touched her own ebony hair. Somehow it made her feel a little bit closer to her twin.

"If you want, I'll give you copies of all the addresses I have for your sister's various foster homes," Judge Bedford offered, "as well as the rest of my records—though some of the information is rather sketchy."

"Yes!" Nora exclaimed, too loudly. "I want everything you've got about her!"

"I suspect the address you'll be most interested in is the most recent foster home I have her listed at," he continued. "It's right here on Long Island. . . ." He looked embarrassed. "Though I have to warn you—it's not the most fashionable neighborhood."

"Margo's here on Long Island?" Nora cried, jumping to her feet again. "She's here? Now?"

"Hold your thoroughbreds, young missy," the judge cautioned. "As you remember, I retired from the bench nearly two years ago. My records end at that point. She's probably long gone from this household—"

"What household?" Nora interrupted.

He consulted the papers again. "The family's name is Logan—Fred and Norma."

Nora took a deep breath. "If Margo isn't there anymore," she reasoned, "maybe the Logans know where to find her. But what if they don't? Can you suggest anywhere else to look?"

Judge Bedford looked up from his file. "Actually, I believe I can. I have a librarian friend—a former paramour of mine." He winked. "I don't have much use for newfangled technology, myself. But Cordelia is a marvel when it comes to searching through this information superhighway thing I keep hearing about." He winked again. "She even knows how to get access to certain records that are, shall we say, not available to the general public."

Optimism swelled within Nora. Judge Bedford had helped Blanche and Junebug make a toddler "disappear" into the system illegally, so Nora wasn't surprised to hear that he had a friend who could hack her way illegally into confidential records. "Do you think she can help me?" she asked.

"I generally don't make a habit of volunteering her services," the judge said, grinning like a small boy with his hand in the cookie jar. "But I like you, young missy. It's not every day that I see a person your age who realizes the importance of family."

Judge Bedford pulled a card out of an address file. "Delia owes me a favor or two," he said. "I'll put in a call and ask her to do one of her special searches. I'll have her send the information to your hotel. In the meantime you can visit the Logan house."

Elizabeth sat on her bed Saturday morning, nearly dressed, and took a deep breath. It was nine o'clock, and she had slept only fitfully since her nightmare. She still found her pulse racing out of control every time she thought of the dream—every time she remembered Margo's cold blue eyes and glittering knife.

"I have to pull myself together!" Elizabeth admonished herself aloud.

On an impulse she selected a hot-pink sweatshirt from her dresser and yanked it on over her jeans. "There!" she exclaimed, appraising herself in her full-length mirror. "I can't help but be cheerful, dressed like this!"

She stood for a moment, eyeing her reflection. Then she gasped. Suddenly it was Margo she saw in the mirror. The pink sweatshirt transformed itself into the strapless fuchsia gown that Margo had worn to the New Year's Eve party—the same dress as the formal of

Jessica's that Elizabeth had worn that night. Of course, Margo had known Elizabeth would be wearing that gown—she had planned it that way.

Elizabeth jumped into her desk chair as quickly as she'd jumped into Lila's Triumph the night before. The need to write in her journal came on her that way at times, with an urgency she couldn't explain.

I had that dream again, she scribbled in her small, neat handwriting. *I had last year's recurring nightmare about Margo in the blue knit cap, by Secca Lake. I never understood then how my subconscious knew that Margo was stalking me—and how it knew that she looked exactly like me and Jessica.*

She stopped a moment, chewing her pen cap, and read over that paragraph. It was still hard to believe that Margo had thought she could get away with murdering Elizabeth and slipping seamlessly into her life, with nobody detecting the replacement—not even Jessica and Todd. It was even harder to believe that Margo had almost succeeded. But she'd admitted to Elizabeth that night that she'd already impersonated her many times, fooling friends and family.

Elizabeth shuddered and returned to her writing.

For the last few hours, I've been too scared

to analyze the dream. I keep remembering the horror of the struggle in the Fowler's pool house. I remember the moment when I looked into Margo's icy gaze and saw envy and loathing. And I remember the moment when I resigned myself to the fact that I was going to die, and I watched with a sick fascination as the knife slashed toward my throat. Then Jessica appeared out of nowhere—a streak of cobalt blue—and threw herself at the blade.

Elizabeth closed her eyes, as if she could shut out the images in her mind.

There's no reason to be afraid now, she wrote. *Margo is dead. This time the dream wasn't an omen. It was a memory—a memory sparked by Todd's near-death.*

So many elements were jumbled together in Elizabeth's mind. She felt as if the orange fireball above the trees was a spark that had set off an explosion of memories and emotions. With the New Year fast approaching, it was only natural that her mind would return to the events of the previous December. But Todd's accident had intensified the horror of those memories; it was a fresh reminder of the collision that had killed Sam.

That's why I had the dream again, Elizabeth realized, puzzling it out as she wrote. *Todd's accident made me think of that other accident, which is linked in my mind to the whole horrible*

Margo incident. Even seeing Todd and Jessica together last night at the hospital must have triggered thoughts of Margo in my subconscious mind—thoughts of being replaced by someone who looks just like me. Maybe that's part of the reason I freaked out about Jess and Todd last night.

As Jessica would say, I have to chill out. The dream is a manifestation of my insecurities about Jessica saving Todd. I have nothing to be afraid of—Margo can't hurt me now, and my sister had no ulterior motives for rescuing my boyfriend.

With her elbows on the desk, Elizabeth set down her pen and leaned her chin on her hands. She couldn't delude herself or her journal. She still felt weird about the dream—and about the tone in Todd's voice when he'd asked to be alone with Jessica. But she couldn't let him or Jessica see what was going on in her head. The important thing now was helping Todd recuperate.

She took another deep breath, stood up, and prepared to face the day.

Nora looked forlornly out the window as she steered the Mercedes she had rented with her fake driver's license and her real credit card. She felt more and more out of place.

"Oh, Margo!" she cried aloud as she

searched for Snyder Street, where Margo's foster family lived. "How could Blanche do this to you?"

The Long Island neighborhood was a bleak one. The houses were too close together, most of them needed paint, and their unkempt yards were littered with beer bottles. A skinny, mangy dog shivered on the edge of the street. Patches of gritty ice marked potholes, and brown-gray slush sprayed up from the tires of the Mercedes. Even the sky looked grimy.

Nora shivered. This place was worse than Georgia.

For an instant she wondered if she'd been wrong to dream of a better place than the fetid South. Maybe the whole world was a big, nasty mess. Maybe her search was futile. There was no pristine, orderly Eden, with manicured lawns and carefully composed views. There was no picture-postcard place where the air was scented only with pure, invisible aromas. There was no New Hampshire. And she would never find her twin.

"No!" she cried aloud. "I can't believe that!" After all, she had felt her twin's presence. She had seen Margo in the mirror. Surely, life would be perfect, and soon. It had to be! All Nora needed was to find her soul mate, and then she would be complete. Everything else would fall into place. With

Blanche's fifty thousand dollars the reunited twins could live happily for some time. They could even go to New Hampshire—or anywhere else that Margo wanted.

Nora's musings ended as she turned onto Snyder Street. She blinked back tears. "Poor Margo!" she cried.

The Logans' street was even worse than the rest of the town. Tattered, greasy clothes, half-frozen, slapped against each other, hanging from a line near one house. Paint was peeling from another, in curling strips like bacon. A disheveled little girl sprang from a barren yard and sprinted across the street, causing Nora to slam on the brakes. She hated small children. They were so . . . unhygienic.

A new thought made Nora's eyebrows shoot up to her forehead: *If Blanche had chosen the other twin, that dirty little girl might have been me.*

Tears sprang to Nora's eyes. She tried to imagine a childhood in such a desolate place. Then a street number on a ramshackle gray house caught her attention. "'Three hundred thirteen?'" she read aloud, alarmed. "'Lewinsky.' How did I miss the Logan house, at three-eleven?"

Nora braked the car and backed up. There was a vacant lot next to the Lewinsky house. And the house on the other side of the lot was 309. Nora parked in front of the vacant lot.

Then she saw that it wasn't exactly vacant. Patches of dirty snow hid something dark. She climbed out of the Mercedes, surprised at the blast of cold wind that chapped her face, and she walked slowly onto the property.

"There was a house here!" she whispered. "Then there was a fire."

She stared at the charred remains of a frame house. All that was left was a cement foundation and the knee-high scraps of one blackened wall. She imagined the smell of the fire—and suddenly, thick, choking, acrid gobs of black smoke were asphyxiating her. She couldn't breathe. And flames roared around her, singeing her skin with the intensity of their heat, even in the snow. She was going to choke. She was going to burn. She was going to die.

Something bumped against Jessica's legs as she trudged down the staircase of the Wakefield home on Saturday morning.

"Oh, it's you, Prince Albert," she said through a yawn. "Are you trying to trip me? It's too early in the morning for practical jokes." She paused, listening for sounds of the stereo playing in the living room, or silverware clinking against china in the kitchen. "That's funny," she said to the dog. "It sounds like nobody else is downstairs yet."

That couldn't be right, she thought. She was

always the last person out of bed in the Wakefield house on a Saturday morning. She didn't know exactly what time it was, but it had to be after nine o'clock—it might even be ten. It was pretty early for Jessica to be up, but she had been born to a family of disgustingly early-morning people, thinking specifically of her sister and parents. The twins' older brother, Steven, was the only other person in the family who knew how to take advantage of a Saturday morning, and he was away at college.

"Yoo-hoo!" Jessica called to the quiet house. "Is anybody up?"

"We'll be downstairs in a few minutes," came her mother's voice from the upstairs hallway. "It was a late night! Let the dog out, will you?—and take in the morning paper while you're at it."

The newspaper! Jim Goldstein, that photographer, had said her picture would be in this morning's paper! She was going to be famous!

Still in her bare feet, she pushed open the front door, scooted Prince Albert out, and pulled her pink bathrobe tighter around her against the chill in the air. She finally spotted the *Sweet Valley News,* stuck in the rhododendron bush by the door. She stood in the doorway, fumbling to unfold the newspaper and ignoring the ink smudges she usually hated to get on her hands. A huge photograph of herself and Todd graced the front page of the newspaper.

Jessica scrutinized her own image. There had been dried blood on her striped sweater (actually, Elizabeth's striped sweater, she reminded herself). Luckily, the stains weren't obvious in the black-and-white photo. Her hair was tousled, but she could live with that. Tousled was "in." And her smile was just right—radiant and brave, but modest.

Todd looked tired but good. In fact, she decided, he was sexier than anyone with a concussion and broken bones had a right to be. The bandage on his forehead was set at kind of a rakish angle. His bare arms had great muscle definition, even with one of them partly encased in a cast. And his eyes shone with gratitude and affection.

Then she read the headline: "Local Girl Saves Her Boyfriend's Life."

Jessica gulped. Elizabeth would have a fit.

Chapter 6

Elizabeth walked into the kitchen at nine forty-five on Saturday morning, rubbing her eyes against the bright sunlight that streamed in through the windows.

"Good morning, honey," her mother said, fitting a filter into the coffeemaker. She eyed her daughter with a frown. "Is something the matter?"

Elizabeth shook her head. "Nothing that a cup of strong coffee won't cure," she said through a yawn. "It was not the most restful night I can remember."

"I'll have some coffee made in a couple minutes," Mrs. Wakefield said. "I think Prince Albert was the only one up early enough to have had a pot brewing this morning."

Elizabeth plopped herself into the seat next

to Jessica, who, surprisingly, was engrossed in the morning newspaper. "We really should teach that dog to run the coffeemaker," Elizabeth suggested. "It's about time he earned his keep."

Mr. Wakefield came into the kitchen a moment later. "It's about time who earned his keep?" he asked with a chuckle. "Not me, I hope! I swear, a guy sleeps late on a Saturday, and . . ." His voice trailed off as he leaned over to give his wife a peck on the cheek. "I'm surprised to see you down here at this hour, Jessica," he remarked, glancing at his watch. "It's not quite morning yet in Jessica Standard Time, is it?"

"Ha ha," Jessica said, not looking up from the newspaper. She was reading with a huge grin on her face, but she held the paper turned away from her sister, so Elizabeth couldn't see what was so interesting.

"I'm surprised, too," Mrs. Wakefield echoed. "After what you did last night, Jessica, I don't think anyone would blame you if you felt like staying in bed until noon."

Jessica looked up. "All in a day's work," she said, not quite concealing her smile.

Elizabeth rolled her eyes. She was sick and tired of Jessica's false modesty. *And everyone seems to be forgetting the fact that it was* my boyfriend *who almost died.*

"Are you all right, Liz?" her father asked as he pulled a bread knife from a drawer. "You look a little tired."

"I'm fine—," Elizabeth began, stopping in midsentence as a ray of sunlight glanced off the knife in her father's hand. The shining blade brought back the memories of Margo—in her nightmare, and at the Fowler's pool house last New Year's Eve. She turned abruptly to her twin, anxious to get her mind on something else—anything else. "Jessica, can I have the front section of the paper?"

Jessica looked up, her eyes wide. "Uh, no!" she blurted out. "I mean, I'm still reading it. Do you want the funnies instead?"

Elizabeth raised her eyebrows. "*You're* reading the front page? I thought the department-store advertisements were the only part of the newspaper you were interested in."

"You know how it is," Jessica said with a shrug. "Mr. Collins said we should keep up our reading over winter break."

Mr. Wakefield smiled. "Alice, is it possible that our daughter was abducted by aliens while we slept and replaced by a Jessica look-alike?"

Elizabeth cringed at the joke, thinking of Margo's sick plot.

The rich, welcome fragrance of coffee now filled the room. Mrs. Wakefield stepped toward the table, holding the pot. As the twins' mother crossed behind Jessica, Elizabeth saw her eyes widen at the sight of something in the *Sweet Valley News*. She set the pot on the table and plucked the newspaper from her daughter's hand.

"Look who made the front page!" Mrs. Wakefield exclaimed, spreading the paper on the table.

Elizabeth felt a rush of warmth and affection. There, on the front page of the *Sweet Valley News*, was the familiar image of Todd's dark head and her blond one close together. Todd looked a little tired, but both faces were smiling and obviously happy to be together. Then Elizabeth looked again. The blond head in the newspaper photograph belonged to Jessica.

Elizabeth read the headline, and her heart landed somewhere near her toes. "Local Girl Saves Her Boyfriend's Life," it announced.

"Her boyfriend?" she whispered.

Jessica at least had the grace to blush. "It was a simple mistake, Lizzie, that's all," she said. "We never told the photographer that. He must have got it from one of the nurses or police officers."

Mrs. Wakefield laid a hand on Elizabeth's shoulder. "I wouldn't worry about it if I were you, honey," she said in an understanding voice. "It'll blow over in no time."

Her husband nodded. "It sure isn't the first time a newspaper has misidentified somebody!"

"I know," Elizabeth said, forcing her face into a smile. "It's no big deal. Everyone who knows me and Jess and Todd knows the truth." Then the phone rang, and she welcomed the opportunity to flee the breakfast table in order to answer it in the living room.

"Hi, Liz! It's me, Olivia!" came her friend's voice a moment later. Elizabeth smiled and relaxed. Like Elizabeth, Olivia wrote for Sweet Valley High's student newspaper, *The Oracle.* Olivia was an artist—and a free spirit. If anyone could distract Elizabeth from her gloomy thoughts, Olivia could.

"I just saw the morning newspaper," Olivia said. Elizabeth closed her eyes and gripped the receiver more tightly. "What a close call for Todd last night!" her friend continued. "I can't believe how brave you were."

"Well, actually, Olivia—"

"Look, I want to play this up in *The Oracle,*" Olivia pressed on. "For the first issue of the new year, I want to do a huge feature spread about how you saved Todd's life! When can I set up an interview?"

Elizabeth felt her face turning red. "Uh, there are some things you need to know about last night," she stammered. "But I can't talk now. Can I call you back in a day or two?"

"Sure," Olivia said, sounding surprised and a little hurt. "We've got plenty of time. I'll talk to you soon."

"Thanks, Olivia," Elizabeth said, trying to make her voice sound friendlier. "Bye."

After Elizabeth hung up the phone, she sank into the couch and leaned her head back against the soft cushions. She closed her eyes and took a deep breath. Obviously, this was not just going to blow over.

Nora shoved aside her room-service lunch and used the butter knife to slit open the thick envelope that had been delivered to her hotel room. Just a few hours earlier, she had been as desolate as the site of Margo's last-known foster home. Now she had trouble swallowing a mixture of euphoria and terror. She stared in disbelief at the papers from Judge Bedford's librarian friend. *Right now,* she told herself— *right here in my own two hands—I could be holding everything I need to locate my sister!*

Discipline was called for. She forced herself to take another bite of her turkey sandwich and to chew slowly and carefully, ten times. She swallowed and ran to the bathroom to scour the turkey smell from her hands. Margo did not appear in the mirror. Then Nora cleared away her tray and left it outside the door, her napkin neatly folded across the plate.

Now it was time. She was about to learn everything there was to know about Margo. But the enormity of that realization was paralyzing.

"OK, OK," Nora cautioned herself aloud. "Let's proceed in an organized fashion." She leafed through the papers. "Chronological order," she decided. "I won't read a thing except the dates until I've arranged all the papers in chronological order. I'll understand Margo better if I do it that way."

The documents included official records and newspaper articles. Some were photocopied; others had been downloaded from databases. Some even contained reproductions of photographs. And the records from the judge's file were still more detailed.

After all the documents were in chronological order, Nora separated them into neat stacks by year. Then she took a deep breath and picked up the first sheet of paper.

Elizabeth stood outside the door of Todd's hospital room Saturday afternoon. "I will be cheerful and upbeat," she promised herself. "Todd has been through a terrible ordeal. It wouldn't be right to give him anything else to worry about."

She shook her head. This wasn't going to work. Images flashed through her mind like a slide show: an orange ball of flame . . . Jessica's hand gripping Todd's bloody one as she helped him into the back of the ambulance . . . and Jessica sitting on the edge of the hospital bed. In the background, like a soundtrack that kept repeating itself, she could hear Todd's voice: "I really need to talk to Jessica—*alone.*"

Alone.

Icy fingers gripped Elizabeth's heart. New images replaced the first set: Margo's cold, vacant eyes as she whipped off the blue ski cap . . . the glitter of Margo's knife in the dim light of the Fowler's pool house . . . and Margo's body on the stretcher, covered by a sheet, with a ragged edge of fuchsia hemline dripping out from below—fuchsia that echoed the shade of Elizabeth's gown.

"I have to stop doing this to myself!" Elizabeth said out loud—too loud, she realized as a nurse turned to stare. She waited for the nurse to move on. "I have nothing to be afraid of," Elizabeth whispered to herself. "Not Margo, and not Todd's gratitude to Jessica."

She placed her hand on the door and resolved again to be cheerful—more like her bubbly twin. Then she pushed open the door and walked into the hospital room.

Nora blotted her tears with a tissue. Her sister's life was so sad. Margo had lived with ten different foster families, and the social-services reports on most of the households were horrifying. One foster mother drank too much. Hospital records reported suspicious bruises on seven-year-old Margo's arms and legs. Junior-high-school records showed high intelligence, failing grades, and a history of behavior problems. There was one arrest for shoplifting at the age of fifteen, but not enough evidence for a trial.

The last entry in the judge's file was from eighteen months ago. Obviously, the fire had taken place since then; the Snyder Street address was the only one listed for the Logans. Nora laid the judge's last few papers aside and reached for the next document, one from Cordelia's search. It was a newspaper article, fourteen months old. Nora held her breath as she began to read.

"Two Children Die in Fire; Foster Parents Called Negligent," blazed the headline. Tears blurred Nora's vision as she raced through the article about the fire that gutted the Logan house. Little Nina had died of smoke inhalation. Her body was found that night while the blaze still lit the sky, said neighbors who watched while rescue workers carried the child out on a stretcher.

Then Margo's name caught Nora's eye, and she pored over the next sentence, horrified: "A second foster child, Margo Black, 16, was apparently in the house at the time of the fire. No body has been recovered, but fire-department sources say the teenager is presumed to be dead."

"No!" Nora screamed. "It can't end like this! My sister can't be dead!" She couldn't bear to read another word. The paper fluttered to the carpet as Nora threw herself onto the bed, sobbing.

Todd pulled himself, painfully, to a sitting position in his hospital bed. He was still a little groggy from the medication. But all in all, he wasn't feeling too bad, for someone who'd nearly died only the night before. At least the throbbing in his head had finally stopped. He looked up when the door inched open. Long blond hair and half of a pretty face peered around the door.

"Todd? Are you awake?" said a cheerful, bubbly voice.

Todd grinned. "Jessica!" he exclaimed, thrilled that the person who had saved his life would take the time to come visit him. "Come on in."

The girl in the doorway hesitated, then stepped forward slowly. He couldn't quite decipher the odd look that seemed to flash across her face. Then it was replaced with a smile.

"It's not Jessica, you dope! It's me, Elizabeth!"

Todd felt his face color. He couldn't remember the last time he'd confused one twin for the other. In fact, he generally found himself forgetting that most people thought they looked exactly alike. "Sorry," he said with a sheepish grin. "You have to excuse my mental lapses. I've been sedated."

"You're forgiven—but only if you promise that you're glad to see me," Elizabeth said, her voice almost unnaturally cheerful.

"Of course I'm glad," he said, taking her hand in his unbandaged one. And he *was* glad that she'd come—though, to his surprise, a tiny little part of him was wishing that his visitor was Jessica. "There's nobody I'd rather see than you!"

"How are you feeling?" Elizabeth asked.

"Great, thanks to your sister," Todd said. "That was awesome, what she did for me last night! I never knew Jessica had it in her."

Elizabeth hesitated.

"What is it, Liz?" Todd asked, noting her pinched forehead and tired eyes. "Is something wrong?"

"Did you see the paper this morning?" Elizabeth asked.

Todd shook his head. "No, I haven't." He grinned. "The room service in this place leaves something to be desired."

Elizabeth pulled a folded newspaper from her backpack. "You made the front page," she said, blinking as if she were trying not to cry. "You and Jessica."

Todd read the headline. "Aw, Liz. You're not mad because the photographer was a little confused, are you?"

"I don't know," Elizabeth said with a shrug. "Should I be?"

"Jessica and I never told him she was my girlfriend, if that's what you mean," Todd assured her. "I was too out of it by the time he came by to tell the guy anything. In fact, I hardly remember having the photo taken."

"I know it was an honest mistake," Elizabeth said, forcing a smile. "It just feels weird, seeing my sister identified as your girlfriend, for the whole town to read."

"I guess I'd feel the same way if I saw your picture in the newspaper, holding some other guy's hand," Todd said, wrapping his good arm around her.

Elizabeth looked into his eyes. "Todd, I saw how you looked at her last night. You can't tell me honestly that you don't feel anything for Jessica now."

"Of course I feel something for Jessica," Todd said. Elizabeth gasped, and he continued quickly. "I feel gratitude," he said, brushing a lock of hair from her face. "And I feel like I owe her one, even if it's a debt I can't repay."

"Is that all?" Elizabeth asked, searching his eyes for reassurance.

Todd felt uncomfortable under her gaze. "Of course, that's all!" he said. "Liz—it's not like you to be jealous! You know I love you."

This time it was Elizabeth who blushed. "I'm sorry for doubting you," she said simply. "I guess I just felt a little insecure. I'm not used to coming so close to losing you."

They both looked up, startled, when the door swung open. A tough-looking nurse bustled into the room, wheeling a cart.

"I'm afraid you'll have to leave now, miss," the woman said. "It's time for the patient's sponge bath."

Todd wanted to die from embarrassment, but Elizabeth only giggled.

"Jealous?" he whispered as she gave him a quick kiss on the cheek.

"Insanely."

But as Todd watched her leave, he couldn't help marveling about how much she looked like Jessica.

Chapter 7

Nora sat at the desk in her Long Island hotel room, reaching again for the stack of documents about her twin sister. She had cried for two hours after reading of Margo's death in the fire—until she realized that a thick pile of newspaper clippings and other records remained from the past year.

"Fire Department Finds No Sign of Teen's Body," proclaimed a headline, dated three days after the fire. Nora's mood rose, like a phoenix from the ashes of the house on Snyder Street. If nobody had found her body, then maybe Margo was alive.

Nora frantically scanned the papers. Fred and Norma Logan were brought in for questioning in what the newspapers began calling Margo's "disappearance." Nora clenched her jaw. If those foster parents had harmed Margo, she would track them down and make them pay for it. But the police had let the Logans go. "Lack of evidence?" Nora whispered. "I'll find the evidence, and then the Logans will be sorry. . . ."

Her voice trailed off as she caught sight of the next document. It was some kind of police report, but it was from—of all places—Cleveland, Ohio. Nora's brow wrinkled. A police detective had looked into a possible link between the missing teenager in New York and the suspicious drowning of a little boy in Cleveland.

"The boy's baby-sitter, a teenage girl who called herself Michelle Snyder" (*Snyder!* thought Nora) "is the chief suspect in the murder of Georgie Smith," said the detective's report. "The girl vanished the day Georgie died. But her description exactly fits the description of Margo Black, who disappeared after a fire in her foster family's home on Long Island last fall. Interestingly, the house was on Snyder Street. A five-year-old girl was killed in the blaze."

Nora's eyes widened. The detective said the police in New York suspected Margo of setting the fire.

"No!" Nora objected aloud. "Margo wouldn't hurt a five-year-old child on purpose. If she did set the fire, she must have had a good reason. She never would have planned to hurt an innocent little girl."

Suddenly the voice of Nora's stepmother rushed to her mind: *"Children were terrified of Margo. She would bite and kick and pull their hair, like a wild animal."*

Nora shook her head. It was all part of Blanche's plot to turn her against her sister.

Besides, the detective in Cleveland had given up on trying to prove a connection between Michelle Snyder and Margo Black. There just wasn't enough evidence in either case. Nora was inclined to agree.

Another murder had taken place, said the next document. An elderly woman was killed in a train station. She had been seen talking to a girl who fit Margo's description.

But the next newspaper clipping sent Nora's pulse racing. A large, grainy photograph smiled at her from a photocopy of the front page of a paper called the *Sweet Valley News*, somewhere in California. The girl in the picture could have been Nora. She had the same heart-shaped face and wholesome-looking features. She even had a dimple in her left cheek. But the girl in the photograph had long blond hair. Of course, Nora thought, the girl in the photograph had to be her twin sister. Margo must have dyed her hair or worn a wig. "Local Girl to Stand Trial," said the headline.

"That can't be right," Nora said, mystified. The newspaper wouldn't call Margo a local girl. Nora's eyes raced over the text. The article said the girl was Elizabeth Wakefield, and that she had been indicted for involuntary manslaughter in the death of a seventeen-year-old boy named Sam Woodruff, who had died in a car accident.

"But Elizabeth Wakefield can't be Margo!" Nora cried. The accident had taken place while Margo was still in New York. The implication hit Nora like a fifth of bourbon: She had a second look-alike! Except for the blond hair, this girl in California resembled Nora exactly—and Margo, too.

Nora ran to the mirror over the bureau, still clutching the newspaper with its grainy photograph of Elizabeth Wakefield. She stared at her reflection, trying to imagine herself with honey-blond hair and a happy, carefree expression like the Wakefield girl's. She couldn't do it. And then it hit her. *Why was this story in the Margo file?*

Dig deeper, her reflection told her. Nora's eyes widened. Margo was in the mirror, looking out at her. *There's more to learn,* Margo said in a low, raspy voice.

"Tell me where you are!" Nora screamed. "Help me find you!"

Dig deeper, Margo repeated. *Do it.* Then she blurred and vanished. And Nora stood staring at her own reflection. She let her head fall forward against the forehead of the girl in the mirror and tried to imagine that it was Margo there—that she could feel Margo's cool brow against her hot one. Then she stood tall, threw back her shoulders, and walked to the desk. Margo had said to keep digging, so she would dig.

Elizabeth Wakefield was acquitted of manslaughter. It was no wonder, Nora scoffed. Elizabeth had a perfect life. A straight-A student, she lived with her parents—an attorney and an interior designer—in an upper-middle-class neighborhood. She had a handsome boyfriend named Todd Wilkins.

Elizabeth would never understand what life was like for someone like Margo—shunted from one foster home to another, unwanted and unloved. She would never even understand Nora's life. Sure, since Dan Chapelle's marriage to Blanche, Nora had always had nice clothes and plenty to eat. But she'd never felt loved, except for when she was alone with her father. She'd never felt wanted. She'd never felt complete. Despite her trial for manslaughter, Elizabeth Wakefield had never suffered. Nora's face tightened into a grim mask. She had never even met Elizabeth, but she hated the girl.

Nora read on. A catering employee had

been murdered, but police had found no motive and no suspect.

A dirt-bike rally was held to honor this Sam Woodruff who'd been killed. And a girl named Jessica Wakefield had helped to organize it. Nora's eyes widened when she saw the photograph that was supposed to be Jessica, hanging on the arm of a dirt-bike racer named James. "Her name isn't Jessica!" Nora cried aloud. "That's Elizabeth!"

Nora thumbed back and forth through the papers, trying to make sense of it. If Elizabeth wasn't Margo's new identity, then maybe this Jessica was. Then Nora's eyes fell on an article in another edition of the *Sweet Valley News,* dated from nearly a year ago. "Murder Plot Foiled," read the headline. Nora's face went white as she read the whole, sordid story.

Margo had sneaked into a New Year's Eve party at a place called Fowler Crest, dressed like Elizabeth Wakefield, with her hair dyed blond. She had tried to murder Elizabeth, with the idea of hiding the body and taking her place in the Wakefield family. But Elizabeth's identical twin, Jessica, had stopped Margo in the act. And three teenage boys appeared a moment later—Elizabeth's boyfriend, Todd, the twins' brother, Steven, and a boy named Josh Smith, who seemed to be a relative of the child who'd drowned in Cleveland. The boys fought Margo, and she fell through a window.

Tears blurred Nora's vision, but she brushed them away angrily and continued to read:

"Unconfirmed reports from eyewitnesses said the attempted-murder suspect—identified as Margo Black of Long Island, New York— appeared to have died instantly. But en route to the hospital, the ambulance she was riding in skidded on the wet road and fell from the Palisades bridge into the rain-swollen Whitewater River. Police later found the drowned bodies of both ambulance attendants, with multiple cuts and abrasions caused by broken glass. Black's body has not been recovered."

So Margo was dead, after all.

Nora couldn't breathe. Her pulse was racing, and her chest felt tight. She knocked the newspaper article to the carpet and ran to the bathroom. Then she hunched over the sink, her eyes watering, and threw up until there was nothing left inside her.

Elizabeth stepped through the sliding-glass doors that led to the Wakefields' backyard patio, admiring the way the late-afternoon sun reflected off the water in the pool. She felt much better about everything, since Todd's reassurances at the hospital a little earlier. She had been silly to feel insecure. They had been in love for a long time, and there was no reason

for her to let Jessica come between them—
especially since all Jessica had done was save
Todd's life.

"Sorry I'm late for the meeting," she apologized to the group gathered around her twin at
the poolside table.

"No problem, Liz," Enid said, looking a little embarrassed. She scooped up an apple from
a bowl that sat on the table and transferred it
awkwardly from hand to hand. "We haven't
even started talking about the New Year's Eve
carnival yet."

"I don't blame you," Elizabeth said, smiling.
"It's hard to believe it's so beautiful today, after
what happened last night." She shuddered, remembering the skid marks of Todd's car on the
pavement.

"Last night is exactly what we were talking
about!" Maria Santelli exclaimed, her dark
eyes sparkling. "Jessica was giving us all the
details."

Elizabeth felt a sinking sensation. "Was
she?" she croaked out. She noticed Enid whip-
ping a stack of papers under the table. But
their eyes met, and Elizabeth knew that Enid
had been trying to hide at least ten copies of
the *Sweet Valley News*.

"Jessica was telling us what it's like to be a
hero," Winston said, unaware of the uncomfortable glance between Enid and Elizabeth. "You

know—brave, quick thinking, and unbelievably humble, if she does say so herself."

Jessica threw him a dirty look. "Well, if you don't want to hear the rest—"

"Don't listen to him, Jessica," Amy Sutton said, tossing her long blond hair behind her shoulders. "He's just jealous because he's never saved anybody's life. We want to hear everything."

"The paper said you pulled Todd out of the window of the car," Lila said. "That must have been pretty grungy. I mean, didn't you get blood on your clothes?"

Jessica shrugged. "Well, yes, I guess I did. But I wasn't thinking about that. I was just trying to rescue Todd before the car went off the side of the mountain." She grinned. "Besides, they weren't my clothes. They were Elizabeth's."

Elizabeth rolled her eyes.

"So, Elizabeth," asked Winston, holding a banana in front of Elizabeth's face as if it were a microphone. "How does it feel to know that it was your sister—and your sweater—that saved Todd Wilkins's life?"

"I'm glad Todd's OK," Elizabeth said, pasting a smile on her face and brushing the banana aside. "I just came from the hospital, and he's recovering quickly. The doctor says he'll be home tonight."

Enid squeezed her hand. "That's good

111

news," she said, clearly having picked up on Elizabeth's discomfort.

"I bet he can't stop talking about what Jessica did!" Amy raved. "It's perfectly normal for someone in Todd's situation to want to give something back to his rescuer," she said in an authoritative voice.

"Would you mind sparing us your Project Youth psychobabble, Amy?" Lila asked. Amy occasionally volunteered to answer phones for a hot line for troubled teenagers.

Amy looked hurt. "All I meant was that it's natural that Todd would feel especially close to Jessica right now—like he wants to do whatever he can to make her happy."

Elizabeth tried to ignore Enid's sympathetic gaze. If she looked at her best friend now, she would lose it in front of everyone.

Jessica grinned. "Dr. Amy is right," she said. "That's exactly what Todd told me last night. He pledged his undying gratitude," she bragged. Elizabeth felt her face turning red. "You can't really blame him, when you think about it," Jessica continued. "After all, if it hadn't been for me—"

Elizabeth turned on her heel and fled into the house. Behind her, she heard Jessica's voice: "What's *her* problem?"

The night smelled of decay, brown and orange and thick. It was cold, and voices rode the wind. Nora was searching—desperately, frantically—while the mist swirled around her like ghosts in the dark.

A wrought-iron gate materialized out of the darkness in front of her. It opened soundlessly as she approached, as if she were being invited to enter. The door glided shut behind her with a muffled *clang*.

The voices of the wind taunted her. Their evil laughs swelled to shrieks and then subsided into hoarse whispers that were somehow even more frightening. The voices carried no words—only menace. But their meaning was clear. Nora must search. She must never give up. But her long black hair hung damp against her shoulders, and Nora shivered, wishing she knew what she was searching for.

Nora stumbled against something white and smooth and knee-high. A gravestone. Suddenly other stones sprang up around her like rows of teeth, smelling of rot and damp marble—and death. The mist that swirled around her was the smell of death. And the voices were at her back, pushing her forward through the mist.

The voices pushed her to a simple granite stone that stood alone, its surface unmarked.

Dig, a voice commanded.

Nora knelt in the moist, sick-smelling peat that stained the knees of her blue jeans as she began to dig.

Nora awoke, panting. Her shoulder was wedged against the curved wall of the airplane. Her pulse was out of control, and her mouth was dry. She wiped the tears from her face, grateful that she had no seatmate in her first-class row, on the red-eye flight to Los Angeles.

She closed her eyes and tried to remember the dream. It terrified her—but at the same time, it held a message. She was sure of it. She'd been searching in the mist, among white rocks. She sighed and shook her head. The details were gone. All that remained was the fear.

Nora looked through the window and drank in the clean, cool darkness outside the jet. She imagined herself floating through that darkness, cradled on the wind, loved and caressed and free. She wondered if Margo was in a place like that—happy and cared for by the peaceful sky, swept slowly along in its blackness.

Then a wave of dark crashed down on Nora, and she knew that she had been wrong. The blackness was inside her, filling her head and her heart like the wet, slimy algae-smell of a lake at dawn. For an instant the ambulance's lights flashed red and blue. Then the wave swallowed them. She was injured but alive. And she was drowning in the blackness. Margo had drowned in the blackness. And her body had never been recovered.

"It never should have happened," Nora whispered to the blackness outside the window. "Margo should be alive!"

She lay a hand on her pounding chest until the turmoil began to subside. She could practically feel her heart hardening as she thought of the wrongs that she and her twin had endured, while those other twins—Elizabeth and Jessica—had led perfect, sheltered, happy lives. She sensed a new power entering her body, as if Margo's strength were pouring into her, becoming part of her.

"Margo should be alive," she whispered again, a new note of grim resolve in her voice. "And the Wakefield twins should be dead."

Chapter 8

Nora stood on the sidewalk early Sunday morning, looking at a ramshackle Victorian-style frame house in the pale pink light of the rising sun. The roof was sagging, the paint was peeling, and the porch was listing to starboard like a sailboat in a hurricane. A green, mildewy stench oozed from every knothole in the wood. And a faded wooden sign hung out front, creaking on broken hinges: PALMER'S BOARDINGHOUSE.

The yard smelled of cat urine.

Nora had just arrived in Sweet Valley, rented a pure white Miata at the airport, and driven to the address she had found on one of the police reports. Her original thought had been to stay in the same boardinghouse where Margo had lived—the same room, if she could manage it. But now she knew she could not.

117

And Margo should never have had to stay in such a dive, either. Nora's heart lurched in her chest at the thought of everything her sister had endured.

Nora tried to guess which window Margo had sat behind when staring out at the world— at the perfect, sun-splashed, tree-shaded, well-manicured world of Sweet Valley, California. Margo had watched the Wakefields' world with longing from one of those dirty, cracked windows. But it was a world that Margo would always be denied.

Rage and loss gathered within Nora like thunder.

"If *you* can't be part of the Wakefields' world," she promised her sister, "then one of the Wakefield twins won't be part of it, either!"

Nora drew a deep breath as the outline of a plan crystallized in her mind—a plan that would avenge Margo's death and pay tribute to Margo's life. At the same time, it would exact a deadly payment from the Wakefields.

"I'll do it for you, Margo!" Nora resolved, her eyes glowing with passion and the sunrise. "I will belong to that world!" Then she corrected herself quickly. "No," she said with quiet force. "*It* will belong to *me*."

Elizabeth's fears dissolved in the warmth of Todd's right hand on hers. His grasp was as strong as always, and it reassured her. She looked into his eyes and smiled. "I'm glad you're feeling well enough to be out tonight," she said, pausing outside the door of the Dairi Burger. "But it's only been one day since the doctors let you out of the hospital. If you're too tired, we don't have to go in."

Todd grinned. "Are you kidding?" he asked. "I know you're worried about me. And I promise I'll let you know the moment I think I've had enough. But right now I can't wait to see the gang. Hospitals are about the most boring places on earth—even worse than Mr. Jaworski's history class!"

"I'll remind you of that the next time we have a test on the American Revolution," Elizabeth promised. She pushed the door open and held it for him, mindful of his injuries. And they stepped into the familiar noise-filled and french-fry-scented ambience of the Dairi Burger.

"Yo, Wilkins! Welcome back to the land of the living!" cried a male voice. Elizabeth spun around, horrified that anyone would make such a comment. Naturally, the source of the remark was Kirk "the Jerk" Anderson, who was sitting in a nearby booth with a group of his tennis-team cronies, including Bruce. Elizabeth opened her mouth to tell him off, but she shut it when she saw that Todd was laughing.

"Don't let it bother you, Liz," he whispered. "Everybody knows that Anderson is an idiot."

"Hey, Wilkins!" called Bruce. "Can I sign your cast?"

Elizabeth glared at Bruce. Then she steered Todd to a booth in the back, where they could have some time to themselves. As hard as she'd been trying to arrange it, Elizabeth hadn't been alone with Todd since their conversation in his hospital room early Saturday afternoon. Now she ordered two root beers and leaned back into the red vinyl bench, holding Todd's hand across the table. It was good to be with him, just the two of them, doing something as ordinary as having a soda at the Dairi Burger.

"Well, the place is packed, and Bruce and Kirk are acting like morons," she said with a sigh. "I'm glad things are back to normal."

Todd nodded. "You said it!" he agreed. "And it's almost a week before Christmas. Another normal holiday in normal Sweet Valley," he said happily.

"Yep," said Elizabeth, "and we're going to see a movie in half an hour. That's normal for us. And if you want, we can go to the mall tomorrow and do some last-minute Christmas shopping together. Shopping at Valley Mall is about as normal as you can get."

"Somehow I find it hard to believe that master planner Elizabeth Wakefield didn't finish her holiday shopping at least a month ago," Todd said with an amused grin. "Shopping at the last minute is definitely not normal, for you."

"You're right," she admitted. "I had my list taken care of by Thanksgiving. But I can help you with yours. With one arm in a cast, you might need an extra pair of hands to carry bags."

"I just might take you up on that," Todd said.

"Or, if you'd like, I could come over to your house and nurse you back to health," Elizabeth offered, running her fingers up his arm.

Todd looked down at the table. "You know, Liz," he said, "no matter what I'm doing, it keeps coming back to me: *I almost died.*" He pulled his hand away and pounded it silently on the table. "It's really a lot to deal with."

Elizabeth's heart went out to him. Along with the physical pain, Todd had a lot of emotional stuff to work through. And as much as she wanted to help him, she knew that he would have to do most of it by himself. She chastised herself for wasting so much time worrying about Todd's gratitude to Jessica. She should be acting like a loving, considerate girlfriend, she told herself. She would give Todd the space he needed to work things out. And if talking with Jessica helped—well, she would have to grin and bear it.

A waiter appeared and set their sodas on the table in front of them. After he'd left, Elizabeth opened her mouth to apologize again for being jealous about Jessica. But before she could say a word, a familiar voice rang out above the noise of the crowd and the song on the jukebox.

"Todd!" Jessica called from a large round booth across the room. "Why didn't you two say anything when you came in?"

Elizabeth waved politely, but Todd stood up.

"It's all right," Elizabeth said. "You don't have to go over. Besides, her table looks full."

"We can squeeze in," Todd said, already edging out of the booth. "Come on! It'll be fun."

Elizabeth gritted her teeth. Spending the evening with Jessica, Lila, Amy, and their dates was not what she'd had in mind when she'd suggested a night out. And normally they weren't Todd's first choice of companions, either. But he was already halfway across the room. So Elizabeth grabbed her drink and followed, a smile plastered on her face.

"Hi, Todd!" Jessica was saying when Elizabeth came up behind him. "Why don't you squeeze in here next to me, in Ken's spot? Ken, you can pull over that extra chair for yourself. With Todd's injuries, I think he'll be more comfortable in the booth."

Ken shrugged and moved the chair.

Amy moved closer to her boyfriend, Barry Rork, to make room for Elizabeth on the other side of the booth. "Thanks," Elizabeth said faintly, her hands clenched. Elizabeth glanced at her watch. She was afraid that the next twenty minutes would pass very slowly. It was Horror Movie Month at the Plaza Theatre. Luckily she and Todd already had tickets to the eight o'clock showing of *The Shining*, and it was seven twenty now. Before long, she'd have her boyfriend to herself again.

"So, Wilkins," Barry began. "I was out of town and missed all the excitement. Jessica was just telling us about the way she dashed to your rescue Friday night. But Jess has been known to, um, *embellish* the truth now and then." Jessica looked down her nose at him. "Come on, Todd," Barry continued, undaunted. "Give us the real story. Tell us what really happened up on the mountain that night."

"Speech! Speech!" cried Amy.

Elizabeth glared at her.

"I just meant that it's important to talk about traumatic experiences," Amy insisted, reverting to her familiar pop-psychology talk. "It helps to get them out in the open." She grinned. "Besides, we're dying to hear Todd's side of it!"

Elizabeth took a deep breath. Then she noticed that Ken was rolling his eyes. She smiled at him. Ken was no more anxious than she was to hear about Jessica's courage again.

"Cut it out, you two!" Ken said to Barry and Amy. "As Todd's best friend, I feel obligated to step in. The poor guy is injured, after all. Let him sit in peace and drink his root beer."

"Todd doesn't mind," Jessica spoke up, flashing Todd a dazzling smile.

"No, I don't mind at all," Todd said. "In fact, I'd be happy to tell you what happened. Besides, Jessica's version probably underplays just how heroic she was."

"Hardly," Lila groaned. She was pretending, as usual, to be above the conversation and slightly bored by it. But Elizabeth could see that Lila was as eager to hear Todd's side of the story as Jessica was.

"Of course," Todd warned, "I was unconscious for a lot of this. So I'm only telling you what I heard later from the police and the doctor. . . ."

As Todd launched into his narrative, Ken shrugged apologetically at Elizabeth. *Thanks for trying,* she mouthed. Jessica and Todd were too caught up in their story to notice.

In her mind Elizabeth pressed an imaginary remote-control button to lower the volume. She tuned out Todd's words and instead watched his face as he spoke. Todd was the same good-looking, sweet boy she'd dated for ages. His forehead was bandaged where he had hit the windshield, and a few cuts still marred his smooth, regular features. But he was still Todd, and he still loved her. And she would just have to remember that. Besides, Amy was probably right about the therapeutic benefits of talking about the experience. And only minutes earlier Elizabeth had promised herself to do whatever she could to help speed his recovery.

She glanced at her watch and saw that it was seven forty.

"Then the T-bird lurched again," Todd was saying. "This time it nearly went over the edge, taking Jessica with it, but—"

"Uh, Todd?" Elizabeth interrupted. "Our movie starts in twenty minutes. We really ought to get going."

"He can't go now!" Amy cried. "It's just getting exciting!"

Todd smiled across the table at Elizabeth. "I'll only be a couple minutes more, Liz," he promised before turning back to the others. Elizabeth bit her lip.

"But Jessica stayed right there by the car until it stopped rocking, even though she could have been killed herself," Todd said. He reached over and squeezed Jessica's hand with his good one. Elizabeth thought she would throw up.

"Jessica tried and tried to pull the door open," he said, "but it wouldn't budge. So she

125

searched around for something to smash the window with."

"Todd," Elizabeth said, pointing to her watch, "I'm sorry to interrupt again, but we have to be out of here in five, or we'll be late. You know how much you hate to miss the opening scene!"

"Yeah, Liz," Todd said absently. "Just a second."

"He could finish a lot faster if you'd stop interrupting him," Jessica pointed out. "Go on, Todd," she urged, as if she hadn't been there herself. "We can't wait to hear what happened next!"

Ken rolled his eyes again.

"Jessica found a piece of a tailpipe," Todd continued, "and she swung it at the window as hard as she could—"

Elizabeth stood up. "I'm going to the movie," she announced.

"All right," Todd said absently. He went on with his story as if she hadn't spoken.

On an impulse Elizabeth turned to Ken. "Would you like to come see *The Shining*?" she asked. She narrowed her eyes in Todd's direction. "I seem to have an extra ticket."

"It sounds like a plan to me," Ken said, rising gratefully. "I've heard this story a hundred times. At least I've only seen *The Shining* once."

❖   ❖   ❖

Nora sat on one of the frilly, ruffled bed-spreads in her room at the Sweet Valley Inn that night. The eyelet lace looked too much like something Scarlett O'Hara would have on her bed. And the scent of potpourri was driving her crazy, with pesky pink puffs circling her head like smoke rings. Quaint was not Nora's style. But at least the inn was clean.

She opened the desk drawer and pulled out a pile of books and folders. They would have to be lined up neatly before she could do anything with them. First, she carefully laid out the packet of hotel stationery, aligning it so that its edge was perfectly parallel to the edge of the desk. Next, she placed the Gideon Bible beside it, and the *Southern California Visitor's Guide* next to the Bible.

Nora winced. The visitor's guide was wrinkled and dog-eared. She picked it up, careful to touch it with only two fingers, and tossed it into the trash can. Then she laid the room-service menu in its place, after the Bible. Last came the Sweet Valley telephone book.

The telephone book!

Suddenly Nora remembered why she had opened the drawer in the first place. She'd been looking for the phone book. But why?

Nora closed her eyes. It wasn't like her to forget things. It wasn't like her at all. But ever since she'd read of Margo's death, she had been able to hold things in her mind for no more than a few minutes. The only thought that stayed with her, like a song that played endlessly in her head, was a burning desire to make the Wakefield twins pay.

The Wakefields. That was why she'd needed the phone book. Nora wanted to look up the Wakefield family address and maybe even call the phone number. She wanted to know who would answer. The twin who picked up the phone would pay for Margo's death, she decided. That made sense. It was symmetrical.

She thumbed through the phone book until she reached the *W*'s. With her finger on the twins' family name, she felt much closer to her goal. "'Wakefield,'" she read, "'Ned and Alice. Calico Drive.'" She punched in the telephone number and waited, breathless, while the phone rang at the Wakefield house once . . . twice . . . three times. The line clicked, and a man answered. "Hello," said a warm, deep voice. "Wakefield residence."

Nora smiled. It was the Wakefield twins' father.

"Hello?" he said again. "Is anyone there?"

Nora dropped the receiver into its cradle. She tried to imagine what Ned Wakefield must look like. He was tall, Nora decided. Definitely tall. And handsome, with dark hair. "Or would he be blond, like the twins?" she asked out loud. For now, it didn't matter. Soon she would know everything there was to know about the Wakefields.

She lifted the receiver again and called the front desk. "Where can I get hold of a map of Sweet Valley?" she asked the concierge. A sly smile played around the edges of her mouth. "I need to locate an address."

Jessica pounded her fist on the kitchen table Sunday night, furious. She glared at the clock on the wall. It was eleven o'clock, she fumed, and Elizabeth wasn't home yet. Elizabeth *and Ken* weren't home yet.

She ran to the front door when she heard a familiar-sounding car pull up outside. She watched through the window as Elizabeth stepped out of the car, waved good-bye to Ken, and then started up the walkway. As Ken drove away, Jessica stormed out the front door to meet her twin.

"What do you think you're doing?" she demanded.

Elizabeth shrugged, her face unreadable in the darkness. "I'm walking into the house. I'm sure you've seen people do it before."

"That's not what I mean, and you know it!" Jessica raged. "You were out on a date with my boyfriend!"

"Come off it, Jessica!" Elizabeth responded.

"It wasn't a date! Ken and I have been friends since elementary school. Todd didn't want to use his ticket to the movie, so Ken came instead."

"I can't believe my own sister would do this to me, after this weekend!" Jessica said, glad that it was too dark for Elizabeth to see the tears of fury in her eyes.

"What do you mean, this weekend?" Elizabeth asked.

"You know very well what I mean!" Jessica yelled. "I save your boyfriend's life, and this is how you repay me?"

A light went on in Annie Whitman's house, next door.

"Come inside, Jessica," Elizabeth urged. "If we've got to argue about it, let's not make it a spectator sport for the whole neighborhood."

"I'll argue about it when and where I please!" Jessica said tearfully, but she followed Elizabeth into the house.

Inside, they both blinked a moment at the bright light of the entrance foyer. "Jessica, you're acting ridiculous," Elizabeth said in an infuriatingly calm voice. "There's nothing between Ken and me anymore except friendship, and you know it."

"You stole my date and took him to the movies!" Jessica yelled. Then she remembered her parents, sleeping upstairs, and lowered her voice. "How could you—especially after what I did for you?"

"What *you* did for *me*?" Elizabeth raged, her calmness shattered. "You mean horning in on my date with Todd?"

"Me?" Jessica fumed. "Me? I can't help it if Todd wants to spend time with other people. He looked like he was enjoying himself once he came over to our table. It's not as though I twisted his arm, or anything."

Elizabeth looked as if she were either about to burst into tears or about to start throwing punches. Jessica glared right back at her, hands on her hips.

Elizabeth broke first. She wrenched her gaze away from her sister's and ran upstairs. A moment later Jessica heard her bedroom door slam.

The smell of death swirled around her again like mist as Nora stepped through the darkened graveyard. Once again the white stones shone, luminescent in the black night. No stars lit the night. No moon hung in the sky. All she could see was sky as black as her hair, mist as gray as her eyes, and shining gravestones.

Voices danced on the wind, pushing her to the one stone that stood alone. At first its surface seemed as smooth and unblemished as white linen. For a moment she thought she could see her reflection in it. Then the stone blurred before her eyes. When its surface recrystallized, two words were carved there, in simple block letters: MARGO CHAPELLE.

Tears streamed down Nora's face, but the cold wind snatched them away. Nora knelt in the dark, rot-smelling peat and began to dig for what seemed like hours.

Nora screamed when something scuttled across her arm. She jerked her hands out of the dark hole and crouched there, breathless, as the wet dirt soaked uncomfortably into her jeans.

Dig deeper, the voices ordered. Then the voices blurred together and formed one voice. Margo's voice. *Dig deeper,* Margo's voice repeated, more insistently this time. *There's more to learn.*

Nora turned back to the hole she had begun, and she dug deeper. Finally her hand struck something hard in the dirt, something smooth and flat that made a hollow sound as her fingers bumped against it. She cleared away the rotting peat from its surface. She groped her way around the hard, smooth object buried in the ground. It was the lid of a coffin. She pried up one side, and it began to open.

The lid was only slightly ajar. But the warm, sick smell of decay engulfed Nora, and she thought she would drown in it. It swirled around her—thick and brown in the black-and-gray night—making her lose her balance and pitch forward into the open grave. . . .

Nora opened her eyes, terrified in the unfamiliar blackness. She groped for a light, and the eyelet-filled room at the Sweet Valley Inn popped into sharp relief, its white lace ludicrous after the darkness and filth of her nightmare. *Eyelet lace*, she thought. *Eyelets. Little eyes.*

Suddenly hundreds of eyes seemed to be watching her, waiting to pounce, like wild animals just beyond the glow of a campfire. "It was only a dream," Nora whispered.

She'd had the nightmare once before—she now realized—on the airplane that had brought her to California. That time the dream had dissipated into the light, like mist, as soon as she awoke. This time it hung in her mind, as heavy as smoke. As heavy as death. And she knew that it would never blow away, that it would weigh her down until she finally accomplished her task and made the Wakefield girls pay for Margo's death.

Jessica stood on a mountain ledge near Secca Lake, admiring the view. The sun shone warmly, and the houses of Sweet Valley dotted distant hillsides like wildflowers. Directly below her, a deep, narrow ravine was filled with jagged white rocks punctuated with black, spindly pine trees. The day was silent—no cars rolled along the nearby road, and no airplanes roared overhead. No bird sang in the woods.

Suddenly footsteps echoed like thunder against the sides of the canyon. Jessica turned and smiled. Elizabeth was coming toward her, feet sliding and crunching on the slippery gravel. Warmth spread through Jessica's body at the sight of her sister. Elizabeth wasn't mad at her. Jessica held out her hand, grateful for her sister's company.

Elizabeth ignored the helping hand. She pulled herself up onto the ledge and stood just behind Jessica, surveying the canyon. Elizabeth looked the same as always—the same as Jessica. But there was a gleam in her eye, a coldness that Jessica didn't recognize. Then there was a hand on Jessica's back, and she was falling off the ledge, into a void. Far below, daggerlike pine trees and jagged rocks tilted and whirled as she tumbled toward them.

"Elizabeth!" she screamed as she fell. But the day turned to the blackest night, and Jessica couldn't see her sister. She was alone. And her body was catapulting through space, to be dashed against shining white rocks in the valley below.

Chapter 9

Jessica was falling into the darkness, toward the white rocks below.

She landed with a thud, and something warm and wet was all over her face. She was dying. She was dead.

Then her mind cleared. Jessica was lying on the floor beside her bed, and Prince Albert was licking her face. She pushed him away and took a deep breath. She was alive.

"It was only a dream," she whispered to herself, trying to catch her breath. "It was only a dream." She was awake now, but her heart was pounding so hard that it drowned out the sound of Prince Albert's gentle breathing, only inches away. Her body was damp with a cold sweat that stuck her nightshirt to her skin and her bangs to her forehead.

She struggled to her feet and switched on the light. Then she sat on the edge of her bed with her head in her hands, trying to control her quiet sobs.

Prince Albert nosed her elbow, and Jessica hugged him tightly, drawing comfort from his warm, familiar body.

Todd flicked a match against the side of the box and watched its flame sputter to life. It was Christmas Eve, and he stood for a moment and gazed into the small, perfect blaze before leaning over the table to light the candles. He cupped his hand around the flame's brilliance and reveled in the warmth that emanated from it. Then he stepped back from the table to admire the effect, feeling a little foolish. Until last week, he had never felt so aware of his surroundings.

Todd had never realized how much he took for granted in his life. He had always enjoyed spending time at the Wakefield house, but this evening was different. It wasn't just that it was the night before Christmas. He'd spent many holidays with Elizabeth and her family. But this one was different, because he was different. Todd looked around the room at some of his favorite people in the world, most of them engaged in last-minute tasks of putting the meal on the table. Mr. and Mrs. Wakefield had always treated him like a second son. Steven, home from college for the holiday, was a good friend. So was Ken. He actually felt a lump in his throat at the thought of how much his friends meant to him.

"Get a grip, Wilkins," he told himself under his breath. Coming close to death had made him appreciate his life more. But that didn't mean he had to get all misty-eyed about everything.

Then the twins bustled in from the kitchen, and Todd watched them with a feeling that bordered on awe. Elizabeth's eyes looked bluer than usual above her soft turquoise sweater.

Jessica leaned over the table for a serving spoon that was just out of her reach, and her hair glimmered like sunshine in the light of the candelabra. Todd picked up the spoon in his good hand and held it out to her. Their fingers touched as she took it from him. The contact lasted for only a second, but a warm glow spread through Todd's body. Their eyes met, and Jessica smiled. *She's beautiful,* he thought, surprised that he'd never fully appreciated her before. Then she looked away, and Todd used his good hand to pull out a chair for Elizabeth.

"I'd like to propose a toast," Ken began a few minutes later, after everyone's glasses were filled with iced tea. "First, to Mr. and Mrs.

Wakefield, for putting up with us here this evening—and for doing it with such style."

"Thank you, Ken," Mrs. Wakefield said after they had sipped their drinks. "And I would like to say how glad Ned and I are to have all of you here tonight." She placed a hand on Todd's arm. "We're especially glad that you're with us, Todd," she said, "after what nearly happened last weekend."

"Hear! Hear!" Steven added. "That was some rebound you made Friday night, Wilkins! Just don't try to slam-dunk any more T-birds anytime soon."

"I wasn't the high scorer in that game," Todd said, rising to his feet and raising his glass. "And I would like to propose a toast to the person who pulled it out in the last second. I have never been as happy to be alive as I am right now, and I owe everything to Jessica." He tipped his glass toward Jessica, seated across the table. "Thank you, Jess, for saving my life."

Mrs. Wakefield patted Jessica on the shoulder proudly. Jessica was beaming at Todd, and he grinned back. Then she made eye contact with her sister. Her smile faltered.

Todd was puzzled by the play of emotions on Elizabeth's face. Her jaw was clenched, her lower lip trembled, and her eyes were full of pain. As Todd watched, Mr. and Mrs. Wakefield exchanged a concerned glance. The temperature in the room seemed to drop by ten degrees.

Steven was oblivious to his sister's mood. "Todd is toasting Jess?" he said, shaking his head. "Now there's a switch."

For a moment it was so quiet in the dining room that Todd was acutely aware of the muffled thump of a tree branch hitting the window.

Then Elizabeth jumped up from her chair. Her arm brushed against Todd's; he drew back from the coldness of her skin. "Excuse me," she said in a flat, dead voice. A moment later her footsteps echoed in the silent house as she ran upstairs.

Nora appraised the Wakefields' dining room with a critical eye, but she found nothing to criticize. The dining room was elegant but not ostentatious. The turkey, stuffing, and cranberry sauce would have been at home on Norman Rockwell's table. Through the archway to the next room, a Christmas tree glittered, laden with ornaments and lights.

A gold-and-green glow filled the room, and Nora knew it was the homey smell of good food and blue spruce, tinged with faint touches of candle wax and lemon furniture polish. She breathed deeply, wishing she could smell it through the window.

The family and the twins' boyfriends were

at the table. Todd had just made a toast. He tipped his glass toward the twin who sat farthest from Nora's window—Jessica, she decided, taking in the dramatic makeup, meticulously tousled hair, and low-cut silk blouse. She had spent the last few days researching and eavesdropping and was beginning to feel as if she knew the Wakefield twins personally. Todd talked for a few minutes in an emotional but happy way. Jessica was beaming.

In her eagerness to see what was happening, Nora tripped over a branch of rhododendron, bracing herself against the window with a soft thud. She held her breath, but nobody had noticed.

Then Elizabeth jumped up from her chair. Nora's first thought was that she had been discovered. But dread dissolved into amazement when she caught her first good view of a Wakefield twin, close-up and in person. Nora's mouth dropped open. Surely, meeting her own identical twin would not have been more startling.

Elizabeth wore a conservative sweater, subdued makeup, and a ponytail. What made Nora stare was Elizabeth's face. It was Nora's face. She was the exact same size and build as Nora, and she even moved the same way. Her hair was honey-blond—the same shade as the wig

Nora had bought that very afternoon. And her eyes were as blue-green as the Pacific Ocean— as blue-green as Nora's eyes, now that Nora had purchased her new contact lenses.

Elizabeth disappeared into another room, and Nora chastised herself. She'd been so mesmerized by the sight of her exact double that she had forgotten to pay attention to Elizabeth's mood and facial expressions.

"No matter," she told herself. "I'll have time for more observation later." Everything she had seen confirmed Nora's belief that the Wakefield family was perfect. The tall, handsome father, Ned, was smiling and relaxed. The proud mother, Alice, looked young enough to be Jessica and Elizabeth's older sister—and looked enough like Nora to be her own mother. Gorgeous Steven, the prelaw student, was the life of the party. And sexy Todd and Ken—the dark-haired basketball star and the blond quarterback—were like boyfriends out of a movie.

Nora sighed. She remembered her vision of Margo standing inside the dilapidated boardinghouse, staring out through a greasy windowpane at a world that would never be hers.

Nora wanted that world—that life. She deserved it. And she owed it to Margo. *I promise to get back at them for you, Margo!* she said in her thoughts.

Nora sighed again, suddenly depressed. It was Christmas Eve, and she was alone. A tear rolled down her face as she thought of all the holidays she and Margo would never spend together. And she made a decision. The next day Nora would find her sister's grave. And she would celebrate Christmas with the only family she had, in the only way she could.

Elizabeth lay on her bed, tears falling onto the pages of her journal as she wrote.

I'm losing Todd, she scrawled in large letters across the top of a page. *The newspaper called Jessica his girlfriend. Soon it will be the truth. I saw the way they looked at each other tonight.*

She paused and chewed on the cap of her ballpoint pen. She remembered the dazzling smile on Jessica's face and the play of candlelight on her hair. Jessica looked beautiful that night; it was no wonder Todd was falling in love with her. Any boy would fall in love with her.

I've never been so jealous in my life! Elizabeth admitted to her journal. *And I've never felt more guilty about being jealous. I should be grateful to Jessica. She saved Todd's life! Now he says it's his responsibility to make her happy. I guess it's working—she seemed awfully happy tonight when he gazed at her over the candles. And I'm sure they'll both be a lot happier after I'm officially out of the pic-*

ture. It can only be a matter of time before he breaks up with me.

What am I going to do? Jessica and I have barely spoken since that incident Sunday night at the Dairi Burger. How can she be so insensitive and self-centered? How can she go on and on about saving Todd's life? She must know that it upsets me! And she keeps passing out that stupid newspaper photograph, despite the mistake. I'm so angry and jealous and confused. I haven't felt this far away from Jessica in a long, long time. In a year, to be exact.

Elizabeth closed her journal with a deep sigh and set it aside. The room was growing dark, but she didn't move to turn on a light. Dark fit her mood. She rolled over on her back and stared at the ceiling, trying to calm her quiet sobs.

Nora knelt in the wet dirt of the graveyard as tendrils of mist curled around her in the dark. The smell of decay surrounded her, as tangible as the smooth white stones that marched in rows as far as she could see. Only one grave marker stood apart, and that was where she dug. MARGO CHAPELLE, the stone said.

Voices blew around her on the wind, wailing and whispering and moaning. *Dig deeper*, commanded one of them. It was Margo's voice, and her words were a threat. *Do it.*

Nora scraped at the hole she was digging, pulling out handfuls of wet peat. Dirt collected under her fingernails, smelling dark brown and thick. Nora longed to wash her hands. Something scuttled across her arm. Nora screamed and jerked her hands away, tears budding in her eyes.

The wind grew colder.

Patience. Margo's voice was soothing now, but it held a sinister secret. *There's more to learn.*

Nora pushed her damp, limp hair behind her shoulders. Then she plunged her hands back into the cold earth and continued to dig. Finally her fingers tapped hollowly against something hard and smooth that was hidden in the soil. She scraped it clear and reached around its rim to feel its shape. It was a wooden coffin. Margo's coffin.

Nora's hands were trembling as she pried open the lid. It gave way with a long, slow creak. A sick, sweet odor engulfed her, like the smell of rotting magnolia blossoms. It swirled around her, thick and creamy white against the black night, and Nora grew dizzy. She bit back her fear and willed her pulse to stop racing.

Do it! commanded the voices on the wind.

Nora raised the lid until the coffin lay open to the night and the mist. The wood of its interior was smooth and flat, gleaming like a mirror in the night. For an instant she thought she could see the ghost of her own reflection, lying in the coffin. She gasped, but the hallucination vanished. The coffin was empty.

There was no Margo.

Chapter 10

Somebody was breathing hard. The panting reached Jessica gradually as she glided upward through layers of sleep. Finally she surfaced in consciousness. Something heavy was moving on top of her feet. She pulled the covers up around her chin and opened one eye. "Go back to sleep, Prince Albert," she told the dog. "Mornings aren't fit for human habitation—or dogs." She squeezed her eyes shut and rolled onto her side.

Prince Albert thumped to the floor. Then he nosed against the side of Jessica's face, as if trying to tell her something.

"Aw, geez, Prince Albert. You're as bad as an alarm clock," she said through a yawn. She squinted at her clock radio. "I don't have to get up. It's only seven thirty, and it's not a school

147

day. It's Christmas break—" Jessica's eyes shot open. "Christmas! Prince Albert, it's Christmas Day!"

She sat straight up in bed. Christmas was always one of her favorite days of the year. Ever since they were kids, she would bound down the stairs early on Christmas morning, trying to beat Steven and Elizabeth in a cheerful race to the tree—and the presents.

At the thought of her sister, Jessica's smile dissolved. Elizabeth had hardly said a word to her all week. She threw herself backward against the pillow. For the first time she noticed the hiss of water in the bathroom that separated her bedroom from her twin's. Elizabeth was up early, as usual, and was already in the shower. Out of habit, Jessica reached for the knob on the radio. Bruce Springsteen's version of "Santa Claus Is Coming to Town" filled the room, drowning out the sound of Elizabeth's shower: *You better not shout. You better not cry. You better not pout. . . .*"

The twins had been doing their fair share of all three lately, Jessica reflected. "It's Christmas morning, and Liz and I are mad at each other," she told Prince Albert, blinking back tears.

Jessica tried to remember when the bad feeling between her and Elizabeth had started.

She knew how angry she had felt on Monday night, when Elizabeth and Ken had gone to a movie together. "I had a right to be mad!" she whispered to Prince Albert. "Liz stole my boyfriend right out from under my nose and went on a date with him!"

She sighed. Elizabeth said she and Ken had gone out as friends. And Ken swore that they had done nothing but watch *The Shining*. Jessica supposed she believed them, but it was still a rotten thing for them to have done—especially in front of Lila and Amy.

Albert gazed at her expectantly. "OK! OK!" she said finally. "Stop with the puppy-dog eyes! I know, there was something wrong even before Sunday. Ever since I saved Todd's life, she's acted like she was mad at me. But I didn't do anything wrong!" she insisted. "Ask anyone. I was a hero!"

Prince Albert was still looking at her as if he expected an answer. "Heck, what do you know?" Jessica asked him. "You're a dog!"

He gave an insulted whine and padded across the room. Then he sat down on a pile of laundry near the door and stared at her.

"What's up with you?" Jessica asked. "Dogs aren't supposed to act this way. You look as if you're trying to keep me from leaving the room—until I figure out why this fight with Liz is my fault." She crossed her arms grumpily.

"Well, it's not my fault! This time Liz, Miss Perfect Twin, is the one who is wrong. I risked my life to save her boyfriend. She's the one who got mad at me for it and tried to steal *my* boyfriend."

Prince Albert was still looking at her. "So I've been getting a lot of attention this week. Well, I deserve it!" she insisted to him. "Liz doesn't have any right to be mad at me. This fight is all her fault!"

Prince Albert cocked his head.

Jessica rolled her eyes. "OK, I admit it!" she said finally. "Maybe I could have been more sensitive. Her boyfriend was in an accident; I should know what that's like, better than anyone." She took a deep breath and continued. "And maybe I went a teensy bit overboard all week, telling everyone about saving Todd's life. And maybe Todd and I were sort of ignoring Liz and Ken that night at the Dairi Burger."

She sighed, even more depressed. It was bad enough to be feuding with Elizabeth on Christmas Day. But now it was partly her own fault. Last year, in the aftermath of Sam's death, had been the worst Christmas of Jessica's life. She and Elizabeth had spoken to each other only when necessary, and then they'd been polite but distant, like strangers. She shuddered, remembering the bleakness

150

of that morning. Surely this year had to be better.

"Well, I guess I'll find out soon," she said. Eager or not, she supposed it was time to get up, brush her teeth, and go downstairs to see what was under the tree—even though she didn't think she could bear to live through another Christmas morning with Elizabeth mad at her.

Elizabeth used a washcloth to rub a clear spot in the steamed-up mirror. From Jessica's room she could hear the sound of Bruce Springsteen singing about Santa. That version had always been one of Jessica's favorite Christmas songs.

Elizabeth stared at her watery reflection and sighed. Some Christmas morning this was going to be. She was losing her sister and her boyfriend in one fell swoop. Jessica and Todd had probably been scheming all week about how to end up under the mistletoe together. How could they do this to her?

"I trusted them!" she said tearfully to her reflection.

With her hair loose and wet and her body wrapped in her bulky terry-cloth bathrobe, she could have just as easily been Jessica, Elizabeth thought with a start, staring at her mirror image. She tousled her hair with her fingers and mimicked Jessica's sexiest smile. In the wet mirror her image looked a little fuzzy. The effect was glamorous, like a soft-focus photograph of a movie star. For a moment she actually felt as if she were looking at Jessica in the mirror.

"What's Jessica thinking this morning, I wonder?" she whispered, wondering if her sister felt even the slightest bit guilty about taking Todd away from her.

Then she shook her head and leaned forward, her hands on the counter. "Who am I kidding?" she said in a small, defeated voice. "It's not Jessica's fault."

Jessica had done a heroic thing. She had saved a boy's life. It was only natural for Todd to feel grateful—to fall in love with her. Elizabeth racked her memory, but she honestly couldn't think of a single thing she'd seen Jessica do on purpose to make Todd love her—except smiling, and that hardly qualified as throwing herself at him. Jessica couldn't help it if she was gorgeous and bubbly and fun to be with. And she couldn't help it if he wanted to repay the wonderful gift she'd given him.

The door from Jessica's room opened suddenly, and Elizabeth stood up straight. Her sister's face appeared around the door and instantly froze. "Uh, sorry, Liz," she stammered, fidgeting with the belt on her pink bathrobe. "I thought you were finished in here. I'll come back later—"

"No!" Elizabeth said. "I'm finished. I was just leaving."

"That's OK," Jessica said, her face coloring. "I can wait—"

"No, it's all right," Elizabeth said, grateful that the steamy bathroom and her wet skin hid her own embarrassed blush and the tears on her face. She turned and slipped out the door to her own room, leaving Jessica alone.

Jessica stood in the warm bathroom, using the hem of her robe to clear a bigger spot in the steamed-up mirror. She frowned at her reflection. "I should have apologized," she told herself. "I will apologize," she decided firmly, "as soon as I'm finished in here."

As Jessica reached for a towel, she heard a tap on the door from her sister's room. "Jessica?" Elizabeth said through the door. Her voice sounded strained. "Can I come in for a minute? There's something important I need to tell you."

Jessica nodded, her eyes wide with surprise. Then she realized that Elizabeth couldn't see her. "Yes," she croaked out, wondering if Elizabeth was going to tell her she never wanted to speak to her again. "Come in."

Elizabeth came in slowly, wearing a blue robe in the same style as Jessica's pink one. Her hair was damp and a little messy. *She looks just like me when she's wet!* Jessica thought, startled.

"Jessica, I—"

"Wait, Liz," Jessica interrupted. "First, let me say—"

"No!" Elizabeth said, a little loudly. "I'm sorry; I'm kind of nervous. But I have to tell you now. I keep remembering last year. I can't stand another Christmas Day of pretending everything's all right between us when it's not."

"Me neither," Jessica said glumly. *This is it,* she thought. *Elizabeth wants to get our fight out in the open. Why bother being distant and polite when you can scream at each other?*

Elizabeth hesitated. Then she took a deep breath, placed a hand on the counter for support, and began. "I'm sorry for the way I've been acting all week," she said.

"You're what?" Jessica asked, incredulous.

"I know, it's lame. I don't expect you to forgive me after the way I've treated you. I mean, you saved Todd's life! And I've acted as if you committed a crime. Then he was so grateful, and I got so jealous every time I saw the two of you together. . . ." Tears sprouted in her eyes.

Jessica managed a watery smile. "You can't apologize to me!" she objected. "I was just working up the nerve to apologize to you!"

A slow smile spread across Elizabeth's face. A second later the twins were laughing and hugging. Then they pulled away and looked fondly at each other. "Merry Christmas!" they said at exactly the same moment. Then they both burst out laughing again. Suddenly the holiday seemed a lot more joyous.

"What do you say we run downstairs and see if Steven has beat us to the presents?" Jessica asked.

Nora opened her eyes and looked at the clock by her eyelet-lace-covered bed.

"Two o'clock in the afternoon," she moaned, sitting up. "What a rotten night!"

The nightmare about Margo's empty coffin had repeated itself all night long, every time she managed to sleep again. By morning she'd fallen into a restless, fitful, but dreamless sleep. Now Nora felt as if the nightmare's mood of terror and scent of decay had become a part of her. Her limbs were too heavy to raise from the bed, as if her body had turned to stone. Smooth white stone, she decided. A gravestone. By herself she was useless—nothing more than a symbol of her twin's absence.

Nora yawned and struggled to her feet.

"Merry Christmas," she said grimly to the empty room.

She squinted to see through the pink haze of potpourri scent that the hotel housekeeping staff didn't see, even when Nora pointed it out. She sighed. Outside the window, the day was drab and overcast, reminding her more of Margo's dreary Long Island neighborhood than of idyllic Sweet Valley.

Thinking of Margo made her remember her resolve of the evening before. She would go to her sister. She and Margo would spend time together on Christmas Day, just as the Wakefield twins were doing.

Of course, Margo wasn't really buried in Sweet Valley. Her body had never been found. But a local support group for troubled teenagers had erected a memorial stone for her in the local cemetery, according to a newspaper article about Margo's death. She would go there, to the cemetery, and listen for traces of Margo's spirit on the wind. Her twin would give her the courage to carry out Margo's plans for the Wakefield family—to complete what had been started the year before.

Nora smiled. It was so . . . symmetrical.

She decided to wear her new blond wig, so that Margo's ghost could see what she intended to do. Of course, that meant she would have to wait until nightfall. She couldn't risk being mistaken for one of the Wakefield twins. Not yet.

Nora stood in front of the bathroom mirror and began to brush her hair while waiting for her sister to appear. Surely, Margo would come this time. It was Christmas Day. And she needed to know that Margo wanted her to continue with her plans. She needed to know that Margo approved. But Margo stayed away, and Nora felt doubt pouring over her like smoke from a campfire. The hairbrush dropped from her hand and clattered on the tile floor.

"This is hopeless!" Nora cried. "I'll never be able to do it!" Tears began to fall from her eyes. "I'll never be able to carry out Margo's plan by myself! I'm not good enough. I'm not strong enough. I'm not Margo!"

Of course she wasn't Margo, she thought. Margo never panicked. Margo never cried.

"I never used to cry," Nora suddenly remembered, staring at her tearstained face in the mirror. "I didn't even cry at my father's funeral." But lately she couldn't seem to help herself—ever since she'd learned of her twin's violent death.

Nora leaned on the counter, sobbing. A part of her was missing, and she would never get it back.

Dig deeper, said a calm, low voice that might have been the rising wind in the trees outside.

Nora raised her eyes to the mirror and gasped. Margo gazed out at her. For a full minute the twins stared at each other through the glass, as if trying to probe each other's souls. Then Nora turned away, with a sudden, depressing awareness that she'd been tested and found wanting. When she looked back at the mirror, only her own reflection stared back at her through red-rimmed eyes.

"No, Margo! Don't leave me!" she screamed, throwing herself against the mirror. "I can do it! I swear I will!" She pounded her fists on the cold, unyielding surface. "Margo!"

Nora stared into her own face and was filled with revulsion and anger. No wonder Margo had left her again. She didn't deserve a twin sister like Margo. Nora took a deep breath through her clenched jaw. Then she pulled back one fist and swung as hard as she could at her face in the mirror.

A loud crack, like a gunshot, splintered her image. Long, jagged black lines radiated outward, slicing through her reflection. And a few shards of glass fell into the sink with a faint jingle.

In the utter silence that followed, Nora lifted her hand and stared at the trickle of blood that ran down her fingers to her wrist. For a moment she watched it, mesmerized. Then her body began to tremble.

Nora twisted the knob on the spigot and thrust her bleeding hand under the purifying rush of cold water. She held it there long after the bleeding had stopped. And her reflection watched the running water through the splintered glass.

Jessica leaned against the couch and sighed contentedly. She stretched her toes toward the fire as she gestured with a Christmas cookie. "I'm so glad this didn't turn out to be like last Christmas!" she said to Elizabeth, who sat beside her on the rug, drinking eggnog. "It's been a great day!" Jessica added, thinking of the quiet, pleasant dinner the family had just shared.

Now Steven was upstairs, talking on the phone with Billie, his girlfriend, and the twins' parents were at an open-house holiday party down the street. For the first time since their reunion that morning, the twins had some time to themselves, together.

Elizabeth smiled and squeezed her twin's shoulder. "This has been the best Christmas," she agreed. "Especially after the way everything was so stilted and twisted between us last year. What a horrible time that was!"

"Yes, it was," Jessica said softly, staring into the fire. A nameless fear rose within her, like the hot gray smoke that glided soundlessly up the chimney.

"I'm sorry, Jess," Elizabeth apologized, her hand still on her sister's shoulder. "I didn't mean to make you think about Sam. It must be terrible, remembering. . . ."

"No, that's not it," Jessica replied. "I'll always miss Sam. But I wasn't thinking about him just now." She lowered her head. "I was thinking about Margo."

"Margo," Elizabeth whispered as her face drained of color.

"Liz, are you OK?" Jessica asked, concerned. "What is it?"

Elizabeth shook her head and gave a weak smile. But with one trembling hand she was twisting the fringes on the carpet into a tight, stiff roll. Then she met Jessica's gaze and shrugged. "It's nothing," she said. "It's just that I've been having that dream again—the one we both had last year."

Jessica's eyes widened. "The one with Margo out by Secca Lake?"

Elizabeth nodded. "Have you had it again, too?" she asked intently.

"No," Jessica said, staring into the fire. She'd had Elizabeth's recurring nightmare only once, and that had been a year earlier. "But I did have another dream about Margo," Jessica blurted out. "It happened earlier this week. I guess I didn't tell you because we were mad at each other."

Elizabeth's eyes were huge, and a perfect, tiny flame was reflected in each blue-green pool. "What happened in your dream?" she asked, absentmindedly reaching for a cookie.

"It was just like something that really did happen, last year around this time," Jessica admitted. "The real thing was kind of unnerving, but I was never sure that I was in actual danger."

"What happened?"

"I was on a picnic with James, in the mountains near Secca Lake," she explained. "We were looking over the edge of a steep cliff, and I started to fall. At the same time, I felt James's hand on my back."

Elizabeth gasped. "He pushed you?"

"No!" Jessica said, too loudly. "Well, maybe. . . . I don't know," she admitted. "He said that I lost my balance, and that he was pulling me back. I guess that was the truth. I mean, James loved me! I'm sure that later, in the end, he was trying to warn me about Margo. And I'm sure it was Margo who killed him before he could tell me."

"So what happened in your dream this week?" Elizabeth asked.

Jessica's voice grew soft, and as she recounted the dream for her twin, she could see it play out in front of her eyes like a movie. ". . . And then a hand was on my back, and the

161

trees and rocks below me kind of whooshed up as I started to fall. And then it got dark all of a sudden. Then I woke up."

"So there was nothing else?"

Jessica gave a tense laugh and took a bite of a wreath-shaped sugar cookie. "Not unless you count finding myself on the floor a second later with Prince Albert licking my face."

"What night did you have the nightmare?" Elizabeth asked.

"Monday," Jessica said. "Just after you and I had that argument about who ruined whose date at the Dairi Burger."

"I'm really sorry about that, Jess," Elizabeth said. "But you know that I was telling you the truth about me and Ken. We went to the movies, but it was perfectly innocent."

Jessica nodded. "I know that now." She grinned. "And Todd's a hunk, but we haven't done anything in the last week except become friends. You've always wanted us to be friends," she reminded her sister.

"I know. I shouldn't have been so sensitive about you and Todd. I was just feeling insecure because he was so grateful that you saved his life." Tears filled her eyes. "He couldn't talk about anything except how brave and wonderful you were, and I was afraid he'd decided that he liked you more than he liked me."

Jessica stared. "I had no idea you were

thinking such ridiculous things!" she said. "Todd loves *you*! There's nothing going on between me and him!" Jessica gulped down a twinge of guilt over a few unsisterly thoughts she'd had about Todd in the past week. But she had no reason to feel guilty. She may have had an occasional romantic thought about Todd that week—and she was almost sure the idea had occurred to him, as well. But thinking about it wasn't a crime. They hadn't *done* anything to act on those thoughts.

Elizabeth nodded. "Let's not ever make stupid assumptions about each other again," she suggested.

"Absolutely!" Jessica said. Then she laughed. "I'm sure Ken and Todd will be relieved to hear we're not upset anymore. They probably think we both lost our minds this week."

"I guess I owe Todd an explanation."

"And I owe Ken an apology for being so wrapped up all week in what happened last Friday night."

"We'll have time to talk tomorrow, when the four of us go to check out the Morginis' carnival."

"Let's promise never to fight again," Jessica proposed.

Elizabeth laughed. "Somehow I don't think that's realistic," she said, taking another cookie.

"Probably not," Jessica admitted. "But we

can at least promise not to have any more really serious fights."

"Agreed," Elizabeth said. "It was our big fight about the prom last year that drove us right into Margo's trap," she remembered.

"Last year the dreams were warnings about Margo," Jessica pointed out. "But Margo's dead. So why are we having nightmares about her again?"

"Yes," Elizabeth said with a haunted look in her eyes. "Margo is dead." She turned away for an instant before resuming. "I think we're having these dreams now because we've been strangers to each other all week. Think about it. I first had the dream about Secca Lake again on the night of Todd's accident. That's when I started being upset about you, after I saw the two of you together at the hospital—"

"And I dreamed about falling off the mountain right after I got mad at you for taking Ken to the movies," Jessica said.

"So these dreams had nothing to do with Margo," Elizabeth decided. "The accident and the time of year just reminded us of last year, and our subconscious minds dredged her up, because we were both mad at someone who looked just like us."

Jessica sighed and finished her cookie. "Now that you and I are friends again," she declared,

"I bet we'll stop having nightmares." She fervently hoped that her words were true.

The night was dark and misty, and Nora thought she must be dreaming again. But the dampness on her forehead was real. So was the brown smell of decay and the prickling sensation at the back of her neck, under the blond wig. This time the night was not a dream.

There was the cemetery entrance, just as she'd seen it so many times, with streaks of moisture gleaming on the wrought-iron scrollwork of the open gate. Something compelled Nora forward, as if she were being sucked through the gate and into a vortex from which she'd never escape. But the gate didn't glide open, as it had the other times. Without thinking, Nora pulled herself up on the scrollwork. Then she dropped soundlessly to the damp earth inside the cemetery.

The wind was cold and full of voices, and they called her forward, through rows of white grave markers that reminded her of dingy teeth.

As in her dream, one granite stone stood apart. Nora's knees were shaking as she stumbled toward it. This small white stone, she knew instinctively, was at the center of her quest. The stone was plain, with no adornment except for a few words carved in simple block letters: IN MEMORIAM was all it said, with the name MARGO BLACK and two dates. The first date Nora knew well. It was the date of her own birth. The date of death was listed as January 1, one year ago.

Nora fell to her knees in the moist, soft dirt. "Merry Christmas, Margo," she whispered to the stone. The granite marker was all she would ever have of her twin sister, Margo—thanks to the Wakefield twins.

"Those girls took you away from me, Margo," Nora whispered, her voice lost in the laughter that rode on the gathering wind. "But they won't get away with it. I'll make the Wakefields pay for what they did to you. I swear, I'll make them pay!"

She closed her eyes and vowed not to cry. "I must be strong," she whispered. "I must be strong."

The wind picked up suddenly, blowing mist around her in mad spirals, like the tattered clouds that blew across the face of the nearly full moon. A dark cloud bank rode into view, and the moon vanished—as suddenly and completely as the tiny flame of a candle in the wind. Nora's heart began to pound in her chest.

Suddenly cold hands tightened around Nora's neck. She tried to scream but could not. The cold, strong hands gripped her throat like bands of steel.

The person behind her was about her height and size, but stronger—and more determined. Nora kicked and twisted and fought. But she knew, deep down, that she couldn't win. She was thrown to the ground, and her face pushed into the thick, dark soil—the same soil where insects burrowed and dead bodies were buried. Nausea rose inside her, and she longed to be clean and dry and warm. Then somebody jerked her to her feet.

The black-and-gray world tilted around her, and Nora struggled against dizziness. She was fainting. She was dying. Vaguely, she was aware of being dragged into a colder, damper place— an inside place, where the smell of wet stone hung heavy in the air, intermingled with the smell of death. A mausoleum, she thought— slowly, stupidly. The horrible pressure on her neck was gone, but she was exhausted and disoriented.

Her attacker whirled her around. As Nora's eyes grew accustomed to the new shade of darkness, the shadowy figure emerged from the fog, the facial features gradually coming into focus.

Nora gulped. She was staring into her own face.

She was hallucinating, she decided, her thoughts moving in slow motion. She'd spent too much time looking in mirrors, and now she was imagining one. But the knife in the dark was real. And it was thrusting toward her throat.

Nora screamed. She grabbed at her attacker's arm. The dark figure reached for Nora's head and pulled her hair back, exposing her naked, vulnerable throat.

Then Nora's blond wig came off in her attacker's hand, and her own hair, as black as the night, tumbled out. Nora's brain began to clear as the knife clattered to the ground.

A cigarette lighter flickered on. Once again Nora stared into a face that looked exactly like her own. But now she knew what it meant, and she could barely contain her joy.

"Who are you?" the girl asked, her gray eyes wide with fear. Her grip on Nora's arm was like a vise, but Nora welcomed the pain.

"Hello, Margo," Nora said, a smile spreading across her face. "I'm Nora Chapelle. I'm your twin sister."

Chapter 11

Nora raised her face to the hot, cleansing stream of water and felt it pouring over her body. After grappling in the dirt with Margo, it was good to cleanse herself of the gritty, death-saturated germs of the cemetery.

She jumped and opened her eyes. The door to the bathroom had just opened. The bloody shower scene from *Psycho* came to mind, but Nora relaxed when she heard her sister's voice.

"Nice setup you got here," said Margo. "Sweet Valley Inn, huh? La-di-da! It sure beats my dump-of-the-month room in somebody's basement. But how did the mirror get cracked?"

"I broke it," Nora said, sticking her head outside the shower curtain. Somehow she knew that Margo would understand. "I didn't like the way it was looking at me."

Margo nodded. "Yeah," she said. "They do that, sometimes. Sometimes you have to take charge."

Nora wrinkled her nose at the dark gray smell that had filled the room when Margo had entered. Cigarettes. Nora tensed up. But Margo was her soul mate, and Margo had been subjected to some terrible, filthy influences during her tortured existence. Nora could overlook a few foul habits for now.

"Sorry the place is such a disgusting mess," Nora said with an apologetic smile, noting that the sink hadn't been wiped since she'd left that afternoon. "I guess I woke up so late today that the housekeeping service skipped the room."

Margo raised her eyebrows. "Are you kidding? This place is so clean, it's almost obscene!" She laughed. "Where I live, clean means that the cockroaches have all scurried out of sight."

Nora was filled with revulsion. At the same time, her heart went out to Margo. She couldn't imagine being able to discuss grimy, nasty cockroaches in such a cavalier tone. She shuddered at the thought. "Uh, I'll be finished in a few minutes, if you want to take a shower," she said. Suddenly she felt guilty. Underneath the cemetery dirt, Margo looked as if she'd started with a base of several days' worth of filth. *It must be hard to keep clean,* Nora thought sadly, *when you have to live the kind of existence Margo has endured.* She chastised herself for not letting her sister shower first.

Margo waved her hand. "Nah," she said, closing the toilet lid and sitting on it. She was wearing an oversize sweatshirt Nora had lent her to sleep in. "I'm so pooped, I don't think I could stand up long enough to take a shower tonight. I'll wait until the morning."

Nora couldn't help but notice a few germ-filled crumbs of black earth that rained down from Margo's sneakers to the snowy white tiles. Obviously, Margo was too tired to see what a mess she'd made. Nora would clean it later.

She ducked back under the shower head to rinse the last traces of conditioner from her hair. She turned off the water and then stopped, dripping and unsure. She bit her lip. She had assumed that she and Margo would be like extensions of the same person—that they would never feel self-conscious together or have secrets from each other. But nobody had seen her without clothing since she was a small child. To her dismay, she was embarrassed to step out of the shower in front of her twin.

"Uh, Margo, could you hand me one of those big bath towels?" she asked, popping her

171

head and one arm out through the shower curtain.

Margo grabbed her arm roughly. "Cool!" she exclaimed.

Nora stifled the urge to snatch it back. "What do you mean?"

"The tattoo!" Margo explained. "I wouldn't have thought you had it in you! Gemini, right?" Her eyes narrowed with suspicion. "But I thought you said you only just found out about us."

"I did," Nora said, accepting the towel Margo finally offered. "Somehow I guess I always knew I was a twin. At least, I always felt like I was searching for part of me that was missing."

"I've been searching, too," Margo said in a soft voice.

Nora stepped out of the shower, the fluffy white towel wrapped securely around her. Her eyes grew round when she saw that Margo was fingering a piece of broken glass that had fallen from the mirror.

"This is about the size of the shard that caught me in the throat last year, after I fell through the window at that rich witch Lila Fowler's party," Margo said in a matter-of-fact tone.

"I still don't understand how you survived that night," Nora said, staring at the glass in her sister's hand. A swatch of Margo's face stared at Nora from the piece of mirror. Then Margo shifted it in her fingers, and the reflection was replaced by Nora's own face. A shiver skated down Nora's spine. She looked away, startled.

Margo shrugged. "It was all in a day's work," she said. "I've practiced for years, holding my breath for a long time. I can last over three minutes sometimes," she bragged as the girls walked back to the bedroom. "If you know how to do it, you can even slow your pulse."

"So you made them think you were dead," Nora said, carefully ignoring an ashtray full of dirty cigarette butts that sat in the center of her own sharply made bed. The other double bed in the room was already rumpled, as if someone had been lying on top of the bedspread.

"Jess and Liz and company never came close enough to really know if I was breathing," Margo said. "I could hear them talking, and they assumed I was dead. The ambulance people knew I was alive. But I broke their radio when nobody was looking, so they couldn't tell the hospital."

"I get it!" Nora said. "You caused the ambulance crash!"

"Bingo!" Margo said, touching her nose. "Stick with me, sis—you'll learn a lot!"

"How did you manage the accident?" Nora asked.

"It's easy to take people by surprise when they think you're on your deathbed," Margo said with a shrug. She grinned.

Nora nodded, impressed.

"I had some pieces of glass from the window hidden under the sheet they threw over me," Margo continued as she climbed into the rumpled bed. "As soon as we turned off the Fowlers' driveway, I attacked the attendants and slashed them good."

Nora picked up the ashtray, holding it as far away from her body as she could, and carefully set it on a table at the far end of the room. She pulled back the covers on her own bed, checked the sheets for cleanliness, and plumped the pillows to exactly the right height. Then she climbed into bed, still wearing her bathrobe, and changed into her nightgown under the blankets. She folded the robe and laid it carefully over the back of a chair near the bed. Margo watched the whole procedure with a bemused expression on her face. Then she laid the shard of mirror on the nightstand and reached up to turn out the light.

"What did you do next?" Nora asked with fascination. She could feel her own strength growing, just from being in the same room with her twin.

"Then I drove the ambulance to the river and crashed through the side of the bridge," Margo continued. "As it fell, I dived out the door."

"Wow!" Nora exclaimed. "You've got more gall than anyone I've ever met!"

"I never had anything else to my name," Margo said, sounding bitter, despite a wide yawn. "I had to make use of my strengths." She leaned up on one elbow and stared at her twin in the darkness. "Nora, the Wakefield twins think they have some kind of psychic connection. I bet we do, too. Do you sometimes hear voices in your head, telling you what to do?"

Nora sat up in bed. "What kind of voices?"

"I don't know," Margo said softly. "Raspy, low voices. Sometimes they make fun of me. Sometimes they just give me instructions. And now and then, especially when I'm getting close to achieving a goal, they kind of . . . become part of me. They talk through me. Does that make sense?"

"Yes," Nora said quickly. "I've heard voices, too, sort of. But it's only happened lately. I've been having this recurring nightmare about the cemetery. The voices in my dream sound like the ones you've heard." She lay back on her pillow and stared up at the darkness, suddenly aware of the thousands of tiny eyes that watched her from the bedspreads and curtains.

"And sometimes," she whispered, "I hear *your* voice."

Margo didn't reply. Nora listened to her twin's slow, regular breathing, and she knew that Margo was asleep.

Jessica gazed around her at the festive colors and happy people as she licked the last crystals of sticky pink sugar from a paper cone. "That's the first time I've had cotton candy in eons!" she said with a grin. "Who said carnivals were only for kids?"

"Actually, I think you did," Elizabeth reminded her with a smile as they tossed their paper cones into a trash bin. "We probably shouldn't have eaten those so close to lunchtime," she added with a glance at her watch. "But what the heck!" she exclaimed, her eyes twinkling. "We have to experience the total carnival if we're going to be able to keep the whole place running five days from now."

"I never thought I'd like research this much!" Jessica said.

Ken put his arm around her shoulders. "What next?" he asked. "Another ride on the Ferris wheel?"

"No way," Todd said, taking Elizabeth's hand. "We already did that. There are more rides and games and concession stands here than we can ever get to in one day. We won't even have time to hit all the highlights if we keep going back for reconnaissance on the same old things."

"Reconnaissance?" Jessica repeated, puzzled. "I thought that was a time in Italy when lots of people painted pictures and things."

Elizabeth shook her head. "Try staying awake in history class next semester," she suggested.

"Why?" Jessica asked with a shrug. "It's a lot easier to let you help me with all the homework assignments," she explained. "Besides, it's good for *your* self-esteem to feel needed."

"Thanks for your concern," Elizabeth said with mock seriousness. Then she grinned and squeezed her sister's hand.

Jessica beamed. It was great to be joking and laughing together again, as though the tension of the week before had never existed. "So what's next?" she asked.

"I think Ken is right," Elizabeth replied. "It's your turn to choose, Jessica."

"How about that little purple tent over there?" Jessica suggested, pointing. "Purple's my lucky color, after all!"

The tent was round, with a graceful point on top, like something nomads would use in the desert, Jessica thought. At least it was like something they would use in the desert in the movies.

"Madame Renata," Elizabeth read from an ornately lettered sign near the entrance. "Get this—'Prophet of the Future, Seer of the Past'!"

Ken grimaced, reading. "'Tarot cards, palm reading, and crystal-ball gazing.'" He rolled his eyes. "It sounds pretty wacky, if you ask me."

"Lighten up, Ken!" Elizabeth urged. "It's all in fun!"

"Besides, nobody's forcing you to go in there," Jessica pointed out.

"Personally," Todd said, "I'm getting hungry for something more substantial than that cloud of pink stuff we just finished." He closed his eyes and touched his head with his fingers. "Wait, I'm receiving a vision now. The Great and Powerful Todd sees hot dogs."

Elizabeth rolled her eyes. "I think he's channeling Oscar Mayer."

Todd ignored her. "I definitely see hot dogs in your future, Matthews," he repeated. "Very big hot dogs."

Elizabeth groaned. "How can you two eat again, after all the junk we've been stuffing ourselves with?"

Ken shrugged. "It's lunchtime," he said, as if that explained it.

"You girls stay here and have your fortunes told," Todd suggested. "Then meet us over there at that concession stand." He pointed. "In the meantime Ken and I will do some research on those foot-long hot dogs. After all, somebody has to make sure they're good enough to serve on New Year's Eve."

"Ugh," Elizabeth said. "But it's very noble of you." She kissed Todd, and he and Ken hurried toward the hot dog stand.

"OK," Jessica said, bouncing on her toes. "You go have your fortune told first, Liz! I'll stay here, and, uh—I'll watch the game next door, where the guys try to pound the bottom of that thermometer thing with a hammer, and ring the bell on top. More research, you know. We have to see which games are the most popular."

"Ha!" Elizabeth said knowingly. "You mean research on those three guys in Marine uniforms who just got into line," she said. "The ones with the big muscles."

Jessica lay the back of her hand against her forehead. "It's a dirty job," she said in a melodramatic voice. "But somebody has to do it."

Elizabeth burst out laughing. "All right!" she said. "You win. I'll go get my fortune told. But if Madame Renata sees foot-long hot dogs in my future, I swear I'm going to be sick."

Nora watched in fascination as Margo started on her third hot dog from room service, a little before noon on Sunday.

179

"What are you staring at?" Margo asked through a mouthful of food. "Haven't you ever seen anyone eat a hot dog?"

"Sure," Nora said, peering through a miasma of sickening hot dog smell. She fought back nausea. "But I've never seen anyone who looks exactly like me eat three of them in a row."

Margo shrugged. "They're good hot dogs," she said. Then she swallowed and grinned. "It is pretty wild, isn't it—the two of us, I mean? It's just like looking in a mirror!"

Nora nodded solemnly. Of course, she had been startled the night before by the sight of her double. But last night she'd seen only her facial features replicated. Now Margo had showered and washed her hair. She was even wearing a pair of Nora's jeans and Nora's red blouse. Her long black hair was as straight and silky as Nora's own. Her skin had the same golden tan.

"I feel as if I've spent my whole life trying to put together a jigsaw puzzle," Nora said. "But there was always this one missing piece. Now I've found it, and it's like I'm complete for the first time in my life. I have my kindred spirit beside me, and finally I'm a whole person!"

"Would you pass me a couple of those ketchup packets?" asked her kindred spirit.

Nora smiled. "Sorry," she said. "You probably haven't been able to afford a real meal in a week—and here I am, blabbing on about kindred spirits."

"It's OK," Margo said. "I know where you're coming from. I told you that I've been studying the Wakefield twins all year. Well, that's how they are—kindred spirits. They have kind of a psychic connection between them, like the way you heard voices in your dream that sound like the voices in my head."

"I thought you were asleep last night when I said that," Nora said, confused.

"I guess I was kind of drifting off," Margo said. "But it was the first thing I thought of when I woke up this morning." She finished off the last of her potato chips, and Nora cringed when she wiped her greasy fingers on the red blouse. "Did you know that the Wakefield twins sometimes have the exact same dreams?"

Nora shook her head. "But how would you know something like that?" she asked. "You can't learn that kind of thing just by watching somebody."

"It depends on how closely you watch them," Margo said with a shrug. She pulled over a dish of chocolate pudding and dug into it. "Personally, I believe in watching very closely," she said with a devious grin.

"For instance, every now and then I borrow Elizabeth's diary for a few hours. I've even got parts of it photocopied, if you'd like to see it."

"Is there a lot of juicy stuff in there about that gorgeous boyfriend of hers?"

Margo rolled her eyes. "Not as much as you'd think. Elizabeth is such a prude, she makes me want to throw up."

Nora cringed at the thought of the three hot dogs and the pink-and-white carpeting.

"I've been researching them, too," Nora said, handing her a file of information she'd collected. "I've seen newspaper articles, yearbooks, and even court records from Elizabeth's trial last year."

"Pretty impressive for one week," Margo said, leafing through the file. "I'd say that we make a good team."

Nora glowed at the praise. "I've also been trying to hang out this week in places where the Wakefields' friends are likely to be," she said. "I've been able to eavesdrop on several useful conversations that way."

"What did you find out?"

"For one thing, Jessica and Elizabeth are in charge of a big New Year's Eve bash at that carnival out at the Ramsbury fairgrounds, a few miles outside of Sweet Valley. Every teenager in town will be there."

Margo's face grew thoughtful. "A carnival, huh?" she asked. "Have you looked into it? What will it be like?"

"They're planning on all the normal carnival things," Nora said. "A Ferris wheel, a Tunnel of Love, games, prizes, cotton candy, a House of Mirrors—"

Margo looked up. "Oooh, a House of Mirrors!" she said, a smile spreading across her face. "Now, that has possibilities!"

"What are you talking about?" Nora asked.

"You said you wanted to make the Wakefields suffer," Margo said with a shrug. "We're almost ready to do it."

Nora stared at her, puzzled. "I came here to avenge your death," she said. "But you're alive, so I don't have to do it anymore."

Margo smiled grimly, dropping her spoon with a clatter. "Oh, yes, you do," she said, staring intently into Nora's eyes. "We both do."

"What do you have in mind?" Nora asked.

"The same thing I had in mind last year," Margo explained. "But doubled. We both know we were gypped out of a happy childhood and a perfect family."

Nora nodded thoughtfully. "You're right," she said. "Jessica and Elizabeth don't deserve everything they have. But we do."

"We can make the Wakefield family pay for that," Margo said, a cold glint in her steel gray eyes. "The Wakefield twins' lives should have been ours. And they still can be."

The smell of incense greeted Elizabeth as she lifted the flap on the purple tent.

"Come in, child," Madame Renata said in a husky voice. The fortune-teller was at the opposite side of the dim tent. Elizabeth stared around her. "This is really good," she said under her breath, impressed by what she could see in the purplish glow of the tent's interior.

The place looked exactly as she would expect a fortune-teller's tent to look. Tiny star-shaped points of white light were sprinkled around the room—cast by several paperweight-sized hollow brass globes, with stars cut into their surfaces and some sort of light source inside.

On her white-blond hair Madame Renata wore a violet turban that was shot through with silver threads, and a complicated arrangement of scarves and robes in the same range of purples as her tent. She sat at a low table that was draped in black. A crystal ball shone softly in its center, like a giant pearl. On a shelf behind her, Elizabeth could see an arrangement of multicolored crystals, clay and fabric figures, and card decks.

"What would you like to see, child?" the fortune-teller asked.

Elizabeth drew closer and saw that the expression on Madame Renata's face was somehow both distant and intense, as if she were gazing deep into another world.

"Oh, I don't know what I want to see," Elizabeth said. "I've never done this before. What do you usually look at—romance and careers? And how do I choose whether I want you to do my palm, the cards, or the crystal ball?"

Madame Renata reached for her hand, and Elizabeth's eyes widened. An electric current seemed to pass through her body at the touch of the fortune-teller's hand. She shivered, and then chastised herself for being caught up in the ambience. *It's just static electricity*, she told herself.

"I will read your palm," Madame Renata decided suddenly, her thinly penciled eyebrows raised. "I feel strong emanations," she added softly, as if speaking to herself. She motioned to a low stool, and Elizabeth sat down nervously.

"Close your eyes and open your mind," Madame Renata said, stroking her palm with a touch that was lighter than a cloud. Then the stroking stopped, and she felt the fortune-teller's hand go rigid.

"What is it?" Elizabeth asked, her eyes popping open.

The woman stared at Elizabeth's hand silently. Her face remained perfectly still, but in her eyes Elizabeth saw surprise, and then fear.

It's all part of the act, she told herself, trying to ignore the goose bumps she suddenly felt on her bare arms.

Madame Renata's chin trembled as she raised her gaze to Elizabeth's face.

"What's wrong?" Elizabeth asked.

"Th-there is more than one of y-you," the fortune-teller stuttered.

Elizabeth let out her breath. "Oh, is that all?" she asked, laughing. "That's because I have a twin sister."

Madame Renata gazed into her eyes, and Elizabeth felt as if the fortune-teller was looking deep into her past—or her future. The fortune-teller's face suddenly looked as pale as her crystal ball in the dim, purplish light of the tent. She turned back to Elizabeth's palm and traced her life line with a trembling finger. "There's more to it than that," she whispered finally, her voice quavering.

"What do you mean?" Elizabeth asked. A part of her still insisted that fortune-telling was only a game. But she couldn't deny the power of the woman's words. "What do you see?" she asked, her voice rising.

Suddenly the tent seemed very cold, and Elizabeth began to shiver as Madame Renata slowly raised her eyes. Elizabeth gasped for air, feeling as if she were suffocating on the smell of incense. She stared into the fortune-teller's still, white face. The woman's eyes had grown huge and were as dark as the blackest night. Suddenly she seemed older than time.

"Be careful!" Madame Renata warned in a deep, rich voice that was potent with meaning. "Be very careful—if you want to reach the New Year alive."

Elizabeth's shivering grew more violent. She shook her head wordlessly, a sense of horror rising within her like bile. Then she snatched her hand away and raced from the tent, wondering if she would ever be free of the thick, choking fragrance of Madame Renata's incense.

Chapter 12

Nora stared at the neat, comfortable-looking split-level house. She and Margo were parked a block away from the Wakefield home, in a sheltered alley just off Calico Drive, and the new-car smell inside their rented Jeep was clogging her throat with greenish fog. She opened the window and stuck her head out, gulping deep breaths of the brisk morning air.

Nora had hung on to her rented Miata, as well—at least for the time being. She and Margo had a lot of work to do. They might need the extra transportation. But the black Jeep, as bad as it smelled, was an important part of their plan.

"The twins' Jeep is still parked in front of their house," Nora said with an impatient sigh when she could breathe again. "I thought those girls we heard at the mall said there was a carnival planning session this morning."

"They did," Margo said, lowering the driver's-side visor to shield her blue-green eyes from the sun. "And Ms. Responsible Twin Elizabeth wouldn't dream of missing it—or of letting her sister miss it. Don't worry. They'll be running out of the house and jumping into their own Jeep any minute now." She stared thoughtfully at Nora. "In the meantime, let's go over some of the basics again, like I've been teaching you. Try this one: What's Jessica's favorite color?"

"Purple," Nora said automatically.

"What did the twins drive before the Jeep?" Margo asked.

"Their mom's old Fiat convertible," Nora answered. She checked the mirror on her own visor to make sure her eyes looked right. She wasn't used to wearing contact lenses, and the left one was itching. But she had to admit—with the blue-green eyes and her hair pulled back in a ponytail, she did look exactly like Elizabeth Wakefield.

"Here come the twins now!" Margo said, pointing.

A block away, Jessica and Elizabeth were walking down the driveway to the street, laughing and gesturing. Nora felt an angry knot in the pit of her stomach. The Wakefield twins had such a happy life together, while the Chapelle sisters had been torn from each other at a young age. It wasn't fair.

They have no right to be so happy, said a low, raspy voice in Nora's head. Her eyes widened. She turned to Margo, who was gazing intently at the Wakefield twins, with fury blazing in her eyes. Margo obviously hadn't heard the voice.

Nora opened her mouth to tell her about it, but Margo spoke first.

"They have no right to be so happy," Margo said quietly.

Nora felt a prickling sensation skate down her spine. At the same time, she felt connected, as if the voices in their heads forged a link between the Chapelle twins. Nora put a hand on Margo's shoulder, and Margo squeezed it in an unspoken pact. Then they turned back to the window and took in every detail of Elizabeth's and Jessica's outfits and hairstyles.

"Our jeans were a good bet," Margo said, patting her own knee. "Both twins are wearing them today."

Nora untwisted her hair from its ponytail and arranged it in barrettes, while Margo ruffled through a shopping bag full of clothes. She had been working for a year on duplicating items in the Wakefield twins' wardrobes. But buying clothes was expensive, and shoplifting them was risky. Now, with Nora's money from Blanche, the girls had been able to add a lot to Margo's collection.

"Jessica's wearing her pink tank top," Margo said, pulling one from the bag. "It's one of my favorites. And here's a white cotton sweater like Liz has on."

"I'm glad she's wearing long sleeves," Nora said, accepting the sweater as she unbuttoned her own blouse. "I'm still working on exactly the right blend of makeup to hide the tattoo on my arm." They pulled the tops on over their heads, and Nora realized that she was no longer self-conscious about dressing in front of Margo. She felt as if she had known her twin all her life. In a way, she realized, she had. They were two halves of the same person.

The Wakefields climbed into their Jeep and sped away down the street. As they disappeared from view, Margo gunned the engine of the second Jeep. "Pop-quiz time again!" she announced as she rounded the corner onto Calico Drive. "What's Lila Fowler's favorite ice-cream flavor?"

"Million-dollar mocha!" Nora shouted out.

"Which Wakefield twin has kissed Bruce Patman?" Margo asked.

"That's a trick question!" Nora objected. "Very sneaky, but you can't fool me—both twins have kissed him. They think he's kind of a jerk, though, even if he is rich and gorgeous."

"Good job!" Margo said, surprised. "You really have been working hard at this. Who's the funniest kid in the junior class?"

"Winston Egbert," Nora answered as the Jeep approached the Wakefield house. "Liz likes him as a friend," she added. "Jessica has better taste. She thinks he's a dweeb."

Margo jerked the Jeep to a stop in the Wakefield driveway, alongside Mr. Wakefield's LTD. "You scored one hundred percent. And that's it for this round of Trivial Pursuit," she said. "Now it's show time!"

A minute later Margo and Nora walked into the Wakefield house through the kitchen door. The warm scent of coffee filled the room with a homey, creamy mist. And Nora's heart raced as she caught her first close-up look at Jessica and Elizabeth's parents—soon to be her and Margo's parents.

"What are you two doing back already?" Mrs. Wakefield said, looking up from her section of the newspaper.

Nora smiled happily. Alice Wakefield wasn't Emmeline Chapelle. But if Nora couldn't have her own, real mother back, Mrs. Wakefield was the best replacement she could imagine. Jessica and Elizabeth's mother was intelligent, sensitive, and beautiful, without a single streak of gray showing in her blond hair.

Even in jeans and a simple blouse, she oozed style.

Tall, dark-haired Mr. Wakefield looked even more handsome today than he had through the window on Christmas Eve. "I thought you two were worried about being late," he said, setting down his empty coffee mug.

"What? Me, worry?" Margo said, in a perfect imitation of happy-go-lucky Jessica. She ran a hand through her loose blond hair. "Worrying gives you wrinkles. Besides, Liz and I are in charge of this fund-raiser. They can't start without us—no matter how late we are!"

Nora rolled her eyes. "Very considerate, Jess."

"Is there a last-minute emergency?" Mr. Wakefield asked. "You're not having trouble with the Jeep, are you?"

Margo sighed. "No, it's not the Jeep," she said. "But it certainly is an emergency. There's a stain on my tank top!"

The Wakefield parents looked at each other and laughed.

"Make fun of me all you want," Margo said melodramatically. "But I can't go out in public like this! What would people say?"

Nora laughed. "They'd say, 'What? Is that Jessica Wakefield—on time, for a change?'"

Both Wakefield parents rose to their feet. "Well, I hope it's a productive meeting, kids—

no matter what you're wearing," Mrs. Wakefield said. "But your father and I have to get going, too. We can't waste all this good vacation time."

Both parents kissed Margo and Nora on the forehead.

"We'll be at the big after-Christmas bazaar downtown," Mr. Wakefield announced. "As for this evening, you girls are on your own. This is the night that Sharon and Sam Egbert invited your mother and me over for dinner."

Mrs. Wakefield began to follow him out, but she turned around in the doorway. "Oh, Elizabeth!" she exclaimed. "Speaking of tonight, I left a note for you on the counter. Enid just called. She said *Invasion of the Body Snatchers* is playing at the Plaza Theatre. Unless you tell her otherwise, she'll pick you up at seven thirty this evening. Jess, aren't you and Ken going to see that one tonight, too?"

Margo smiled. "Yep," she said. "You know how guys are about horror movies." She rolled her eyes. "Body snatchers! How dumb. Personally, I'm a lot more interested in *Ken's* body."

After Mr. and Mrs. Wakefield went out, Margo and Nora listened for the sound of the LTD revving up and driving away. Then they turned to each other, grinning triumphantly. "We did it!" Margo exclaimed. "We fooled

Jessica and Elizabeth's own parents!"

Nora chose a mug from the counter and inspected it for cleanliness. Then she sat carefully at the kitchen table, already feeling as if she belonged there.

Margo slid into the chair next to Nora's, put her feet up on another chair, and helped herself to some coffee. "What did you think of your first experience at being a member of the Wakefield family?" she asked. "Do you still want to go through with this?"

Nora nodded, suddenly serious. "I want this life at any price," she declared quietly, gazing at the sparkling, sunlit kitchen. "And no one's going to stand in my way."

"You'll have it," Margo promised. "We both will."

"So what next? Do we stick around here for a while?" Nora asked hopefully.

"For a while," said Margo. "I'd like to nose around Elizabeth's latest diary entries, for one thing."

"The way I see it," Nora said, "the only way this can work is if we divide and conquer."

"What do you mean?" Margo asked.

"Well," Nora reasoned, "we're going to be popping in and out of their lives, stirring up trouble and manipulating things until it's time to make our final move, right?"

"That's the plan."

"No matter how convincing we are at impersonating them, they're going to know something's up if they can compare notes."

Margo nodded. "You know, you're getting good at this!" she said, her eyes narrowed. "Almost too good. I thought *I* was the criminal mastermind of this operation!"

Nora laughed. "You are. But you're a good teacher."

Margo looked at her thoughtfully. "The other reason we have to get them mad at each other is because they'll be more vulnerable that way," she continued after a moment. "If they're not spending time together, one twin won't realize something weird is going on when we get to the other one first, kill her, and dispose of the body."

Nora nodded. A month earlier, talking about killing people and disposing of their bodies would have frightened her. But that was the old Nora, the incomplete Nora. Now such conversations gave her a rush of power. Now she was strong. She had Margo by her side, and the same silent, raspy voice spoke to them both, connecting them. Through her blouse she traced the Gemini tattoo on her arm. "Fourteen years ago you and I were torn apart," she said in a low voice. "Now we will tear the Wakefield twins apart. It's what they deserve."

Margo beamed. "It's also the most fun part of the plan!" she said gleefully. "I love seeing the golden girls miserable! And I know just where to start," she added, jumping up and running to the phone. "Elizabeth is going out with Enid tonight, is she?"

Nora followed her and leaned in close to listen while Margo dialed a number.

"Quiz time!" Margo said. "Whose phone number was that?"

"Todd Wilkins," Nora answered instantly just before he answered.

"Hi, Todd," Margo said into the phone, in a voice that was Elizabeth's. "What are you doing tonight?"

Todd smiled uncertainly as Elizabeth answered the door Tuesday night, wearing a blue blouse that brought out her eyes. He waited, hesitantly, for her reaction. Elizabeth had been acting more like herself since Christmas Day. At least she wasn't bursting into tears for no reason and running out of rooms anymore. But he still detected an uneasiness in her anytime he and Jessica were in the same room together—and anytime anybody mentioned his accident.

This time there was nothing to worry about. Elizabeth's eyes lit up when she saw him on the doorstep. He opened his mouth to greet her.

But before he could say a word, she placed her hands on his shoulders and gave him the warmest, most passionate kiss they'd shared since before the accident.

He smiled back at her, glad that she finally seemed to be getting over whatever had been making her so crazy. "What was that for?" he asked softly as soon as he'd caught his breath.

"To let you know I'm sorry about being so manic lately," she said.

"Sometimes I wonder if we should argue more often," Todd said, wrapping his good arm around her and feeling her soft, smooth hair against the side of his face. "Making up is always so much fun."

"Hmmm," Elizabeth sighed. "Can't we make up without arguing first?"

"Sounds good to me," Todd said. Suddenly he pulled back and looked her over from head to toe. He laid a finger against his chin. "Something's different," he announced, "but I'm not sure what it is."

"Different?" Elizabeth asked. "What do you mean? Oh, I know. It's the blouse. It's new."

"No," he insisted. "It's more than that. You look a little different. Did you get your hair cut or something?"

"Don't be silly," Elizabeth replied. "I'm exactly the same as I've always been."

She reached up to kiss him again, and Todd

lost himself in the feel of her lips against his. Whatever she might have changed about herself, he approved.

"Elizabeth!" Todd said, reluctantly pushing away from Nora's eager kiss. He squinted to see the time on the dashboard clock of his BMW. "It's eight o'clock. The movie's starting!"

Nora shrugged. "No, it's not," she said, tracing the outline of his face with her finger. "The previews, remember? We've got at least another five minutes."

"It's not like you to cut it this close," he said.

She kissed him on the earlobe, grateful that his hair smelled as if it had been freshly washed. Of course, Elizabeth would never date anyone who was unclean.

"You're the one who said you like making up," she reminded him. "And I feel like we have a lot of lost time to make up for." *Sixteen years of misery,* she thought, *while Elizabeth has had a perfect life, with people like Todd to love her.*

"Well, if you insist," he murmured, leaning in close for another kiss.

A few minutes later she glanced over his shoulder and shifted her wristwatch into the light from the window. She sighed, pretending to be reluctant. "I guess we should get going," Nora said. "The movie's probably about to start."

She straightened out the blue blouse she and Margo had found, an exact duplicate of one Elizabeth had bought the week before. It was the same blouse that Jessica had borrowed to wear that night on her own date with Ken.

"I don't know," Todd said with a grin. "I was kind of enjoying these previews."

They entered the darkened theater a minute later and stood in back while their eyes adjusted to the dimness. Nora scanned the crowd and spotted Elizabeth and Enid exactly in the center of the fourth row. Jessica and Ken were supposed to be there, too. But they were nowhere in sight.

"Let's sit in the front," she whispered into his ear as the opening credits began to roll. "It's easier to get good and scared that way."

Donald Sutherland held his girlfriend's weakened body in his arms. "Elizabeth, I love you," he cried. But he couldn't wake her. He was too late. Her eyelids fluttered and were still. The old Elizabeth was dead. Sutherland held her close. Then he shrank back, aghast. Her head was beginning to sink in on itself, and her body to crumble and wither.

The other Elizabeth—the one who was sitting, mesmerized, in the fourth row of the movie theater—jumped in her seat. She couldn't remember feeling so spooked by a movie. And it didn't help that the main female character had her name.

A little voice in her head always told her that horror movies were stupid, that she was too intelligent to be taken in by the outlandish story line. But as usual, once she was sitting in the darkened theater, she was hooked.

Suddenly the spell was broken. In the first row of the theater, a couple shifted position. Part of the girl's head blocked Elizabeth's view.

"Not again!" Elizabeth whispered as she scrunched closer to Enid to see the whole screen. "I don't mind a little necking in the movies, but this is ridiculous!" Even in a movie that was so engrossing, it was distracting to be sitting behind a girl and boy who obviously thought they were alone in the theater.

"They must be scuba divers," Enid whispered back. "I don't think they've breathed at all since the first scene."

Elizabeth forced her attention back to the screen and was again swept up in the plot and special effects.

Sutherland heard a voice and whirled around. He gasped. Elizabeth was standing behind the trees. But her smile was vacant, and he knew this was not his Elizabeth. The body and face were as lovely as before. But inside, she was different. Her soul was no longer her own. The pod people had taken her.

He backed away from his girlfriend's empty beauty. Then he turned and ran.

Sutherland ran through the dark warehouse district, and Elizabeth felt as if she were running with him. Fire blazed in the background as the pod people chased him. They would steal his identity and replace his body with a replicate whose heart was evil and whose mind was not his own. Elizabeth clutched Enid's arm as Sutherland darted through an alley toward the pier. Then he shot underneath it and froze, crouching silently on the rocks, waiting.

Nearby, the waters of San Francisco Bay lapped against the pilings, but the noise of pursuit was intensifying. Then the footsteps of the pod people echoed on the wood of the pier, directly overhead. Elizabeth held her breath. A man knelt over a hole in the pier and shone a flashlight into the cavern below. Sutherland ducked behind a piling.

"We'll get him," somebody said. "He can't stay awake forever." When you slept, you became vulnerable. That was when the pods slipped up behind you and took you for their own.

Elizabeth was shaking. She jumped when a

voice spoke in her ear. "Are you OK?" Enid whispered in the dark.

"I'm fine," she choked out.

By the last scene of the movie, Elizabeth was crawling out of her skin, she was so tense. Sutherland met a friend, one of the last few people in San Francisco who still had her own mind and soul. She needed his help. Bagpipes played an eerie version of "Amazing Grace" in the background as Sutherland opened his mouth and emitted the deafening, mechanical-sounding scream of the automatons. The pod people had won.

Chapter 13

Elizabeth forced herself to breathe normally as the last of the credits rolled by on the screen. She stood up slowly and fought the urge to look over her shoulder.

"That gave me the creeps," she confided to Enid with a shudder. "It was much scarier than *The Shining*." Then she noticed Enid's chalk white face. "You, too?" she asked with a laugh. "Well, I'm glad I wasn't the only one—"

She followed Enid's gaze to the couple in the front row who had been necking throughout the movie. Elizabeth froze, aghast. The boy's back was to her, but she would know Todd's wavy, dark brown hair anywhere. A cast covered his left forearm and wrist. And his arms were around a girl with a heart-shaped face and long blond hair. Jessica.

Elizabeth gulped. Her original suspicions had been right. The twins' happy Christmas together had been a farce. Todd was in love with Jessica.

Elizabeth's eyes met Jessica's, and Jessica held her gaze steadily, her face a mixture of surprise and triumph. Elizabeth shook her head, disbelieving. Her lower lip began to tremble. Then she fled up the aisle, in tears.

Forty-five minutes later Jessica stood on the front step of the Wakefield house, humming an off-key version of "Amazing Grace" to herself as she watched Ken climb into his car. The memory of his good-night kiss still tingled on her lips. She didn't remember much of the movie, but it had definitely been the best date she'd had all month. Ken was the sweetest, most exciting guy in the world. And the best kisser. Best of all, he adored her.

She reached for the doorknob and then stopped, sure she'd heard something rustling in the rhododendrons near the front door. She peered into the darkness, but she couldn't see anything. "Probably just a bird," she murmured to herself. She smiled dreamily as she opened the door and let herself in.

"How dare you?" Elizabeth screamed, charging down the steps.

"How dare I what?" Jessica asked, mystified.

She was sick of Elizabeth's on-again, off-again hysteria. "Whatever I did, can you criticize me for it tomorrow? I just had a great date, and I'm in too good a mood for you to spoil it now."

Elizabeth's mouth dropped open. "I don't believe this!" she sputtered, her face twisted with anger. "How can you stand there and brag about your great date, knowing what you did to me tonight?"

Jessica grimaced as realization washed over her. "Oh," she said. "I did sort of borrow your brand-new blouse," she admitted, stroking the soft blue fabric. "I'm sorry I didn't ask first, but you weren't home yet, and my purple one needed ironing—"

"Don't play dumb with me!" Elizabeth demanded. "You took a lot more than my blouse tonight. Jessica, I saw you at the theater!"

"Look, Liz, whatever I did, I'm sorry. Can we talk about it tomorrow? I want to go upstairs and fall asleep remembering what a wonderful night I had, so I can give Lila all the details in the morning."

"My God, Jessica! What was all that about on Christmas Day? You sat in front of the fire and told me nothing was going on between you and Todd—"

"Is that what this is all about?" Jessica exclaimed, rolling her eyes. "Geez, Elizabeth, I was telling you the truth when I said that. Read my lips: *Nothing is going on between me and Todd!*"

"You vowed that we would be friends forever, and that we'd never have another real fight!"

"You're the one who started this fight," Jessica pointed out. "I still don't even know what we're fighting about!" She sidestepped Elizabeth and headed toward the stairs. "And frankly, I'm not listening to another word!"

Elizabeth grabbed her shoulder and whirled her around. "Oh, yes, you will!" she screamed. "You don't know what we're *fighting* about? You sit through an entire movie, necking with *my* boyfriend, and then you have the nerve to tell me *I* started this fight?"

"Your boyfriend?" Jessica said, shaking her head. "I necked through the whole movie, all right—but it was with *Ken.*"

"Don't treat me like a complete idiot!" Elizabeth yelled. "I saw you!"

"If you did, then you saw me kissing *Ken.*"

"You were sitting in the very first row, wearing my blue blouse, and you were kissing Todd! Don't you think I know my own boyfriend?"

"You don't even know your own twin!" Jessica shot back. "Yes, I was wearing your blouse. But I was sitting in the back row of the balcony! And I wasn't kissing Todd! I was kissing Ken!"

"Good try, Jessica, but it won't work this time," Elizabeth said, her voice rising. "I'll never believe another word you say! I hate you! And I'll never forgive you for this! Never!"

Elizabeth pushed past her twin, wrenched the front door open, and stomped outside. The door slammed behind her with a crash that reverberated through the empty house.

Nora flinched as the outside wall of the Wakefield house vibrated with the slamming of the front door. Through the rhododendron branches she saw Margo turn away from the window. Just a few feet away Elizabeth stormed down the front steps and disappeared into the night.

"Well done," Margo whispered, slapping Nora on the back. "You fooled Todd, and you incensed Liz. There's no way that her relationship with Jess will survive this!"

Nora smiled at her twin's approval. "Thanks," she said. Margo checked to be sure nobody was watching. Then she slipped out of the bushes. Nora followed, cringing as the rhododendron leaves brushed against her skin, slightly sticky.

"Now that I've played Elizabeth," Nora said as they walked toward the Jeep, "I'm ready for the ultimate challenge—Jessica. Todd's cute, but I like blond guys."

"You can't be Jessica," Margo argued. "I'm Jessica!"

"Why do you get to be Jessica?"

Margo shrugged. "Because I was Elizabeth last year. Now it's your turn."

"But that's exactly why you should be Elizabeth!" Nora pointed out. "You've got more experience being Liz. Since you took her place last year, I assumed that you would become Liz permanently."

Margo shook her head. "No way!" she objected. "That's one of the reasons it didn't work last year. I'm not convincing as Liz."

"You did a great Liz on the phone to Todd today!"

"But not in person," Margo said, her hand on the door of the Jeep. "Look, Nora, I'm too much of a partyer to be that Goody Two-shoes. She doesn't know how to have fun, she doesn't stay out late, and she's been dating Toddy-boy forever."

"I thought you liked Todd!"

Margo shrugged. "I do, but not for months and months! Did you know that in all this time Todd has never even managed to get Elizabeth out of her clothes? It's positively sick!"

"I'm sure *you* could convince him to."

"That's not all," Margo said. "Elizabeth

helps with the *housework,* for God's sake! You're the neat freak of this duo, not me! I'm even more of a slob than Jessica. Sorry, but this is the way it has to be."

Nora climbed into the Jeep, crestfallen. She and Margo were two halves of the same person. Life was supposed to be perfect now that they were together. So why was a knot of tension building in her stomach? She had never imagined herself arguing with her soul mate.

On the other hand, Nora had her heart set on becoming Jessica Wakefield—not Elizabeth.

"Margo, you have to understand," she said in a low, fervent voice as she drove to the hotel. "All my life, Blanche tried to get me to act like Elizabeth—quiet, polite, and responsible. I didn't want to fit that mold then, and I don't want to do it now."

Margo stared at her thoughtfully. "But this Blanche witch was into all that debutante stuff, right? You said she was always trying to make you wear the right clothes and go to the right parties."

Nora nodded. "So?"

"You said it was too superficial," Margo reminded her. "Well, Jessica spends her whole life worrying about the right clothes and the right parties. So you'd be playing right into Blanche's hands if you became Jessica."

"That's different," Nora objected.

"Besides," Margo continued, "you've got that tattoo on your arm. We can hide it better if you're Elizabeth. She wears long sleeves more often than Jessica does."

"But we can't hide my tattoo forever!" Nora objected, stopping the Jeep at a red light. "Sooner or later Mr. and Mrs. Wakefield are going to see my arm. I'll never convince them that Elizabeth would get herself tattooed! If I'm Jessica, they'll be ticked off—but at least they'll believe that I would do it."

Margo shook her head. "This is my show," she said. Nora detected a hint of menace in her voice. "The cast includes me in the role of Jessica, and you as Elizabeth. There are no understudies."

Nora turned the Jeep into the parking lot at the Sweet Valley Inn. Then she sat for a moment, leaning glumly on the steering wheel as she gazed at the Pacific Ocean, its waves gilt-edged in the moonlight. A few palm trees were silhouetted against it, their trunks glistening. It was so beautiful here in Sweet Valley—not as she'd imagined brisk, pine-scented New Hampshire to be, but just as perfect in its own golden way. For the first time since she'd been reunited with her twin, Nora felt like crying.

"Please think about it," she urged Margo in

a tiny, dejected voice. "We don't have to decide right now."

Margo shook her head. "We're not deciding right now," she said. "The decision was made almost a year ago. And I'm Jessica!"

"All right," Nora said with a shrug.

Margo stared at her, as if surprised that she'd given in so suddenly.

Nora sighed and stared at the full moon, lovely and unreachable. She hated going against Margo's wishes. But she wasn't ready to give up her dream. Not by a long shot.

Sweet Valley was breathtaking, even at night. Elizabeth walked the dark streets, watching the black silhouettes of palm trees against the midnight blue sky. The moon illuminated well-manicured lawns—in front of tidy split-level and ranch-style homes that blended into larger, more luxurious residences as she walked out of her own neighborhood. The night looked perfect—romantic, even. But it was all a facade. Her tears fell freely as she walked.

The accident was when the trouble had started, when Jessica and Todd had forged some secret bond. She'd sensed it right away, but then she'd allowed her sister to convince her that she'd imagined the whole thing.

Of course, she realized, it was possible that

Jessica and Todd had decided to cool things off between them right around Christmas. Maybe her few recent happy days with Todd had been real. But now it was clear that Jessica and Todd were unable to suppress their love. Jessica had saved his life, and now they belonged to each other.

"They're the two people I trusted more than anyone else in the world," Elizabeth sobbed, standing still and alone on the sidewalk. "How could they do this to me?"

When she looked up, she realized she was in front of the Wilkins home on Country Club Drive. She stared up at it, overcome with grief and anger. The moon scudded behind a cloud, and the front lawn grew dark, but the massive pillars shone white in the night, and Elizabeth could make out the windows of Todd's bedroom, between the two pillars farthest to the right.

On an impulse she bent over, found a handful of pebbles, and dashed them as hard as she could against the window she knew was closest to his bed.

A moment later the windows shone with light. The shade snapped up, and Todd's head and upper body appeared in one of them. His hair looked tousled, and he was wearing striped pajamas. Todd ran a hand through his hair as he peered outside. Then he shook his head in surprise and opened the window.

"Elizabeth? Is that you?" he called out, his voice hushed. "It's after midnight! What's going on?"

"As if you didn't know!" she challenged.

"Shhh! You'll wake my parents!" he cautioned. "Stay there. I'll be right down."

Elizabeth had gone stark, raving mad, Todd decided as he stomped to the front door. She'd been a maniac ever since the night of his accident—first acting as if she was grateful he was alive, and the very next minute treating him as if she'd like to kill him. He never knew anymore if she'd be sad, angry, casual, affectionate, or completely neutral.

"But this really takes the cake," he muttered to himself as he switched on the light near the front door. "She couldn't get close enough to me at the movies tonight, but now she comes to my house in the middle of the night and talks as if she wants to break my kneecaps."

He clenched his jaw, swung the door open, and stepped outside to meet her. He was fed up with being patient and understanding. It was time for Elizabeth to get her act together.

"What are you doing here?" he asked, pulling her arm. He was hoping to steer her toward the summer house on the west lawn. At least that would get her out of his parents' earshot.

Elizabeth wrenched herself free. "Don't you dare touch me!" she yelled, crossing her arms in front of her as if she were rooted to the front walkway, directly in front of the house. "Not after what you did to me tonight!"

"What did I do to you tonight?" he asked, utterly at a loss. He said a silent prayer of thanks to the architect who had placed his parents' bedroom at the back of the house. "What are you talking about?"

"How can you even ask me that?" she exclaimed, outraged. She stepped toward him, and he backed up as if he were being pushed. "I was there, Todd. I saw you!"

Now he was genuinely worried. Elizabeth looked the same as she always did. It was the same body, the same face, and the same voice. But this was not the Elizabeth he knew. For a moment he thought of the pod people in the movie, taking over the bodies of normal human beings. But that was only a movie. This was real life.

"Elizabeth," he said in a gentle voice. "You're beginning to scare me. Let's talk about this rationally. Tell me what's wrong now. You looked like you were having a perfectly good time earlier tonight."

"Oh, I did, did I? So you knew I was there, and you—" She stopped, seething. Then she continued in a quiet, tense voice. "I don't want to be rational!" she hissed. He took another step back until he was standing in the doorway. "It was bad enough, behind my back—but out in front of everyone! How could you?"

"Elizabeth, I have no idea what you're talking about," he said. "Why don't I come pick you up first thing in the morning? We'll drive somewhere quiet and figure out what the misunderstanding is."

"Misunderstanding? Misunderstanding?!" she screeched, loud enough to make him glad that both his parents were heavy sleepers. "There is no misunderstanding after tonight," Elizabeth continued. "Now I understand perfectly. I understand everything!"

Tears were streaming from her eyes. Part of Todd longed to take her in his arms and hold her close. But he didn't dare. He stared at her wild eyes and disarrayed hair, and worried if something was seriously wrong with her.

"Elizabeth," he began, "I had such a good time at the movies tonight—"

He stopped, shocked, as Elizabeth raised her hand and slapped him squarely across the face. Then she spun on her heel and stormed away, into the night.

Todd stood frozen on the front step, his hand on the side of his face. For a moment he wondered if he should catch up with her and force her to accept a ride home. It wasn't safe for a girl to be out alone after midnight. You never knew what sort of psychos lurked in the dark.

Then he shook his head. If Elizabeth met any psychos while she was in her current mood, the psychos were the ones who would need protection.

Jessica tucked her purple blouse into her black jeans and eyed herself in the bathroom mirror, trying to decide if the blouse was too wrinkled. She loathed ironing. Normally, she would have borrowed something of her sister's to wear to the New Year's Eve carnival—or even cajoled Elizabeth into ironing the purple blouse for her. But Elizabeth hadn't spoken to her in nearly two days. Not since Tuesday night, after the movie.

Jessica couldn't help thinking about another New Year's Eve when Elizabeth had been angry with her. "Exactly one year ago tonight," she whispered, remembering.

Both twins had been dressing for Lila's party. Elizabeth had just discovered that Jessica had spiked her punch before the accident that killed Sam. And Jessica had been overwhelmed with guilt and grief—and about as excited about going to Lila's party as she was about this carnival. She sighed. The carnival was a benefit, and she was one of the co-chairs. She would have to go and smile and greet the New Year, as if she really had something to look forward to. As if her sister didn't hate her.

"No!" she objected, still eyeing her reflection. "I'm not going to let her ruin my evening! This time I have nothing to feel guilty about. I may have felt a little attracted to Todd. But I never did anything about it!" She took a deep breath. The current cold war wasn't her fault. But this time, she resolved, she would take the first step toward making up with Elizabeth. "I'm not going to give up my sister without a fight!" she whispered to her mirror image.

She squared her shoulders and knocked on the door of Elizabeth's bedroom.

"What do you want?" Elizabeth asked harshly, holding the door open a crack. Her hair wasn't brushed yet, and she was wearing her bathrobe.

"I want to talk," Jessica began earnestly. "I keep thinking about what almost happened last New Year's Eve, and I can't stand the thought of us starting next year all mad at each other—"

219

"Learn to live with it!" Elizabeth said, just before slamming the door in her face.

A tinny jingle echoed around Jessica as the bathroom mirror vibrated on the wall, shaking her reflection in the purple blouse. She sighed heavily. She had tried.

"Oh, well," she whispered to her image in the mirror. "I have nothing to feel bad about. I didn't do anything wrong." She shrugged. Elizabeth had been acting strangely ever since the night of Todd's accident, she reminded herself. *Maybe if I just leave her alone for a while, she'll be back to normal soon.*

The doorbell rang.

"Jessica!" her father called up the stairs. "Ken's here for you!"

"Thanks, Dad!" she yelled back. "I'll be right down!"

Jessica grabbed her purple-and-gold earrings and threaded them through her ears. She smiled at her reflection. Then she frowned, considering her blouse again. She tried to smooth out the wrinkles with her hand.

"If you can't beat 'em, distract 'em," Jessica said to the mirror as she undid her second button and then the third. The girl in the mirror did the same and grinned back at Jessica, satisfied.

She turned off the bathroom light and ran downstairs to greet Ken with a kiss. He, at least, still loved her.

But as she turned to close the front door behind her, a strange sensation overtook her. Jessica paused on the doorstep, feeling a tingling at the back of her scalp. A faint voice inside her head told her to stay home, but Jessica brushed the thought away. "I'm having a flashback," she told herself under her breath. She'd heard that same, tiny voice exactly one year earlier as she had left for Fowler Crest. She should have listened to it then. But tonight the voice was only a memory.

"Bye, Mom! Bye, Dad!" she called.

Then she stepped outside into the twilight and shut the door behind her.

Chapter 14

Elizabeth tapped her foot outside the main tent at the carnival, waiting for Enid. She would have preferred to be home with the television set and her own private bowl of popcorn. But she was one of the organizers of the New Year's Eve carnival, and she couldn't let the hospital fund down.

So far, the carnival seemed to be everything she and Jessica had dreamed of when they'd first come up with the idea. At eight thirty in the evening the place was already crowded—mostly with teenagers and a few of their parents and siblings. The air smelled of popcorn and candied apples. The multicolored tents and costumes were cheerful, though a little garish in the bright lights. Laughter and excited conversations mingled with the music of the calliope.

And the Ferris wheel turned in the sky overhead, its sparkling lights making it look like a huge constellation in the night sky.

She was glad that people seemed so happy to be at the carnival—and to be on the verge of a New Year. But she didn't feel as if she had anything to look forward to. Jessica and Todd loved each other, leaving Elizabeth all alone. She had never felt so lonely in all her life. She sighed miserably, wishing Enid would show up.

Elizabeth glanced around for her friend—and froze. Todd was standing a few feet away, watching her hesitantly.

"You haven't answered my calls," he said as he came toward her. "I think we need to talk."

"We have nothing to talk about," Elizabeth snapped, turning her back.

For a moment she sensed him standing there, gazing at her. She could practically feel his eyes on her back as she blinked away her own tears. Then she heard him sigh softly and move off into the crowd.

Todd left Elizabeth and wandered toward the main gate of the carnival. He wished he could leave—just go home and spend New Year's Eve in his driveway, shooting baskets in the dark with his one good hand. But he was on the organizing committee for this carnival. He was obligated to be there.

Elizabeth was mad at him for no apparent reason, and she wouldn't even tell him why. He had corralled Jessica as she and Ken had arrived at the carnival earlier, but she was just as much in the dark—and in the doghouse—as Todd. All she had said was that Elizabeth was possessed and wouldn't speak to her either.

Well, he decided, *I'm not going to stick around and watch all the other couples kissing at the stroke of midnight.* Obligated or not, he would head home before that final countdown began.

Suddenly Enid emerged from a crowd of people near the entrance. Todd's eyes lit up. Enid seemed to be about the only person Elizabeth could tolerate these days. Maybe Enid knew what was wrong.

He edged through the crowd and tapped her on the shoulder. "Am I glad to see you!" he said. "Look, Liz is totally ticked off at me, and I don't know what for. I was wondering if you had any clue—"

Enid's green eyes narrowed as she glared at him. "You have to be kidding," she said finally, her hands on her hips. "What an absolute creep! You've got the nerve to play dumb? After what you did to her?"

"That's just it!" Todd cried. "Enid, I haven't the slightest idea what I did to upset her! We were at the movie that night, and—"

Enid's mouth dropped open. "You mean you even have the gall to admit it?" She shook her head. "I never would have believed it, Todd, if I hadn't seen you with my own eyes!" She stalked away, toward the dance tent where Elizabeth waited, leaving Todd staring up at the lights of the Ferris wheel, feeling even more mystified than before.

"That was great!" Jessica cried, jumping down off the Ferris wheel with Ken. "You can see all the way to the ocean from up there." She linked her arm around Ken's. "You know, I thought I was going to have a lousy time tonight."

"Why would you think that?" Ken asked. "This whole night was your idea!"

Jessica shrugged. "Oh, it's not the carnival," she said. "It's Elizabeth. You know, after the last New Year's Eve party, I thought we'd know better than to ever let another year end with us hating each other."

"You don't hate her, do you?"

"No, but Elizabeth sure hates me," Jessica said.

"I doubt that's true," Ken objected.

Jessica smiled. "Maybe not, but she certainly *thinks* she hates me, which is just about the same thing. The weird thing is that I don't have any idea why she's acting so possessed."

Jessica stopped, blushing. For some reason she didn't want Ken to know that Elizabeth thought Todd and Jessica were in love with each other. *OK*, she admitted to herself, *there was kind of an attraction between me and Todd at the hospital after the accident. But that's all it was! I didn't do anything to be ashamed of!*

Suddenly she really did feel guilty. She had withheld the truth from Todd when he'd tracked her down just inside the main gate earlier. The poor guy was dying to know why he was on Elizabeth's hit list. But Ken had been standing right there, and Jessica was too embarrassed to let Ken hear what Elizabeth thought she saw at the movie theater. So she had allowed Todd to wander off, looking as if someone had run over his dog. She vowed to catch up with him later that evening and tell him about Elizabeth's hallucination, or whatever it was.

"This is getting much too serious," Ken said. "Let's do something fun."

Jessica wrapped her arm around his waist. "How about the Tunnel of Love?"

"Jessica!" he cried. "You are insatiable. We've been through that thing at least four times this evening!"

Jessica laughed. "OK, so what about the House of Mirrors? We haven't done that yet."

"No, I don't think so," Ken said, shaking his head. "You identical twin types might be used to seeing your reflection walking around without you. But not me! Those places always give me the creeps."

"Then you pick something!" Jessica said with mock impatience.

"Cotton candy," Ken said decisively. "And then we'll go into the big tent and dance the rest of the night away, until the countdown to the New Year." He checked his watch. "We have a little over two hours until the stroke of midnight."

"That sounds like a plan," Jessica said. "But look—there's Lila over by Madame Renata's tent. I bet she'll go in the House of Mirrors with me, while you wait in that long line for cotton candy. I'll meet you outside the dance tent afterward."

Ken leaned down to kiss her, but Jessica allowed him only a peck on the cheek. "No time for more than that!" she said. "I can't let Lila get away. Besides, I'm saving my lips for a really good kiss on the stroke of twelve."

"My lips can't wait to wish your lips a happy New Year," Ken said.

Jessica watched him saunter away, his broad shoulders swinging as he moved easily through the crowd. She felt a sudden urge to scramble after Ken and stay close beside him until after the start of the New Year. Then she shrugged off the impulse and ran toward the fortune-teller's tent instead, to catch up with Lila.

"Go with me to the House of Mirrors," Jessica urged her best friend. "It'll be fun."

Lila rolled her eyes. "Come off it, Jess. That's for kids."

"Since when?" Jessica asked. "I thought mirrors were your favorite things in the whole world. It'll be even better than the full-size, three-sided mirror you've got in that ballroom you call a closet."

"Very amusing," Lila said. "But as you can see, I'm waiting in line here so that Madame Renata can"—she read the ornately lettered sign—"'prophesy my future and see into my past.'"

"What's the big secret?" Jessica asked. She put her fingers to her temples, closed her eyes, and spoke in a deep, throaty voice. "In your past I see a wardrobe to die for, a great house, and tons of money," she intoned. "In your future I see a wardrobe to die for, a great house, and even more money." She opened her eyes and spoke in her normal voice. "See? Now you don't have to spend all night waiting your turn. There isn't any line at all at the House of Mirrors. I guess all the kids are at that puppet show near the bandstand."

"Forget it, Jessica," Lila said. "I want to wait

for the fortune-teller. This Madame Renata must be good. You said she even had sensible, down-to-earth Liz shaking in her Reeboks the other day."

"Sensible, down-to-earth Liz has turned psycho," Jessica said. "So I wouldn't take her recommendations too seriously."

"Get Ken to go with you," Lila said. "Aren't boyfriends supposed to indulge your every childish whim?"

"Nope," Jessica said. "Boyfriends are supposed to stand in line for half an hour to buy the cotton candy. It's best friends who are supposed to indulge childish whims. Face it, Lila. It's in your job description."

"Then I'm taking a leave of absence," Lila said. "Besides, what do you need me for? The place is full of mirrors; you'll have company in there, even when you're all by yourself."

"OK, OK," Jessica said. "I guess one of you is about all I can handle at once, anyway. I'll see you in the dance tent later."

"Fine," Lila said. "I'm meeting Tony Alimenti there at eleven."

A few minutes later Jessica stepped through the door into the House of Mirrors. As it closed behind her, she jumped, startled at the sudden silence. The cheerful sounds of the carnival had been extinguished, like a flame.

She walked forward, her eyes adjusting to

the purplish light, and she almost screamed as a figure stepped toward her. Then she stopped, chuckling at herself. It was a blond girl in slim black jeans and a violet blouse; she was looking into a mirror! She groped her way along its smooth, flat surface and suddenly found herself in another room, with more images of herself on every side.

"At least my hair looks good," she said, arranging her bangs. But she could see why Ken hadn't wanted to come in there with her. It was pretty unsettling, seeing herself reflected a dozen times, fragmented, and at crazy angles. The silence really was kind of spooky, she thought. There must be other people in this maze of mirrors, but she hadn't seen or heard anyone. And the place was a whole lot bigger on the inside than it had looked from the outside.

She turned around and around, trying to remember where she had entered the room, and realized that she had no idea which direction she had come from. On all sides of her a girl in a violet blouse turned around and around as well, until all the Jessicas seemed to blend into the purplish light of the mirrored hall. Jessica stopped, dizzy, and stared at each reflection, one by one.

Some of the reflections looked exactly like her in every detail. Others were distorted.

231

Some were wavy; some were dark. Some were twisted into grotesque, evil-looking caricatures of herself. Fear clutched at Jessica's stomach. For a minute she had the scary sensation of not being sure which Jessica was the real one.

"This is so weird," she said. Only afterward did she realize that she had whispered—as if she were afraid that the reflected Jessicas would overhear her. Jessica shuddered. She had to get a grip on herself. She had to get her bearings. But suddenly she felt as if she couldn't breathe.

In a panic Jessica ran toward what she thought was a corridor. But one of the purple-shirted Jessicas was running, too. She and her reflection merged as they both slammed into a wall of glass, their purple-and-gold earrings clanking together. Jessica leaned against the mirror, her hands pressing the cool glass, trying to catch her breath. Then she opened her eyes and gasped. She saw herself reflected to infinity. A girl in a purple shirt stared back at her, blue-green eyes unnaturally bright in the bizarre light. Another girl in a purple shirt was reflected in the mirror behind that girl, and still another reflected girl stood behind her, with the pattern repeating far into the distance, each blond head smaller than the one before.

Jessica was used to seeing an exact replica of

herself, but this was giving her the creeps. There were just too many of them. Her heart was pounding in her chest.

She skidded around a corner and found herself in another room. Reflected Jessicas glided forward on all sides as she walked, and were replicated even in the ceiling and floor. Jessica's face went white, and so did a hundred faces around her. She shuddered. One part of her brain knew she was being silly. She was at a carnival. This was supposed to be fun. But she couldn't shake the feeling that the other Jessicas were watching her, from every side and every angle.

"Of course they're watching me," she said aloud. "I'm looking in the mirrors, so my reflections are looking back." If she didn't look, they wouldn't watch her, she reasoned. But if she didn't look, she'd never find her way out of this maze. She stopped for a moment to try to get her bearings when terror clutched at the pit of her stomach. At the very corner of her eye, one of the reflections had kept moving.

Nora paced across her room at the Sweet Valley Inn, nine strides each way. It was after eleven o'clock, and she had been pacing for more than an hour. By now she knew those nine steps inside and out.

"What happened to Margo?" Nora demanded of the quiet room. "Where is she?" There was no reply. Margo had been out all evening, but she hadn't said where she was going. Now only a faint trace of her dark gray ashtray scent remained.

Obviously, Margo had chosen to spend New Year's Eve terrorizing the Wakefield twins on her own. At first Nora had been hurt. Then she began to pace faster. She balled one hand into a fist and pounded it against her other palm. She and Margo were partners. Margo had no right to operate solo.

Suddenly Nora stopped in midpace, almost falling forward from the momentum. She folded her arms in front of her and stared around at the thousands of spying eyes in the bedspreads and curtains. "She doesn't think I'm up to it!" she realized, furious. "After all I've done, I thought I had proved myself—to myself and to Margo," Nora whispered, striding to the bathroom to gaze at herself in the cracked mirror over the sink. "And she still doesn't think I can do it!"

The hotel manager had tried to move her from this room until the broken mirror could be replaced, but Nora had refused to leave. Except for the eyelet lace and potpourri scent, she liked this room. And she liked the mirror, with its ugly black spiderlike cracks. It reminded her that she was the one on the outside of the mirror. She was the one who was in charge.

She stared into her own eyes, blue-green with her new contact lenses. She'd given up the blond wig and had dyed her hair, pulling it back in barrettes to look just like Elizabeth's.

Nora's pulse began to pound in her chest as she gazed at her image in the mirror—Elizabeth's image. "No!" she screamed. She yanked the barrettes from her hair, tousled her golden waves with her fingers, and unbuttoned the first two buttons of her nightgown. Her expression transformed slowly, her eyes lighting with mischief as the corners of her mouth tilted upward in an I-know-a-secret smile. Jessica stared back at her.

Yes, said the voice inside her head. *This is your destiny.*

"I'll show Margo," she vowed. "I'll show everyone! I'm going to make the ultimate move, and I'm going to do it tonight." Her voice dropped to a whisper. "Good-bye, Nora," she breathed, her eyes a more intense blue-green than the contact lenses alone could account for. "Hello, Jessica."

Elizabeth stood against the inside wall of the big tent, watching her classmates dance by. The room was dim, but a huge mirrored ball rotated

235

overhead, catching glittering fragments of the dancers' images and reflecting them back around the tent like circling butterflies of light and color. Everyone was laughing and talking and singing along with Dana Larson, who led The Droids in a cover version of "When Will I Be Loved?"

Elizabeth picked up a clipboard and inspected the band's play list. After all, she told herself, she was the organizer here. She had a responsibility to make sure everything went well. But she couldn't keep her mind off the words Dana was belting out: *"I've been cheated, been mistreated. When will I be loved?"*

She gazed around the festive scene, telling herself she was just making sure everyone was having a good time. *I am not checking to see if Todd's here,* she tried to convince herself. *I don't care who he's dancing with, even if she does look just like me.* She couldn't pick out Todd anywhere. But he was probably there, hidden with Jessica in some dim corner that didn't catch any of the spots of reflected light from the mirrored ball. *Poor Ken. Poor me.* She checked her watch. Midnight was only fifteen minutes away. Soon her own sister would be on the receiving end of a New Year's kiss that should have been Elizabeth's.

*"I've been made blue. I've been lied to.
When will I be loved?"*

Elizabeth jumped when a hand touched her
shoulder.

"Well, well, Elizabeth," Lila Fowler began
in her usual haughty tone, "where were you just
now, outer space?"

Elizabeth gestured with the clipboard. "Uh,
I was just checking to see when the band's next
break is scheduled," she said, trying to make
her voice sound official. "Can I help you with
something?"

"Your clone was supposed to meet me here
ages ago," Lila said. "Have you seen Jess?"

Elizabeth pursed her lips and forced her
eyes back down to the clipboard. "I'm not her
keeper!" she retorted, willing herself not to cry.
It was none of her business if Todd and Jessica
both happened to be missing just before midnight. But she couldn't help imagining them in
a secluded spot somewhere—maybe in the
Tunnel of Love—creating their own private
New Year's celebration.

"Well, excuse me for living!" Lila said. "But
I'm not the only one who's wondering about
Jess. Ken is looking for her, too. Your mirror
image was heading toward the House of
Mirrors almost two hours ago. Nobody's seen
her since then."

"I told you, I don't know where she is!"

Elizabeth snapped. "And frankly, I don't care."

"I've always admired the close relationship you two sisters share," Lila replied.

"Sorry, Lila, but I've got work to do here," Elizabeth said, pointing to her clipboard again.

"Oh, that's right," Lila said, rolling her eyes. "It's a quarter to twelve on New Year's Eve, so naturally you're wondering if it's time for the band to go on break. Now that would make a whole lot of sense, wouldn't it?"

"What would make a whole lot of sense?" Jessica asked, appearing out of nowhere, her violet shirt dappled with reflected colors from the mirrored ball.

You're not with Todd! Elizabeth wanted to blurt out. But she held her tongue. Of course, she realized, Ken was still Jessica's boyfriend, officially. And he didn't know about Jessica and Todd yet. So, naturally, Jessica had to be back in the big tent in time to usher in the New Year with him.

"What happened to those cute purple-and-gold earrings you were wearing?" Lila asked Jessica.

Jessica shrugged. "I somehow managed to lose one in the House of Mirrors," she admitted, patting her purse. "So I had to take off the other one, too."

"Oh," Lila said. "Are you sure you don't want to spend the night at my house with me and Amy after this? The invitation is still open."

"Thanks, but I'm a little tired already. By the time I say good-bye to Ken tonight, I think I'll be ready to crash. Speaking of which, where are Ken and Tony?"

"Last time I saw them, they were both over there, with Amy and Barry."

"So what are we waiting for?" Jessica asked. "Let's dance!"

Jessica and Lila moved off to find their dates, and Elizabeth was left alone. She stared at the mirrored ball high above, trying to expel from her mind the image of Todd and Jessica, holding hands in the Tunnel of Love.

"I wish she had never saved his life!" Elizabeth declared under her breath. Then she froze, aghast. What kind of a person was she? How could she even think such a horrible thought?

The stage lights dimmed, and the mirrored ball reflected blue-green glimmers throughout the room as Dana began on a classic tune from The Who: *"Nobody knows what it's like to be a bad man, to be a sad man—behind blue eyes."*

Elizabeth shook her head and backed into a dark corner. She couldn't take one more minute of being single and full of dark thoughts, in a room full of happy, carefree couples.

"The heck with staying late to help with the

cleanup!" she muttered under her breath. "Olivia and Enid will cover for me. I'm going home now, and I'm going straight to bed."

As far as Elizabeth was concerned, the New Year could start without her. If she was lucky, maybe she could sleep through the entire twelve months.

It was a few minutes after one o'clock when something brushed against Nora's leg on the dark staircase of the Wakefield house. She clamped her mouth shut to keep from crying out. Of course, it was only Prince Albert, begging to be petted. "Some watchdog you are," Nora whispered to him, trying to pet him without letting too much of her hand touch dog hair. She wondered whether it was true that dogs have fewer germs than people. Then she stopped, feeling her face draining of color. The big dog usually slept in Jessica's room. *That will change*, she couldn't help thinking. But why was he roaming the house? Did it mean that Jessica was still up?

Nora listened for any sounds coming from the twins' rooms. No, she was sure Jessica was asleep. Jessica had come home a half hour ago and gone straight to bed almost as soon as Ken had dropped her off. Nora had waited outside in the bushes until the light in her window flicked off. And Elizabeth wasn't even home yet. She had planned to be at the carnival until about two o'clock, helping with the cleanup work.

Mr. and Mrs. Wakefield were out, too, and Nora figured they'd be out for a long, long time. If their friends' parties were anything like the New Year's Eve parties Blanche and her father used to attend, everybody would be too drunk even to sit up until at least three o'clock. With Steven back at school for a party at the university, this was the perfect time for Nora to end Jessica's old life and begin a new one for her. *As her.* The old Jessica—the undeserving Jessica—was alone in the house. And she was asleep and vulnerable.

Nora shooed Prince Albert downstairs. Then she slipped Margo's long, glittering knife from underneath her black leather jacket. A finger of moonlight reached down the staircase from a window on the upstairs landing, and Nora saw a distorted reflection of her own face in the blade. Her expression was hard—almost ugly. With a start she realized that the image looked exactly like Margo. She almost expected Margo to speak from the knife blade—the way she had spoken from the bathroom mirror.

Nora's mouth went dry. For a moment she wondered if Margo was right. Maybe she really wasn't up to this. Maybe she should wait and let Margo run the show. Margo was the expert.

But if Margo ran the show, then Nora would be stuck being Elizabeth.

No! whispered a raspy voice inside her head. *Jessica is your destiny. You will be Jessica. You are Jessica.*

Nora smiled Jessica's I-know-a-secret smile. Of course, the old Jessica couldn't keep a secret if her life depended on it. But the new Jessica could. And her life did depend on it.

Nora resumed climbing the steps. She gripped the knife like a talisman. She was strong now. Her powers were complete. She would succeed.

Jessica's door was ajar, the room dark beyond it. That explained why Prince Albert was up and about. Nora paused and listened to Jessica's slow, regular breathing. Jessica was asleep, all right. Nora pulled the door closed behind her to keep the dog out while she was completing her mission.

Inside the room Nora steeled herself against the disarray. Clothes and CDs littered the carpet; notebooks spilled across the desk. *Jessica's personal habits might change a bit in the next few months,* she thought. Nothing too drastic or too fast. Just a gradual evolution to a more orderly existence, while retaining the characteristics that made Jessica so appealing—her rebelliousness, her adventurous spirit, and her disregard for rules imposed from above.

Nora gazed down at Jessica's peaceful face—so much like her own, but so young and innocent in sleep. Her mouth was open slightly. One arm was tossed casually over the blanket, which had uncovered the first line of loopy, cursive print on her nightshirt: "Sweet," as in Sweet Valley. *She's sweet, all right,* Nora thought. And revenge was even sweeter. Revenge for a lifetime of happiness bestowed on the wrong twins.

One pillow had fallen to the floor, and Nora leaned over silently to pick it up. She weighed it in her hand as she took a slow, deep breath. She raised the knife in her other hand, aiming for the word "Sweet." Then she hesitated. Jessica looked exactly like herself, Nora. She was about to plunge a knife into her own chest, to watch the life drain from her own body. For a moment she wondered if she was killing the right person. Maybe the person in the bed was herself. Maybe she, standing with the knife in her hand, was the impostor.

It's time, the voices told her, rising to a crescendo in her head, like a hurricane-force wind. *Do it!*

In one fluid motion Nora pressed the pillow against Jessica's open mouth—while with the other hand she stabbed downward with the knife at Jessica's Sweet Valley High nightshirt. As she stabbed her victim repeatedly, a faint, sweet scent danced along the edge of Nora's awareness, tantalizing her with tendrils like mist.

Suddenly she recognized the smell. Magnolia. It was not logical. But somehow it made sense. It had symmetry.

Nora smiled, understanding. The old Jessica Wakefield was dead. A new Jessica Wakefield was about to be born.

Chapter 15

As Nora gazed triumphantly at the still form of the old Jessica Wakefield, a frightened voice whispered something incomprehensible. Nora froze. The voice came again, as soft as a dove's coo. It was not a voice from inside her head.

Then realization crept over her like a rash. Elizabeth was home. And she was in the next room. But she was only murmuring in her sleep, probably roused by the rustle of Nora's stealthy movements or of Jessica's weak flailing. If Nora remained quiet, Elizabeth would stay in bed.

She lifted the pillow from Jessica's face. Even in the faint glimmer of moonlight, Nora could see the blank expression that was frozen on Jessica's white face. Blood was soaking into the bedsheets, staining them with scarlet splotches. Nora had succeeded. Now she could slip through the looking glass and enter Wonderland. Exhilaration coursed through her limbs. In killing Jessica, she had killed her own past. She had set herself free.

Something scratched at the door. The old Nora would have jumped, panic-stricken. The new Nora merely turned and shook her head. "Go away, Prince Albert," she whispered in Jessica's voice—her own new voice.

The dog whined once more and then was silent. Nora was silent, too. The next stage of her plan involved disposing of the body and hiding the bloody mess until she could burn the sheets.

Then a cry sliced through the night.

Jessica was crying, but Elizabeth didn't want to hear her. She was mad at Jessica for something, but she couldn't remember what. It had something to do with a mountain road and a steep, high cliff. A girl whipped off the cap on her head, and long black hair tumbled out, flying behind her on the wind like a flag. It was Margo, and a knife glittered in her hand.

Jessica struggled, and now Elizabeth was afraid. Her sister was in trouble. "Help me, Lizzie! I need you!" Jessica cried.

Elizabeth's pulse was pounding, and her

sheets were drenched with sweat. She knew it, and she tried to wake up, but she couldn't. She couldn't help her sister.

A silent explosion destroyed her world, and an orange fireball rose above the trees, like a beacon. But it was too late. Jessica was covered with blood, and she was falling from the cliff to the white rocks below.

"Jessica!" Elizabeth cried. She sat up in bed, breathing hard. Jessica was in trouble. Elizabeth felt it—knew it. Her body felt paralyzed, but she forced her terror-stricken limbs to move. She half fell out of bed and staggered across her room and through the twins' bathroom.

"Jessica?" she called, pushing open the door to her sister's room. As she did, an arc of light from the bathroom reached across the cluttered carpet. Jessica, dressed in black leather, was scrambling out the window, silhouetted against the moonlight. A knife glittered in her hand, and its blade was wet with blood.

Elizabeth's eyes met the eyes of the girl in the window, and terror rose through her body like a fireball lifting through the trees. The eyes were not Jessica's. They were ice-cold.

Margo was back.

Outside the bedroom door, Prince Albert began to howl, breaking the grasp of those cold blue eyes. Elizabeth ran to the bed, screaming.

Tears streamed down her face as she held her sister's limp body. Jessica's eyes were closed, and the sheets were slick with blood. The girl in black leather slipped through the window. Then she was gone, her blond hair flying out behind her like a flag.

A sick, sweet smell filled her mouth and nose. Elizabeth grew dizzy. Elizabeth's hands dripped blood, and she felt as if she were falling off a steep, high cliff. Somewhere a dog was howling.

Then everything went black.

Mrs. Wakefield laughed and took a deep breath of the cool, clear night air that whooshed in through the car window. "That was some New Year's Eve party," she said, chuckling. "But I thought Cindy Santelli was going to fall off the couch when Sam told that atrocious joke!"

"I can see where Winston gets his sense of humor," Mr. Wakefield remarked. "It was good to see Bert Wilkins and his wife again, too," he continued. "I hadn't had the chance to talk with them since Todd's accident."

A block from the Wakefield house, Alice leaned out the window. "Ned, what is that awful noise?" she asked. "Something is howling."

Her husband laughed. "There haven't

been any wolves in this neighborhood in about a century," he said. "So I guess it must be a dog."

"A very sad dog," Alice said as the car reached the Wakefield house. "I don't think I've ever heard such a mournful sound—"

She gasped. A dark figure leaped from the drainpipe of the house, sprinted across the yard, and disappeared into the night. At the same time, she recognized the howling dog's voice as Prince Albert's.

"Call nine-one-one!" she screamed to her confused husband. The car was still moving when Mrs. Wakefield jumped out and ran to the house, choking back her fear.

When she opened the door to Jessica's room a minute later, Prince Albert pushed past her and ran toward the bed. She flicked on the light.

"Ned!" she screamed, sinking to the floor beside her daughters. "Ned!"

Jessica and Elizabeth lay on the carpeting beside the unmade bed, their arms around each other. Both girls were covered with blood, and the sheets were drenched with it. Jessica's face was a ghostly white. Alice lifted Jessica's hand to check for a pulse. And Prince Albert nosed both girls urgently, as if trying to wake them.

*   *   *

Thousands of lacy eyes spied on Nora as she paced—nine steps across her hotel room and nine steps back. She hated the eyelets in the lace bedspreads and curtains. They had wanted her to fail, and now they were mocking her.

She cursed herself for her impatience. What would Margo say to her? What would Margo do to her? She shuddered and felt a cold, oily sweat breaking out on her forehead. For the first time since the Chapelle twins had met, Nora admitted to herself that she was afraid of her soul mate.

"I should have waited!" she told herself. "I should have done it by Margo's plan!" She spoke the words in rhythm with her heavy strides. Margo had not returned. One sniff told her that. A dark gray layer of air still hung near the ceiling, the residue of cigarette smells from Nora and past occupants of the room. But it was thinner. The pink potpourri puffs were winning.

Jessica was dead, and her family knew it. Now Jessica could never be replaced. Not by Margo. Not by Nora. Not by anybody, ever. She'd heard sirens approaching as she'd jumped into the white Miata, which she had parked a block off of Calico Drive. Margo had taken the Jeep that day, and Nora still had no idea where she was.

And then there was one, said a raspy voice.

Nora thought it was the eyes. But the eyes could not speak. They watched and mocked her in silence. She ran to the mirror, and her fragmented image gazed back at her through the cracks in the glass.

And then there was one, repeated the voice, louder. The voice was not in the mirror. And it wasn't Margo. The voice was in her head, and its vibrations jarred her skull. But Nora didn't know what the voice wanted—what it meant.

And then there was one twin! her image in the mirror told her. It didn't seem strange to Nora that her reflection was moving and talking on its own now, as if it didn't know that it was broken in the splintered glass. Outside the mirror Nora stood, still and silent, shattered into glittering pieces like knives. Jessica wasn't dead. Jessica was in the mirror.

Elizabeth, said the voice in Nora's head.

Elizabeth! said the reflection in Nora's mirror.

Nora grabbed a rubber band from the counter and coaxed her hair into a ponytail. She shrugged off the leather jacket, wiped the bright lipstick from her mouth, and smiled thoughtfully into the mirror. This time it was Elizabeth who smiled back.

"If I can't be Jessica, I'll be Elizabeth," Nora

251

resolved. It was the only logical solution. Jessica's place in the family was permanently filled—even if the occupant was a memory. The only spot left was Elizabeth's, boring or not.

But what would Margo say about Nora's new plan? The reflection in the mirror became a snarling, silent Margo, who caressed a shard of glass with her fingers. *Margo won't like it*, said the voice in Nora's head.

"I don't care," Nora decided, hardening her eyes against her long-lost twin and soul mate. "I will join the Wakefield family," she resolved. "Nothing and nobody will stand in my way. Not even Margo!"

Bloodred flashes lit the darkness behind her closed eyelids. Voices spoke nearby, and sirens screamed. Somebody was asking her if she was awake, but Elizabeth didn't want to be. Something horrible was happening—a waking nightmare. As long as she stayed asleep, it wasn't real.

"Elizabeth, honey? Can you hear me?"

It was a woman's voice. Her mother's voice.

"I think she's coming around," said another woman. Gentle fingers touched Elizabeth's wrist, and the nightmare was back. Blurred images crowded her mind—images of bloody sheets and Jessica's still, white face. She re-

membered a thick red smell and felt dizzy
again.

None of this is really happening, she told
herself. It had all been a dream. Now she
thought she was half lying in a narrow, cramped
space, her head in someone's lap. But that
didn't make sense. She would open her eyes,
and she would be in her warm, comfortable
bed, with Jessica running into her room to borrow a blouse. The rest was all a nightmare. She
almost sighed with relief.

Elizabeth opened her eyes. Her mother's
face came into focus, strained and desolate.
This was no dream. Elizabeth was lying in the
backseat of a car—a police car that was parked
in front of the Wakefield house. Elizabeth's
head was in her mother's lap. A woman in a
uniform was in the doorway, bending over her
to feel her pulse. "Don't worry about anything," said the woman, her voice kind and
gentle. "I'm a paramedic, and you can take it
from me—you're going to be just fine. You're
not hurt, are you?"

Elizabeth opened her mouth to say yes. The
hurt was devastating, paralyzing. She felt as if
half her body had been torn away. She wasn't
going to be just fine. She would never be just
fine again.

"No," she whispered, shaking her head. "I'm
not hurt." There was blood on her hands, and a

253

red smear on her mother's blouse. But she wasn't injured.

From the front seat a police officer leaned over to scrutinize her. "In that case I'm afraid we're going to have to ask you some questions," he said.

Elizabeth's mother whirled on him. "Not now!" she hissed. "Can't you see she isn't ready?"

Elizabeth sat up weakly. "Mom?" she asked, needing to know the truth. "Is Jessica . . ."

Mrs. Wakefield closed her eyes for a few seconds before answering. "We don't know anything yet," she said, staring tearfully at Elizabeth. "They're just loading her into the ambulance now—"

Elizabeth struggled past the paramedic and jumped from the car. The ambulance doors were closing, with her father in the back. Their eyes met, and his expression looked numb. Then the ambulance sped away, lights flashing red.

Forty-five minutes later Elizabeth was pacing. Her tears marked a path across the shiny white floor of the emergency room waiting area. She was vaguely surprised to notice that she was still wearing her terry bathrobe, thrown hastily over her blood-spattered pajamas.

A hand touched her shoulder. "Liz, sit

down," said her father. "The doctors will tell us as soon as they know anything for sure." His face was weary and lined, and Elizabeth felt a numb kind of surprise. She had never thought of him as old before.

"She's dead, isn't she?" Elizabeth asked. "I held her in my arms, and she wasn't breathing. And there was blood everywhere . . . so much blood."

Her father put his hands on her shoulders. "Elizabeth, listen to me," he ordered. "We can't give up hope. The paramedics couldn't revive her at the scene, but Dr. Morales hasn't given up yet. He said there could still be brain activity. . . ." He stopped, his eyes filling with tears, and turned away.

"I think we could all use something hot to drink," Mrs. Wakefield said, walking over with three cups. She forced Elizabeth to accept a cup of hot chocolate. As she took the cup, Elizabeth noticed that her own hands were no longer bloody. But she couldn't remember when she had washed them. Her mother led Elizabeth and her father to an orange vinyl couch.

Elizabeth sipped her favorite drink mechanically, not tasting it. "Why is it taking so long?" she asked tearfully. "I can't stand not knowing!"

"I know, honey," her mother said. But the

strain of waiting had forged deep lines in her forehead, as well. "But it hasn't been that long."

"If only I'd woken up sooner!" Elizabeth exclaimed, absentmindedly twisting off bits from the rim of her hot-chocolate cup. "If I'd come into her room a few minutes earlier, then maybe—"

Mr. Wakefield shook his head. "This is no time for guilt," he told her. "Jessica needs all of us to be strong for her right now."

"This isn't your fault, Liz," her mother said, taking her hand. "There's no way you could have stopped it. Whoever did this to Jessica would have hurt you, too."

"It was Margo," Elizabeth said in a loud, sure voice. "I saw her climb out the window." Over her head her parents exchanged a troubled glance.

"Let's not think about that right now," Mrs. Wakefield said, squeezing her hand. "There'll be plenty of time to straighten it out in your mind later, when the police take your statement."

"Your mother's right," Mr. Wakefield said. "We should all be thinking about Jessica right now."

Elizabeth burst into anguished sobs. "I was mad at her!" she cried. "I had hardly spoken to her in days!"

"Elizabeth, you are more important to your

sister than anyone in this world," Mrs. Wakefield reminded her. "All siblings argue from time to time. I'm sure she knows you didn't mean it."

"But I did mean it!" Elizabeth cried. "She tried to make up with me tonight, before the party," she said. "She came to my room and reminded me about last New Year's Eve. She said she didn't want us to start out the year mad at each other." Elizabeth stared at her hot-chocolate cup, her sobs quieting. "I wouldn't listen to her," she concluded in a small, numb voice. "I wouldn't listen. . . ."

A door swung open, and all three Wakefields jumped to their feet. Dr. Morales walked slowly into the room, running a hand through his thinning hair. He stood for a moment, looking at them.

"Oh, no!" Elizabeth whispered. Suddenly she was trembling so hard that her hot chocolate was sloshing over the sides of the cup. She barely noticed when the doctor gently took it from her hand and led her back to the couch.

"We tried everything," he said quietly. "But the internal damage was too extensive. She had lost too much blood." He shook his head and turned his face away. "I'm terribly sorry," he said a moment later, "but we couldn't save her. Jessica is dead."

Enid leaned against Todd's shoulder as they sat on the cold front steps of the Wakefield house in the dark. A few feet away, Olivia was sobbing quietly. But Todd felt strangely isolated, as if he were looking at them both through the wrong end of a telescope. Enid was shivering. Automatically, he pulled off his letter jacket, jerking it over the cast on his wrist. He wrapped the jacket around Enid's shoulders. But she never looked up—just kept staring at her hands, clenched tight in her lap.

Todd gazed at the stars until they blurred. He drew his good hand across his eyes. There had been no stars on the rainy night when Jessica had saved his life, exactly two weeks earlier. Now he was alive, thanks to her. And Jessica was dead. None of it made sense.

"Where's Ken?" Enid asked in a hushed voice.

"I think he wanted to be alone for a few minutes," Todd answered, his voice sounding strained, even to himself. "He's around the side of the house."

She squinted at her watch. "It's three thirty," she said. "How long do you think it will be before Elizabeth and her parents come home?"

Todd shook his head. "There's no way of knowing," he said, choking on a sob as he thought of the grief and horror Elizabeth must be feeling. He took a deep breath. "When I called the hospital, Mr. Wakefield said they had to go to the police station so Liz could make a statement."

A car screeched to a halt in front of the house, and they jumped to their feet. It was a lime green sports car—Lila's Triumph. Todd sat down again. His body suddenly felt very heavy.

A minute later Lila and Amy were running toward the house. They stopped short, in a pool of moonlight, when they recognized Todd, Enid, and Olivia on the front steps.

Lila began to tremble. Her shoulders slumped, and her face crumpled as she buried it in her hands. "Then it's true about Jessica?" she asked faintly, her voice quavering.

Enid's face looked stricken. "Yes, it's true," she whispered.

"No!" Lila wailed, sinking to her knees on the sidewalk. Seeing Lila lose her composure rattled Todd more than anything else had that night. He felt as if he should comfort her, but he was too numb to move. Olivia stepped forward instead and put an arm around Lila's shoulders.

"Does anybody know what happened?" Amy asked, tears streaming down her face in the moonlight. "All we heard on the radio was that she was killed by an intruder in the house."

"That's all we know, too," Olivia said. She gulped. "She was stabbed to death."

Lila's wrenching cries grew louder. "She was only sixteen!" she wailed.

Todd couldn't watch her—couldn't watch any of them. He didn't want to see his own horror reflected in their eyes. It would be more than he could handle. Instead, he looked at his hands. There, just below his left thumb, he could make out a big, loopy signature on his cast: *Jessica Wakefield.* The *i*'s were dotted with circles.

Todd looked away. He took a deep breath, and then another. Somehow his lungs seemed too small.

"Do the police have any idea who did it?" Amy asked.

"Elizabeth may have seen the person climbing out the window, but she was too upset earlier to describe what happened," Enid said. "Maybe she'll remember something later that will give the police a lead."

"Maybe we should go to the hospital," Lila said through her anguished sobs. "Maybe we could help—"

Todd shook his head. "Mr. Wakefield asked us not to," he choked out. "He said to come here instead of creating a mob scene at the hospital."

"Where's Ken?" Amy asked, looking around.

"He'll be back in a minute," Enid said.

"Elizabeth and her parents may be home soon," Olivia said, swallowing a sob. "We have to get ahold of ourselves. Liz will need us to be there for her."

Todd shook his head helplessly. "I don't know if I can," he whispered. "Besides, Liz might not even want me here," he admitted. "She's been so angry at me for most of the last two weeks."

Enid turned to cast a tight-lipped glare at him, as if she had just remembered that she was supposed to be mad at him, too. Todd didn't even care why anymore. Jessica had saved his life, and now she was dead. And the person he loved more than anyone in the world was suffering through the worst night of her life. He had never felt so useless.

"Elizabeth loves you," Ken reminded him, materializing out of the darkness, his blond hair glinting in the moonlight. "Whatever had her ticked off before, it won't matter tonight."

Amy took Ken's hand. "How are you holding up?" she asked.

Ken nodded but didn't speak. Even in the dim predawn, Todd could see the anguish in his eyes.

"Jessica had such a good time tonight," Lila said with a brave, tearful smile. "Didn't she, Amy? I think she went on every ride and played every game at least once."

"She seemed so happy at the dance," Ken said in a low, calm voice as he stared into the darkness. "She said she was sure it was going to be the best year of her life."

"And now it will be the worst year of Elizabeth's life," Todd concluded. Cold seeped through his jeans from the concrete step, numbing the back of his leg. He wondered if he would ever feel warm again. Todd heard somebody else begin to cry. Then he realized that it was himself. He felt Enid's hand on his arm and clutched it gratefully, wishing the night would end.

Detective Gail Pappas of the Sweet Valley police sighed heavily. "All right, Elizabeth," she said, pacing across the interrogation room where Elizabeth, her father, and another detective sat at a conference table. "Let's go over it once more, but this time I want you to start a few minutes earlier. What made you go into your sister's room in the first place?"

Mr. Wakefield patted Elizabeth's hand. "Take it slowly, honey," he said in a numb, faraway voice. "And try to say it exactly the way you remember."

Elizabeth stared at her hands. The whole scene reminded her too much of her interrogation a year earlier, when she'd been charged with involuntary manslaughter after the accident that killed Sam. Detective Marsh, taking notes at the table now, had been one of the arresting officers then. The pale green cinderblock walls and the scarred tabletop were the same. The room even smelled the same—stale with sweat and cigarette smoke. Her father had been there then, as well. She looked at him now, and he nodded at her.

"I had a nightmare, I guess," she began. "Well, it was sort of a nightmare, but it must have been mixed up with sounds I was hearing from Jessica's room."

"What kind of sounds?" asked tall, red-haired Detective Pappas, leaning over the table to watch her face.

Elizabeth looked away. "I-I don't know," she stammered. "Jessica was calling me. She said, 'Help me, Lizzie, I need you.' But I don't think that was real. It was part of my dream. I knew she was in danger, and that part was real."

"And how did you know she was in danger?" asked Detective Roger Marsh, looking up from his legal pad.

"I just knew," Elizabeth said lamely, "like I always do."

Detective Pappas sighed again, still leaning over the table and glaring at Elizabeth. "Ms. Wakefield, please stick to the facts of the case."

"He asked me a question, and I answered it!" Elizabeth cried, an undertone of hysteria in her voice. "Jessica was in trouble in my dream, and I knew she was in trouble in real life!"

Her father held her close for a minute. "My daughters are"—he closed his eyes—"*were* identical twins," he explained. "I know there's no logical explanation, but this isn't the first time one has known when the other was in danger."

Detective Pappas rose to her full height of six feet. As she turned to resume pacing, Elizabeth noticed that she rolled her eyes in disgust. "And you said that you and Jessica had been arguing?"

Elizabeth nodded. "It seems so stupid now," she admitted. "I thought she was after my boyfriend. But we weren't arguing," she whispered. "We weren't even speaking to each other."

"Did you hear anything else before you went into your sister's room?" asked Detective Marsh.

"Prince Albert—our golden retriever—was whining," Elizabeth said numbly. "And there was something else, like somebody moving around or struggling. But it was soft. I can't be sure."

"Could that sound have been in your dream, as well?" Detective Pappas asked sharply.

"I don't think it was," Elizabeth said carefully.

"But Margo was in my dream. She whipped off her blue knit cap, and her hair flew out like a raven. And it was black." Her voice went up an octave. "Jessica was falling off a cliff, and there was an explosion, like with Todd's accident." The detectives looked confused, but Elizabeth raced on. "And then I opened the door," she said. "And Margo was climbing out the window. But her hair was blond, like mine—and Jessica's!"

Detective Pappas whirled. "Margo again!" she cried, raising her voice. "Ms. Wakefield, I know you have gone through a terrible ordeal. But, frankly, I am losing my patience!" She ran a hand through her thick red hair, so that it stood on end. "We already showed you the death certificate of Ms. Margo Black, aged sixteen."

"But you never found her body," Elizabeth pointed out, "because she's not dead!"

The tall woman clenched her jaw. "As I understand it," she said, "you were actually there, on the scene, when Margo Black died one year ago today. Your own statement at the scene said that you saw her body! You may have dreamed about Margo this morning, but she was not in your sister's bedroom!"

"Margo was there!" Elizabeth insisted, bursting into tears. "I saw her!" Mr. Wakefield handed her a handkerchief. "I know I did!"

"Elizabeth," said Detective Marsh in a

gentle voice. "You had just had a nightmare about Margo, one year after she tried to kill you. Then you saw that your sister had been stabbed. It was dark in the room. It's only natural that your mind would play tricks on you and make you mistake the person at the window for Margo—"

"It was Margo!" Elizabeth screamed. The room swayed, and she gripped the table to steady herself.

"This is getting nowhere," Mr. Wakefield interrupted in a weary voice. "It's nearly four o'clock in the morning! Can't you see that my daughter is on the verge of a breakdown? I want to take her home."

"Mr. Wakefield," Detective Pappas began, "a teenage girl—your daughter—has been murdered. And Elizabeth is an eyewitness!"

Detective Marsh spoke up. "Please, Mr. Wakefield," he said. "As an attorney, you know how important it is for us to get Elizabeth's statement now while the events are still fresh in her mind."

Mr. Wakefield looked at Elizabeth. "I'll try," she whispered, nodding. "But they don't believe what I'm telling them!"

"Elizabeth, it's not that we don't believe you," Detective Marsh said. "I believe that you did see your sister's murderer at the window. That's why we're grilling you so hard on this

266

point. Let's try this again. This time don't inter-
pret or give me your impressions. Just tell me
exactly what you saw—not *who* you saw."

Elizabeth noticed vaguely that her thumb
was beginning to bleed where she'd been picking at the nail. "It was a girl about my age, in a
black leather jacket. She was holding a knife
with blood on it. The moon was shining on her.
I could see long blond hair and cold blue eyes."
She shuddered. "They were Margo's eyes!" She
dissolved into hot, stinging tears.

"Maybe you should bring my wife in," Mr.
Wakefield said in a helpless voice, a hand on
Elizabeth's shaking back. "I think Elizabeth
would feel better with her mother here."

"Your wife is giving a statement about what
she saw from the car," Detective Pappas said. "I
don't want to compromise her testimony by al-
lowing her to hear Elizabeth's statement before
she's finished with that."

"Elizabeth, Margo Black is dead," Detective
Marsh reminded her quietly. "I think you know
that."

"All I know is what I saw!" Elizabeth insisted. "I don't know how, but I know that she's
alive! And she was in Jessica's room tonight!
Why doesn't anyone believe me?" Her body
convulsed into spasms of painful sobs, but
Elizabeth's eyes remained dry. She had no tears
left. "I saw her, Daddy," she whispered, implor-

267

ing her father to believe her. "They think I'm crazy, but I'm not! I saw Margo! I saw her!"

Mr. Wakefield's eyes were filled with pain. "Honey, don't you remember last year?" he asked. Elizabeth's heart sank. Her father was talking to her in a voice he would use with a six-year-old. "You were there when Margo died."

Elizabeth stared at the tiny smear of blood on her thumb. "Yes," she whispered. "And I was there last night, too—when Margo murdered my sister."

Elizabeth closed her eyes and pretended she wasn't there. She couldn't deal with any of this—not the cinder-block walls, the skeptical detectives, or even her father. She didn't want to think or feel or see. Jessica hadn't deserved to die. Jessica had saved Todd's life; she was a hero.

"Why couldn't Margo have killed me instead?" Elizabeth asked herself under her breath. "It should have been me!"

She hardly noticed when her father led her from the room.

Nora woke suddenly and sat straight up in her eyelet-covered bed at the Sweet Valley Inn. Sunlight streamed through the window like blood pouring from a wound. For a moment she wondered what had awakened her. It had been a voice. She was sure of it.

"Margo?" she called, her heart gripped with tension. "Are you there?"

And then there was one, said a voice. But the voice was not Margo's. The voice was in Nora's head. And it smelled like magnolias.

"And then there was one," Nora repeated. There was only one Wakefield twin left. She would dispose of Elizabeth in a more careful way, a more orderly way. Then she would take Elizabeth's place in the Wakefield family. She would have a perfect life—well, almost perfect, Nora amended. She would have no sister to make her feel complete.

Her sister. Margo would have the same plan, as soon as she knew what Nora had done to Jessica. Margo would try to kill Elizabeth, too.

And then there was one! insisted the voice in her head. Nora felt a shivery feeling down her spine. The voice wasn't talking about one Wakefield twin. The voice was talking about one Chapelle twin. Margo wanted to be a Wakefield, too. And Margo would do anything to get what she wanted.

Nora's eyes widened as she thought of all the people Margo had killed. Her little foster sister in Long Island. The boy she was baby-sitting in Cleveland. A woman in a train station. A temporary catering employee in Sweet Valley. James, the boy Margo had hired to spy on the Wakefields for her, who had died when he'd tried to warn Jessica. Margo had even killed two ambulance attendants who had worked to save her life.

Suddenly a chill numbed Nora, down to her bones. She knew why Margo hadn't come back to the hotel room.

"Margo knows!" Nora said aloud, trembling. "She knows everything, and she's planning to kill me next!"

She jumped from the bed and began pacing the hotel room. "How could Margo know?" she asked the empty room. Her glance fell on the lacy bedspreads and curtains. "Eyelets," she remembered. "Little eyes." She had guessed that the thousands of eyes were spying on her. Now she knew the truth. They were working for Margo. And Margo was coming to kill her. All at once, the smell of blood hung thick around her, ruddy and grotesque—like red smoke, choking her. She had a sudden vision of Jessica's crumpled body, on sheets spattered with scarlet. Only it was not Jessica's body. It was Nora's.

Suddenly her path seemed clear. "I have to find Margo. And I have to kill her—before she kills me."

Her eyes focused on the mirror's surface instead of her reflection in its murky, shining depths. She ran her gaze over the stark black spiderweb in the glass, and she studied the daggerlike voids where splinters of mirror had fallen, sparkling, to the sink. For now, it was her own face behind those dark, violent slashes. But soon it would be Margo's face, and it would be for real.

After Margo was dead, Nora would go after Elizabeth. In the end, there could be only one.

Chapter 16

Elizabeth lay on her rumpled bed, staring at the ceiling. She didn't know how long she'd been there—it could have been ten minutes or ten days. But the afternoon sun was streaming through her window, as if this were a normal day—as if her world hadn't ended. She wished it were gray and drizzling—or stormy, with thunder and lightning. With Jessica dead, the cheerful weather seemed mocking—obscene.

Her friends had been waiting at the house when Elizabeth and her parents had arrived home in the cold predawn. But Elizabeth had been too numb to speak. Lila and Ken appeared to be in shock. Todd had reached out for her, but Elizabeth had shaken her head. She had stared, wild-eyed, into her friends' tearstained faces. Then she had run upstairs to be alone.

Only now she felt more alone than she'd ever been—or had ever conceived of being. She and Jessica had had their share of arguments; from time to time they'd been separated by distance or conflict. But through everything she'd always known, deep down, that Jessica was there for her and always would be. And now she wasn't. Part of Elizabeth's nightmare rushed back at her. But this time Elizabeth was the one who was falling through the black, empty void, utterly alone.

The door opened, and her brother's head appeared. With it came a rush of hope, as tangible as a breeze.

"Steven!" Elizabeth breathed, sitting up. "You're home."

Steven's face was pale and lined with grief. He crossed the room in two strides and sat down beside her. "How are you doing, kiddo?" he asked, his voice thick with unshed tears.

Elizabeth shrugged. "I don't know," she replied honestly. "I just don't know." Her voice dropped to a whisper. "I can't believe she's gone."

Steven wiped his eyes with his fingers. "Neither can I," he said. "I almost walked into her room a few minutes ago, just to feel her presence. But I couldn't do it. I couldn't go in there."

"Me neither," Elizabeth admitted. She hadn't been able to cry for hours, but now the tears began gliding down her face, hot against her skin. "Mom and Dad felt the same way. They said we should wait a week or so before we even try to go through her things. . . ." She gestured toward the bathroom. "I keep waiting for that door to burst open, and for Jessica to run in, begging me to lend her a pair of socks, or to make dinner even though it's her turn." She squeezed her eyes shut.

Steven patted her hand. "I know," he said. "The house seems so quiet without her gabbing on the phone to Lila and playing her stereo too loud."

"Have you talked to Mom and Dad?" Elizabeth asked. "How are they? I guess I haven't been much help to them today."

"Nobody expects you to be," Steven assured her. "This is a nightmare for all of us. But we all know it hits you worse than anyone."

"I saw Lila and Ken and the other kids when we got home this morning," Elizabeth said. "Everyone was devastated, Steven. It was awful."

Steven sighed. "Todd and Enid have both

been calling all day, Mom said. I wanted to get you, but she said you didn't want to come to the phone. Maybe you should talk to them, Liz. It might help."

"I know," Elizabeth said, shaking her head helplessly. "But I can't talk to anyone else about it—not yet. Maybe tomorrow."

Steven took a deep breath. "Liz, Dad told me what happened at the police station. He's pretty worried about you. And so am I."

"I know what I saw!" Elizabeth insisted, her lips tightening into a stubborn line.

"I know you were sure last night," Steven said. "But you were traumatized, almost hysterical. Now that you're calmer, I was hoping you'd be able to remember more clearly—"

"I do remember clearly!" Elizabeth said. Her lower lip began to tremble. "I wish I didn't."

"I hate to ask you about it at all," he said gently, "but you're the only lead the police have. You're the key to figuring out who did this to Jessica."

"I know who did it!" Elizabeth said. "It was Margo! I saw her! But the police don't believe me. They think I'm losing my mind, and so does Dad." She noted the fear and concern in her brother's brown eyes and dropped her voice to a whisper. "And so do you."

Steven grasped her shoulders. "Elizabeth, listen to me! I don't care what the police believe. But *I* don't think you're losing your mind."

"But you don't believe me, either."

"I believe that you're feeling upset and alone and scared," Steven said carefully. "Your brain is confusing images from your nightmare with images that you really saw—"

"Spare me your Psychology one-oh-one lessons," Elizabeth interrupted bitterly.

Steven continued as if she hadn't spoken. "If you can separate the real memories from the dream images," he said, "you might be able to point the police toward a suspect."

"I did point them toward a suspect! I told them exactly who it was!" Elizabeth cried. "Dammit, Steven, Margo is still alive—and she's out there somewhere, gloating about this. You have to help me convince the police! You have to!"

Her brother's eyes looked apologetic as he searched for the words to reply. Elizabeth's heart sank. Steven was not going to help her. She truly was alone.

Before he could reply, the door opened. Mr. and Mrs. Wakefield walked in, with Prince Albert padding along at their heels, his tail practically dragging on the carpet. More than anyone's, he had been Jessica's dog. Elizabeth was shocked at her parents' faces. Her mother's eyes were puffy and red, her skin chalky. Her father's expression was tense and weary.

"Elizabeth and Steven, we need to talk to you," Mrs. Wakefield said, slowly pulling out the desk chair and sitting down. Her husband stood behind her, shuffling his feet.

"We've been making plans for the funeral service," Mr. Wakefield said in the same lifeless, professional voice that he might have used to ask a judge for a continuance. "It will be Monday morning—the day after tomorrow."

"We thought the two of you would want some part in the decisions about readings and so forth," Mrs. Wakefield said, staring at her hands. A single tear fell, sparkling, to her lap.

Elizabeth began to tremble. A funeral seemed so final. It made Jessica's death seem so . . . irrevocable.

Steven tightened his arm around her shoulders. "Where will the funeral be held?" he asked.

"We're planning for a service at Reed's Funeral Parlor, near Jackson's Bluff," Mrs. Wakefield replied. "Then we'll go to the cemetery for—"

"No!" Elizabeth cried, rising to her feet. "No funeral parlors!"

Her mother winced. "Elizabeth, honey," she began, "I know how hard this is for you. But—"

"Jessica would have hated that," Elizabeth said with absolute certainty. "It's too depressing—a stuffy funeral parlor with a lot of big, ugly flower arrangements and people in conservative clothes. It isn't what she would have wanted."

"Liz, this is the way these things are done," her father told her. "It will be all right. Trust me."

"No, Dad," Elizabeth insisted. "It's not all right. It's all wrong!"

"What would you suggest, Liz?" Steven asked. "Where would you hold the service?"

"At school!" Elizabeth answered instantly. "In the auditorium of Sweet Valley High, on the same stage where she starred in *Macbeth* and *Splendor in the Grass* and all the talent shows and other productions."

"Elizabeth," her father objected, "I hardly think Mr. Cooper would consent to—"

"He has to!" Elizabeth cried. "Don't you see? Jessica loved that school more than any other place in the world. That's where I want to say good-bye to her," she concluded, her determination melting into tears. "That's where she would have wanted to say good-bye to everyone."

Mr. and Mrs. Wakefield exchanged a glance.

"Mr. Cooper already canceled school on Monday, because of Jessica," Mrs. Wakefield said in a weary voice. "So it might not be a problem to schedule it at the school."

Mr. Wakefield thought for a moment and then nodded. "All right, Elizabeth," he said. "I admit that I have my doubts, but I can't refuse you something like this. I don't think they'll allow us to bring the coffin to school, but there's no reason why we can't hold the memorial service there—if you believe that's what Jessica would have wanted. I'll give Mr. Cooper a call right now."

Nora pulled her sweater around her shoulders. It was a chilly Saturday night, but devoid of wind. The smells of dirt and decay hung in the air, silent and heavy, darker than the black of the surrounding night. Except for the smells, the night was clear. A few cold, distant stars shimmered above, alongside the waning moon. No swirling mist enshrouded the stark white gravestones.

The gravestones. Nora spun frantically, her eyes piercing the darkness. Margo could be hiding behind any of the smooth white stones. She could be waiting to pounce on Nora, wielding a long, glittering knife. Her presence was everywhere, unclean, like the presence of death. Margo had not appeared in the hotel room. She had not materialized out of the shimmering depths of the murdered mirror. Nora had waited outside the Wakefield house for hours, but Margo did not return.

She's playing with me, Nora thought. *She's trying to break me, to catch me off guard.*

Margo had ambushed her once before, wielding the knife. And that had been at the cemetery on Christmas night. Nora didn't want to go there again—didn't want to make herself vulnerable in a place where Margo clearly held power. But she couldn't help herself. Her feet had drawn her there inexorably, as if Margo were reeling her in. The voices had demanded it.

Nora stopped in front of her sister's memorial stone, trembling with fear and rage.

Dig, commanded a voice inside her head. For a moment Nora prayed that none of this was real—that she was trapped inside her recurring nightmare. The smells were the same. But there was no wind, and the night was clear. This was real.

Dig! a chorus of voices repeated, more insistently.

Nora shrank back in horror. She suddenly knew what the voices intended. The grave she was being asked to dig would be her own.

She would not do it. The voices couldn't make her. Now she knew the truth: Margo ruled the voices. Margo had heard the voices first, had implanted them in Nora's brain. Now Margo was using the voices to scare her. She was hiding, waiting for her chance to draw the glittering knife along Nora's white vulnerable throat. Then the blood would pour out of her, scarlet in the moonlight. And a dog would howl.

"No!" Nora screamed. "I won't let you do this to me!"

Nora was stronger now, she reminded herself, as strong as Margo. She would kill Margo first. And then she would go after the remaining Wakefield twin.

"Margo!" she called into the darkness. "Come out and face me!"

The stage of the school auditorium was filled with flower arrangements for Monday morning's service. For the rest of her life, Elizabeth realized, the smell of flowers would remind her of death. She was standing in the wings, to the left of the stage, peering out from behind the thick curtains as Lila spoke onstage.

Through her tears Elizabeth gazed in awe at the more than two thousand people who were crowded into the auditorium for Jessica's memorial service. She knew Jessica had been popular, but she hadn't realized that her sister's life had touched so many people. Her parents and Steven sat in the front row, their expressions poised on the edge of tears. Todd and Enid sat with them, their faces just as sorrowful. Elizabeth bit her lip. Todd had tried to talk to her earlier, but she had asked him to wait until after the service. She couldn't risk breaking down before she had taken her turn at the microphone.

Elizabeth mouthed *"Thank you"* to Lila, who had just finished speaking and stumbled backstage, her face as white as the magnolia blooms in an expensive arrangement that somebody had left near the podium. Lila laid a hand on Elizabeth's shoulder. Elizabeth had never had much in common with vain, snobby Lila. But their love for Jessica united them. Elizabeth hugged her tightly. Then Lila ran toward the stage door, sobbing as if her heart was broken.

Next, it was Ken's turn to speak. With tears shining in his eyes, he leaned over to kiss Elizabeth on the forehead. "You look so much like her," he whispered to Elizabeth, his voice quavering, before he walked out onstage. A portrait of Jessica sat to one side. In front of it he laid a bouquet of two dozen red roses tied with a purple ribbon. Then he stepped to center stage and spoke into the microphone.

"I'm not very good at public speaking," Ken said, his voice husky. "Not like Jessica was. Jessica could talk to anybody, about pretty much anything. She loved being the center of attention—and it's a good thing, because that's exactly what she usually was. Jessica was so beautiful and so full of life that people couldn't resist her. They wanted to be around her. We all wanted to be around her—"

Elizabeth tried to listen to the rest, but she knew she would burst into anguished sobs if she did. She took a deep breath and pulled out the tear-blotted sheet of paper on which she'd written her own contribution to the service, a poem to her sister.

When Ken finished speaking, he came backstage and hugged her again. He pulled away, and the shoulder of her black dress was wet with his tears. She squared her shoulders and stepped onstage, calling on Jessica's courage and confidence to see her through.

"I'd like to read a poem I wrote for my sister," she said, feeling the tears starting already. "It's called 'The Girl in the Mirror.'" She took a deep breath and began reading:

> Reflection, soul mate, sister, friend,
> Half of what I am is you—

A vibrant smile, a helping hand
A love that always pulled us through.

You, who so loved life, are gone
The life I loved is torn apart,
And I am left to carry on
My mirror empty as my heart—

In the front row of the auditorium, Todd's seat was empty. Her parents were weeping in each other's arms, and the sight of their sorrow was more than she could stand. Grief, horror, and guilt washed over Elizabeth like a waterfall. She gripped the podium, feeling as if she were drowning in the scent of magnolias. She bit her lip to keep a sob from escaping and closed her eyes as if she could hold back the tears.

The rest of the poem went on to describe her sister and the closeness they shared. But Elizabeth knew she would not be able to read any more of it.

"I love you, Jessica," she whispered into the microphone. "Please forgive me." Then she limped offstage, blinded by her tears.

Nora knew that it was dangerous for her to be at Jessica's memorial service, but she had no choice. Surely, Margo couldn't resist showing up for such an event. And Nora had to find Margo—before Margo found her.

Backstage, she peered out from behind a piece of scenery left over from a school play. The scenery was dusty, and she took care not to lean against it in her simple black dress—an exact replica of Elizabeth's.

She was too far away to hear what Elizabeth had said to Lila and Ken. But their sniveling voices from the podium came through loud and clear. And she could see the swirls of floral scent that nobody else seemed to notice, though they turned the stage lights pink. White tendrils of magnolia smoke wound through the pink haze, emanating from the arrangement Nora had brought. She wasn't sure why she had felt compelled to bring magnolias. Her reason was elusive, like the faintest whiff of an unnamed memory, triggered by a powerful scent. But she knew instinctively that she had made the right choice. It had symmetry.

Nora sensed Margo's presence somewhere close by. Nora looked deep within herself, trying to examine this vague intuition that hinted at a third twin who hid in the dark, as if behind a smooth white gravestone. Nora felt her twin—could almost smell her. But when she scanned the crowded room, Margo was nowhere to be seen. All she could see were rows and rows of people crying for

Jessica Wakefield. Jessica didn't deserve their grief.

Nora chuckled. She reveled in the power of being the only person in the auditorium who wasn't blubbering and swollen-eyed. They were weak, and she was strong. Crying was sloppy. And Nora had vowed never to get sloppy again.

Elizabeth was onstage, shrouded in pink floral scent. She was reading a poem into the microphone, her voice on the verge of weeping.

"The girl in the mirror," Nora whispered, rolling her eyes as she repeated the title of Elizabeth's poem. "What sentimental nonsense!" Nora had been through the looking glass, and she knew that the mirror was broken. The girl inside the mirror was a fantasy. Twins were a fantasy.

In the end, we are alone, a voice whispered to her. Life was tidier that way.

Elizabeth's face was ashen in the stage lights as she began struggling through her poem. Todd's heart went out to her. He had never seen anyone in so much pain. He slipped from his seat and ran backstage to be there for her when she finished. He wasn't sure if she would want to see him, but he had to make the offer.

Elizabeth limped offstage, and Todd caught her as she collapsed, crying. "That was beautiful," he whispered, holding her tightly. "Jessica would have loved it."

"Oh, Todd!" she cried, tears dampening his shirt. "I'm sorry for everything!"

"I love you, Elizabeth," he told her. "And I'm sorry we've been so distant. I don't know what you think I did, but I didn't do it. Anyway, it doesn't matter now."

Elizabeth gazed into his face, looking more beautiful and delicate than he could remember, despite her tearstained face and watery eyes. "I know you didn't do it," she said softly. "It wasn't Jessica with you that night. It was Margo."

Todd felt his veins turn to ice water. Steven had said he was concerned about Elizabeth's fantasies about Margo. But Todd hadn't believed how serious her condition might be. "Liz," he whispered gently, steering her toward the stage door, "what are you talking about? Margo is dead. Remember, honey? You were there with me last New Year's Day when we saw her die."

"No, Todd," Elizabeth replied, her voice soft but unwavering. "We only thought we saw her die. Margo is not dead. She kissed you, and she killed Jessica, and she's somewhere nearby, right now. I'm sure of it."

"Don't think about that right now," Todd told her, wrapping his arms around her protectively. "Let me drive you to the cemetery."

Elizabeth sighed, grateful for Todd's familiar and reassuring presence, even if he didn't believe her story about Margo. Maybe she could convince him later. She leaned against him as they passed through the stage door and into the school hallway.

Suddenly Elizabeth froze, her eyes wide.

"Liz, what is it?" Todd asked. His voice was full of concern.

"It's Jessica," Elizabeth whispered. She couldn't explain how, but her sister's presence suddenly overwhelmed her, as surely as if Jessica had been standing beside her.

Todd's hand was trembling as he held hers, but Elizabeth felt completely calm.

I'm alive, said her twin's voice in Elizabeth's head. *Help me Lizzie—I need you!*

"Elizabeth!" Todd said, shaking her. "Elizabeth! Tell me what's wrong!"

Hope rose in Elizabeth's chest. "Nothing's wrong," she said. "I just felt Jessica. Todd, maybe she's still alive."

Todd bit his lip. "Liz, I know how upset you are," he said. "But you saw Jessica's body yourself. Just like you saw Margo's last year. Jessica's dead, Liz. She's gone."

Thoughts were percolating in Elizabeth's brain, like puzzle pieces that wouldn't quite fit together. They were trying to tell her something. She just had to dig deeper. Then she would understand.

A hand rested on her shoulder, and Elizabeth spun around, half expecting to see her sister. But it was Lila, with a confused expression on her face.

"Liz?" Lila began, looking around her as if she expected to see somebody else.

"Is everything all right, Lila?" Todd asked.

Lila shook her head as if to clear it. "I guess so," she said. "But how did you get her out here so fast? I swear, Liz, I was sure I just saw you backstage."

Elizabeth gasped as one of the puzzle pieces in her brain nearly shifted into place. She slipped from Todd's grasp and ran backstage, searching frantically in the gloom behind every backdrop and every piece of dusty scenery. Nobody was there.

Chapter 17

Steven sat at the kitchen table, his head in his hands. He was listening with growing alarm to Elizabeth's voice as she paced back and forth across the Spanish-tiled floor.

"She needs our help," Elizabeth muttered. "I have to go to her."

Steven reached for her hand, stopping her in midstride. "What in the world are you talking about, Liz?" he asked. "You're scaring me! Please sit down and tell me about it."

Elizabeth shook her head. "I can't!" she said, pulling her hand away. "You would never believe me! You didn't believe me about Margo, and you won't believe me about this, either."

"Please, Liz," her brother said, "I promise I'll listen with an open mind this time."

Elizabeth resumed pacing, moving her lips

as she walked. Steven could see her wrestling with something in her head, as if she were trying to put together the clues to solve a mystery. Again he grasped her hand, but this time he didn't let go. After a moment she allowed herself to be led to the table.

"Elizabeth, you've been acting strangely ever since we got back from the cemetery," he said. "Please talk to me. Tell me what's going on in your head."

Elizabeth looked up at him, her beautiful blue-green eyes brimming with tears. But this time he saw something new there, something that confused him. Hope.

"Steven, this is going to sound crazy, but I could feel Jessica at the memorial service today."

Steven sighed sadly. "I know, Liz. I could feel her, too. You were absolutely right when you said the school auditorium was the best place to hold the service. It's exactly where she would have chosen to say good-bye."

"No, Steven," Elizabeth objected, shaking her head impatiently. "That's not what I meant!"

Steven was beginning to have serious doubts about Elizabeth's sanity. Had her twin's death pushed her over the edge? He wondered if she was on the verge of a nervous breakdown of some kind. "Then what do you mean, Liz?" he asked gently, squeezing her hand. "Describe what you felt."

"It was the same as what we always called 'twin's intuition,'" Elizabeth explained. "Like I felt Friday night, just before I ran into Jessica's room."

"You mean you felt her spirit with you?" Steven said. "I can understand that, as close as you two always were."

"No!" Elizabeth objected, pounding her hand on the table. "I didn't feel her spirit. I felt *her*! She was at the school, and she was calling to me, Steve. She was all alone, and she needed my help." She took a deep breath. "I believe that Jessica is alive."

Steven felt a prickling at the back of his neck. He had thought the family's life had hit rock bottom with Jessica's death. Now he was afraid it was about to get worse. Was he losing his other sister, too?

"I know how difficult it is, Elizabeth," he told her softly. "You haven't slept in days, and you're not thinking straight. I believe that you're still in shock about what happened. But you don't have to face this alone. We'll help you find a way to deal with the grief."

"I don't need help!" Elizabeth screamed. "Jessica is the one who needs help! Steve, we have to find her!"

He took her by the shoulders and shook her

gently. "No, Liz. You have to come to terms with reality. Jessica is dead."

Elizabeth shook her head. "I don't care what you say," she said quietly, staring at the table. "I don't understand what's happening, but I know that I felt Jessica today. And I'm going to find a way to help her." She looked up at him, and Steven saw a new intensity in her eyes. "But you're right about one thing. I'm not thinking clearly."

"No, Liz, you're not," he said.

"That's why I'm going upstairs to get some sleep," she said. "After that I'm sure I'll be able to put the pieces together so I can solve the whole puzzle. Then I'll know what to do."

Everyone was gone, and the dark hallways of the school were quiet. Nora had followed the mourners to the cemetery and watched the ceremony there from behind the old willow tree. She felt exposed at the cemetery, during the light of the day. At any moment she had expected to feel Margo's knife at her back. Jessica's casket was lowered into the ground. But Margo hadn't come.

The voices had come, though. They had whispered to Nora as she'd crouched behind the tree, reminding her that she'd felt the presence of an unseen twin during the service at the school. Margo was at Sweet Valley High.

Nora knew it, deep in her bones. Margo was waiting there among the lockers and classrooms, waiting to pounce on her and drain the life from her body.

But Nora was onto her. Nora was almost ready for her.

She glided down the corridors, as quiet as a snake. Here was Elizabeth's locker. There was the door to the *Oracle* office, where Elizabeth spent so much time writing and editing for the school newspaper. Nora tried to imagine herself breezing through these hallways every day, shuffling through the books in that locker, greeting Mr. Collins as she opened that door.

She heard a faint banging sound and whirled around. Was that a movement, near the door to the newspaper office? She began to feel a presence—faint and indistinct, like a reflection of her own thoughts. But she knew what it was. It was Margo. Her evil twin was dogging her footsteps, hiding in classrooms, and waiting for her chance to spring.

"Margo?" Nora called hesitantly. "I don't want to play anymore. If you're there, come out in the open where I can see you! Let's settle this, once and for all!"

Nora spun around again to look behind her. In the process she slipped on the freshly polished floor and skidded into a locker, scraping her shin. The clamor echoed through the deserted hallways like an explosion.

Nora pressed her hands to her ears. "Stop it!" she screamed. "Stop making that noise!" She began to run, but the noise was coming from in front of her now. She scrambled back in the other direction, but she knew it was useless. She couldn't escape Margo. She had never had a chance.

Suddenly she realized that the echo was getting louder. She froze near the stage door to the auditorium, listening. She heard a metallic banging, like the sound of her own body crashing against the locker. But this noise wasn't an echo. It was no reflection. It was real, and it was coming from somewhere nearby. She heard a faint rustle and hurled herself across the hall, against another door. This door led downstairs, and it was marked FURNACE ROOM. The noise had come from down there. Nora was sure of it.

As she listened at the door, Nora suddenly knew without a doubt that this was where Margo had been staying. This was where the evil emanated from. Little by little, the evil slipped out, around the cracks in the door and through the keyhole. Reddish black filaments of evil oozed from the basement when nobody was looking. Margo was sending them out, to find Nora and to bring her there. And now

Nora had come. But maybe she still had an advantage, she thought. Maybe Margo didn't know that Nora had found her and was standing at the entrance to her lair.

Nora could hear only silence from the room below. But she could feel her sister down there. Her presence was overpowering, like the scent of flowers that was seeping out of the auditorium and into the hallway to choke her.

The smell of roses triggered a memory—and a realization. Nora froze, finally understanding the truth. Margo's voice was in her head, but it wasn't the only one. One of the other voices had been Blanche's, all along. Blanche of the cabbage roses. Blanche of the razor-sharp fingernails, dripping in bloodred polish. Blanche, who had torn her away from Margo when they had been babies, when there had still been hope.

Blanche had tried to destroy her, but she had failed. The voices were in Nora's head. So Nora had control. She threw back her shoulders and breathed deeply. Attar of roses gave her strength—Blanche's strength. Her stepmother would never be able to hurt her again.

Now Nora was ready. She reached for the doorknob to let herself downstairs. Then she cursed under her breath. The door was locked.

But Nora would not be defeated that easily. She would find a way to get in, and she would be back—after dark, when her powers were at their full strength. A locked door wouldn't stop her. Nothing could stop her.

The key, said Jessica, her face shimmering like a reflection in wavy glass. *Find the key to unlock the secret.*

Elizabeth was frantic. "What do you mean?" she asked. "How do I do it?"

Dig deeper, Jessica urged. *You're almost there.*

Then Jessica vanished under a sphere of orange flame that rose like the ball in Times Square on New Year's Eve. In her place was a girl who looked just like Jessica, who whipped off her blue knit cap and brandished a knife— as her long black hair flew out behind her, covering the sky.

Elizabeth screamed and ran down the shoreline of Secca Lake. But there was the girl again, dressed in black leather. Her knife glittered like silver in the moonlight, and her eyes glittered, too, a glacial blue-green, cold enough to burn.

Elizabeth spun around, but the first Margo was there, laughing at her, the blue knit cap still in her hand. Her eyes were the same color as Jessica's eyes, but they were cruel.

"Jessica!" Elizabeth screamed. "Where are you?"

I'm alive! Jessica called. *Help me, Lizzie! I need you!* But she was falling off a high black cliff, to the white rocks below.

Elizabeth wanted to run to her, to break her fall. But the two Margos were descending on her, mocking her with their cold laughter. Elizabeth tried to run, but her legs were frozen in place. She could only watch helplessly while they swung their knives in glittering arcs. . . .

Elizabeth sat up in bed, breathing hard. Drops of sweat beaded on her forehead, but she was shivering. *I'm alive,* Jessica had told her in the dream. Now Elizabeth was sure of it, more than ever.

Find the key, Jessica had urged.

Elizabeth tried to calm her racing pulse. "I have to think this through rationally," she whispered. "The key to unlock the secret is in my dream. But what is the key? Why are there two Margos? Is that the secret?" She blinked back tears of frustration. "Why can't I understand?"

One puzzle piece was still missing, she thought. That was Jessica's key.

Suddenly Elizabeth's mind flashed back to her nightmare. Jessica was tumbling from the steep cliff, through the cold, thin air. She was falling toward the white rocks below. Before long she would be crushed against them. Jessica was alive, but her time was running short.

Elizabeth was gripping the edge of her sheet so hard that it tore. She stared at it in surprise, remembering the blood-soaked sheets on Jessica's bed. She knew without a doubt that Jessica would die again if Elizabeth couldn't solve the puzzle soon—and that this time Jessica's death would be for keeps.

"Where is the key?" she asked aloud, her voice rising to a fever pitch. "Where do I find it?"

Forty-five minutes later Elizabeth took a deep breath and followed her mother into the living room. Detectives Roger Marsh and Gail Pappas had arrived with more questions for Elizabeth and her parents.

"We're sorry to trouble you again," Detective Marsh said, folding his lanky body into a chair as Elizabeth sat on the couch between her parents. "But we didn't get everything we needed at the station Saturday morning."

"We thought you all might be a little, uh, calmer today," Detective Pappas added. She was already beginning to pace the length of the room, just as she had at the police station.

Elizabeth nodded. "I'll help however I can," she said in a resigned voice. Internally, she wanted to scream. She knew whom she had seen climbing out of Jessica's window, but nobody wanted to believe her. And now she knew Jessica was alive, though she couldn't explain how it was possible or why she was so sure. But even her own brother didn't believe that; it was a sure bet that the police would think she was crazy.

"Let's begin with some routine questions," Detective Marsh said, pulling out his legal pad. "I know that you and Jessica were very close. Who else was Jessica close to, outside the family?"

"Her best friend is . . . uh, *was* Lila Fowler," Elizabeth began. She knew that she sounded vague, but inside, she felt sharp and lucid as her mind searched for the puzzle piece that would make the big picture come clear.

"Fowler as in Fowler Crest?" Detective Marsh asked.

"Yes, that's right," Mrs. Wakefield said. "Jessica and Lila have been best friends for years."

With part of her brain Elizabeth was listening to the questions and responding politely and truthfully. In fact, she was surprised at how aware she felt—as if Jessica had appeared in her dream to open Elizabeth's eyes, so that she'd see the missing puzzle piece when it appeared.

Detective Pappas was pacing. She spun around when she reached the opposite side of the room. As she turned, her coppery hair swung out around her face and her navy blazer flapped open, revealing a glimpse of glittering metal in a shoulder holster. To Elizabeth's eye, every detail of the detective's appearance—every detail of the room—stood out in sharp relief.

"I heard that Jessica had a steady boyfriend," Detective Pappas said, her expression unreadable. "I saw their picture in the newspaper—" She consulted a small notepad. "Todd Wilkins, correct?"

Mr. and Mrs. Wakefield both glanced uncomfortably at Elizabeth. A week ago the question would have sparked fury, or at least self-doubt. Today Elizabeth only shook her head. "No," she said evenly. "That was a misprint. Todd Wilkins is *my* boyfriend. Jessica had been dating Ken Matthews for a couple months."

Both detectives looked surprised. "How was Jessica getting along with this Ken Matthews?" Detective Marsh asked.

"Great," Elizabeth said with a shrug. Her mind flashed on an image of Todd kissing a blonde in the movie theater, but now it brought no pain. Elizabeth knew now that the girl had been Margo, no matter what anyone else said. "Jessica and Ken went to the New Year's Eve carnival together that night. I heard they had a great time."

Detective Pappas wrinkled her forehead. "You *heard*?" she asked. "But I thought you were at the carnival, too. Didn't you see them?"

Again Elizabeth's parents glanced at her uneasily, but, again, she only shrugged. "Not really," she said. "There were hundreds of people there, and I was one of the organizers of the event. I was pretty busy."

Elizabeth's mind raced through her memories of the carnival. Lila and Ken had both been looking for Jessica shortly before midnight. *"Your mirror image was heading toward the House of Mirrors almost two hours ago,"* Lila had said. *"Nobody's seen her since then."*

"Wasn't Jessica also on the organizing committee?" asked the tall, red-haired detective. "Shouldn't she have been working with you?"

Mrs. Wakefield smiled tearfully. "If you knew Jessica, you wouldn't have to ask that," she said, biting her lip. "Jessica was never one to slave away at administrative tasks when there was a party going on. She was full of ideas. But she was content to let more responsible heads—like her sister's—prevail when it was time to implement them."

The House of Mirrors? Elizabeth thought. Was that a clue? Somehow it seemed important, but she wasn't sure how it fit in. If the House of Mirrors was Jessica's missing key, then Elizabeth hadn't found the right keyhole. Suddenly Jessica's face appeared before her, just as it had in Elizabeth's dream—shimmering, like a reflection in wavy glass. *Wavy glass, as in a House of Mirrors?* Elizabeth wondered.

Dig deeper, Jessica urged. *You're almost there.*

After more than an hour of questions, Elizabeth was feeling restless. The living room was warm, and perspiration stood out on Detective Pappas's forehead as she paced between questions. Finally she stopped at the far side of the room, pulled off her navy jacket, and searched around for a place to lay it. Then she stepped through the archway into the darkened dining room and laid it over a chair.

"Was there anyone you didn't recognize at Jessica's memorial service?" Detective Marsh asked.

Mr. Wakefield shook his head. "There were two thousand people there," he began. "I doubt I would have noticed if—"

Elizabeth's gaze was drawn to Detective Pappas's handgun, looking so shiny and lethal as it sat in its holster, hugging her large, solid body. *Margo could make use of a weapon like that,* Elizabeth thought. She shivered, despite the stuffy room.

The detective's eyebrows shot up, and she glanced from her holster to Elizabeth's face. *She thinks the gun is making me nervous,* Elizabeth realized. *I guess it is, in a way, but not for the reasons she thinks.*

"I don't understand," Mrs. Wakefield was saying. "Why does it matter who was at the memorial service?"

"It's not uncommon for a murderer to show up at a victim's funeral," Detective Marsh explained. He went on to say why, but Elizabeth's mind flew back to the school. The only unexpected presence she'd noticed at the service was Jessica's—alive. Suddenly she knew that she had to go back there, tonight. Jessica was all alone, and she was falling through a black void. Elizabeth had to save her before she hit the rocks below.

But what if Margo was at the school, too?

With a nod toward Elizabeth, Detective Pappas unbuckled her shoulder holster and set it on the dining-room table. Then she turned and paced back toward the Wakefields and Detective Marsh.

Elizabeth eyed the handgun that shone in the gloom of the next room, reflecting the lights from the living room and kitchen. She noticed that the tall redhead's back was to the gun. And an idea began to formulate in her mind.

"You've all given us a lot of background," Detective Marsh was saying. "And it's useful information. But I'm afraid we're going to have to go back now to the period around one in the morning, on New Year's Day."

"Is this really necessary?" Mrs. Wakefield asked.

"Yes, it is," he replied. "I'm sorry to put you through the same questions again. But we have no leads at all in this case. We're hoping you might be able to remember some detail that slipped your mind at the station the other day."

Mr. Wakefield sighed. "I really don't think upsetting my daughter again is going to do any good."

Detective Pappas opened her mouth to reply—probably unkindly, Elizabeth guessed from her expression—but the other detective spoke first. "No," he said with a sharp glance at his colleague. "Elizabeth has been through enough for now. We are not going to question her about that night—unless she's prepared to tell us anything different from what she said in her statement."

Elizabeth shook her head. "I'm sorry," she said, her voice rising despite herself. "But what I told you at the police station is still exactly the way I remember it. I know you don't believe me—nobody believes me! But I saw a teenage girl standing at Jessica's window that night. She wore a leather jacket, and she was blond," she insisted. "And if she wasn't Margo Black, then she must have been Margo's twin sister!"

Jessica's shimmering image appeared in her head. This time Jessica was beaming. *Margo's twin sister!* Elizabeth thought, breathless. *Of course! Why didn't I, of all people, think of that before?*

Elizabeth heard the almost audible snap of a puzzle piece fitting into place. Two Margos were descending on her, swinging their knives in glittering arcs. Two Margos!

With one part of her mind, Elizabeth knew the explanation was preposterous. There was no logical reason to believe it—except that it was the only explanation that allowed Jessica to still be alive. One Margo was dead; the other Margo had killed her. And Jessica was somewhere else—alive. *But in terrible danger,* if Elizabeth could trust her intuition.

"Well, I see no point in grilling you any further about it," Detective Marsh said with a sigh. "But we may eventually request that you speak with a police psychologist; he's an expert at bringing out suppressed memories of traumatic events."

"We'd be willing to consider that option," Mr. Wakefield said with a concerned look at Elizabeth.

Detective Pappas turned to Elizabeth's mother. "Mrs. Wakefield, you also saw a person we assume is the murderer," she said. "I think we're finished with Elizabeth for a while, but perhaps you can help us by describing the figure you saw on the lawn."

Elizabeth stood up quickly. She knew she looked agitated, but that would probably only help her case. "Do you mind if I leave, then?" she asked. "I, uh, think I forgot to eat today. I'm feeling a little faint."

"Are you all right, honey?" her father asked.

"I'm OK, really," Elizabeth assured him. "I'll just grab an apple or something and then go upstairs to lie down for a while." She forced herself to walk slowly through the lighted hallway to the kitchen as Detective Pappas began questioning her mother.

Once in the kitchen, she crept through the other door—the one that led into the dark dining room. She waited until Detective Pappas paced toward the archway. Then the detective wheeled to face her audience in the living room, a new question on her lips.

And Elizabeth lifted the gun from the table and tiptoed out the kitchen door.

Chapter 18

The corridor outside the auditorium was lit only by the school's dim, yellowish emergency lights, which stayed illuminated all the time. Nora worked by feel, rather than sight, as she slipped a chisel into the crack between the basement door and the jamb.

She had bought the chisel at Valley Hardware that evening, peering carefully down every aisle to be sure Margo wasn't waiting for her among the tools and sharp instruments. Now Nora slid the chisel up and down, applying pressure exactly where the voices said to. After a minute she was rewarded with a metallic click. The door opened, and she looked down a deep staircase that descended into a black void. From the top of the stairs, she couldn't see the basement below.

But she was a creature of darkness now. The cemetery winds had filled her with their strength. Blanche and Margo had added to her powers, without meaning to. And Jessica's life had poured into her soul like blood. The stale-smelling dark didn't scare her now. It couldn't hurt her. Only Margo could hurt her. But Nora wouldn't let that stop her. She had to confront her evil reflection. Only one twin would triumph and would earn a life as the sole remaining Wakefield daughter. Only one of them would emerge from the furnace room alive.

Nora listened to the gloom. The voices were silent. Somewhere below, water dripped, beating a low, steady cadence, like a death toll. And in a far corner of the basement, someone was breathing slowly, as if in sleep. It was Margo, she knew. Margo's evil presence whirled around her like the blackest scent of death and fear. She might be pretending to sleep, but Margo never slept. Margo was always ready.

From beneath her leather jacket Nora pulled a long, glittering knife. She stopped for a moment, removed the jacket, and hung it neatly on the doorknob. She would move faster without it. Then she squared her shoulders and stepped into the void.

The brakes screeched to a halt as Elizabeth parked the Jeep under a streetlamp in the parking lot of Sweet Valley High. She leaped from the vehicle and sprinted to the main entrance, the heavy gun in its too-long holster banging at her waist. She struggled with the doors, but they were locked.

"The auditorium!" she cried aloud. That was where she had sensed her sister so strongly. It was the best place she could think of to start. She ran around the building to the ticket-office entrance and then stopped short. The door was not only unlocked—it had been propped open.

Her twin's presence engulfed Elizabeth like smoke. But Jessica hadn't left this door open. If Jessica was free to open a door, she would have come home by now. The winter term had been postponed until Wednesday, so nobody else had any reason to be there. Nobody except Margo. Elizabeth felt a chill run down her spine. She considered turning back. She could drive home and somehow convince the police detectives to return with her.

But Jessica was alone and scared, in some dark corner of the big, empty school. And Margo was in there with her.

Elizabeth took a deep breath. There was no time to get help. She would have to help herself—and her sister. She reached under her jacket to pull the gun from its holster. She had already checked to see that it was loaded. Now she held it in both hands as she slipped through the door.

The auditorium was pitch-black, except for the red EXIT sign over each door. Elizabeth reluctantly unclenched one hand from the pistol in order to feel her way along the seat backs, down the long center aisle. The loaded gun shook in her trembling hand, its barrel chattering like teeth against a ring she wore on her finger. Something sighed behind her, and Elizabeth whirled, thrusting the gun out in front of her. But everything was silent, except for the faint echo of the slow-moving door that had finally eased shut behind her.

She took a deep breath and continued down the aisle. She could feel Jessica, and she could feel Jessica's fear intensifying. Jessica was in the dark, but she was not alone. Elizabeth gulped. That morning her sister's presence had been strongest in the hallway, just outside the stage door. That's where she would go.

Nora held her knife in front of her like a challenge. Margo was waiting in a shadowy corner of the furnace room, ready to pounce. But Nora was strong now. She would pounce first.

The room was black—both with the darkness and with a sour, dank smell that reminded Nora of the soil under her fingernails as she had dug deeper, toward her sister's casket. That had been a dream. But now Nora had a strange conviction that her dream was coming true. It was all there—the descent into the earth, the swirling dark, and the shapes emerging out of the night.

"No," she told herself silently. The still, fetid air bore no trace of the cemetery winds that had emboldened her. The faint shadows and dull metallic glimmers that loomed out of the blackness around her were not tombstones. They were furnaces and hot-water heaters, electrical cables and plumbing fixtures. A few hummed warnings. But above their low roar Nora heard the soft breathing, growing faster.

Suddenly a dark shape shifted position ahead of her. Margo! Nora rushed at the gray movement with her knife. A hand tightened on her arm, and Nora slashed downward, her blade whispering harmlessly through something soft, like fabric. The hand still gripped Nora's arm, and she couldn't maneuver the knife. She lashed out with her foot instead, kicking at what she hoped were her twin's legs. Margo clamped short a scream. Then she twisted Nora's arm backward, and red pain replaced black night.

Nora's knife fell, clattering, to the floor. A reflection in the blade's surface gleamed momentarily, and Nora threw herself after it. Margo followed, wrenching Nora's arm cruelly. Nora heard her own shirt rip. And the knife blade flashed again—this time in Margo's hand.

"I'm not afraid of the dark," Elizabeth reminded herself under her breath as she groped her way through the dark area backstage. "I'm not afraid of the dark!" Then she stumbled against a piece of scenery. She cringed as it tottered and fell, echoing like thunder in the silent auditorium.

Had Margo heard?

Elizabeth took a deep breath. She was overreacting. The noise hadn't been that loud; her fear had amplified it.

She focused her attention on a lighted red EXIT sign that hung over a door she couldn't see—a door that led to the hallway. It was everyday and tangible and so somehow comforting. She was at Sweet Valley High, and she had to find Jessica before Margo did.

Then she froze. From somewhere nearby came thumps and crashes—the sounds of a struggle. She turned from side to side, trying to pinpoint its source. But the noise seemed to be all around her. Suddenly she realized that

316

something else was all around her, too. Jessica's presence was there, and Jessica was in trouble. Earlier that day Elizabeth had felt her sister in the hallway, just past the EXIT sign. So she ran toward the lighted red rectangle, hoping nothing stood in her way.

She emerged into the hallway and gasped. Across the hall, the door to the furnace-room stairs was ajar. The clamor was coming from below. And a black leather jacket hung over the doorknob.

"Margo!" Elizabeth said aloud. She knew now with a growing sense of urgency that light was more important than stealth. Running to the nearest switch, Elizabeth flicked on the hallway lights. Then she bounded down the stairs into the basement, clenching the gun in both hands.

Jessica leaped clear as the glittering knife slashed toward her. She couldn't see her assailant, but she knew who it was. Who else but Margo would be trying to kill her? Margo was the only person who even knew where Jessica was—unless Elizabeth had experienced one of her famous premonitions about her twin.

Somehow Margo had survived her supposedly fatal injuries of the year before. She had kidnapped Jessica from the House of Mirrors at the New Year's Eve carnival—days ago, Jessica guessed. She had dumped her into a Jeep that looked just like Jessica's Jeep. And she had brought her here, to the cold, dark cellar of Sweet Valley High.

As if she held a baseball bat, Jessica swung her arms at the place where she guessed Margo's stomach to be, her hands balled into fists. The ropes around her wrists constricted painfully, and Jessica yelped. But she found her target. Margo grunted and began to double over. She recovered quickly and slashed again with the knife.

Jessica's wrists were still tied together, limiting her mobility. She had also been tied like a dog on a leash—with just enough cord to walk four feet to a tiny alcove that contained a foul-smelling toilet. But Margo had miscalculated her first knife thrust. Instead of stabbing Jessica, she'd sliced through the leash.

Now Jessica dived and rolled on the cement floor. She'd had rusty-tasting water since she'd been there, from the steady dripping of a leaky water heater into a metal pail. But she was weak from hunger and fear. Margo was strong and quick. Jessica felt her shoulders slamming, hard, against the floor as Margo's body landed on top of hers. "Now it's time to die," whispered Margo, her face close to Jessica's but invisible in the gloom. For an instant the blade shone above Jessica's throat.

Then an arc of yellow light spilled down the stairway. Jessica felt relief flooding through her. Elizabeth had come to save her. It had to be.

The next minute passed as if in slow motion. Margo flinched, as if the light were an enemy. Jessica saw her attacker's face and shuddered. Margo was her exact duplicate, but she appeared distorted by evil—as if seen through a carnival mirror.

Footsteps clattered down the stairs, and Margo whipped around, momentarily off balance. Jessica took advantage. She threw her shoulders forward and twisted, knocking the other girl to the floor. The knife clanked to the cement a few feet away. Both girls, half sitting, lunged for it.

Suddenly another girl stood in front of the two, casting a monstrous shadow that thrust across the floor toward them. Her face and body were backlit, but it was clear that she looked exactly like both Jessica and Margo. Except that she was holding a shining pistol.

Jessica's hand stopped in midlunge, and so did Margo's. "Elizabeth!" Both girls screamed at the same time. Both were breathing too hard to say more.

Elizabeth held the gun on them, her eyes wide with panic as she shifted her aim from

Jessica to Margo and back. *She doesn't know which is which!* Jessica realized in horror. She desperately tried to croak out a few words to identify herself. But Margo was trying to speak, as well. Both eyed the knife, lying just out of reach. Elizabeth's finger moved toward the trigger.

Elizabeth hoped nobody could see how hard her hands were shaking as she held the gun, first on one girl and then the other. One blonde was Jessica; the other was Margo, or Margo's double. One was her sister; the other wanted her dead. One wore a low-cut black top; the other, a purple blouse. Jessica owned both. But Elizabeth couldn't remember what her sister *should* be wearing. She shifted the gun back and forth, but she couldn't think. Her brain seemed paralyzed by fear. And she couldn't imagine shooting at anyone at all, much less a girl whose face was exactly like her own.

Sirens whined in the distance, and hope leaped like a flame in Elizabeth's chest. But both of the identical girls on the floor were tensing to spring for the knife. There was no time to wait for the authorities. Elizabeth made a split second-decision and trained her gun on her target.

❖ ❖ ❖

Jessica let out a sigh of relief as the gun barrel pointed squarely at her attacker.

"Stay away from that knife!" Elizabeth cried as the other girl's hand inched toward the glittering blade. "Jessica, pick up the knife and keep it away from her."

"Oh, Lizzie!" Jessica breathed. "You don't know how glad I am to see you!" She slashed through the ropes that bound her wrists, nicking the edge of one purple sleeve in her eagerness to be free. But that was all right. After wearing the blouse for days on end, Jessica didn't care if she never saw it again.

Elizabeth still held the gun on the other girl. "Not half as glad as I am to see you, Jess," Elizabeth said, her eyes still leveled on the face of the girl in the black top. "But right now I need you to grab that piece of rope that's lying there and tie her hands."

"Gladly," Jessica said. "How did you know I was down here?" she asked as she knotted the rope. "Did you know it was Margo, alive again?"

"You're not Margo?" the girl on the floor gasped, staring at Jessica.

Jessica scowled. "Good try, but you can't trick my sister!" she warned the girl. "We know *you're* Margo!" She turned to Elizabeth. "She's Margo, all right. Who else but Margo could have kidnapped me and brought me down

321

here? It's not as though there are dozens of teenage girls running around California looking exactly like us."

"Not dozens of them," Elizabeth said, raising her voice to be heard over the rising sirens outside. "But there were two. Now there's only one." And then she directed a question at her target. "Who are you?"

"I'm Nora," said the girl on the floor, staring from one twin to the other as the realization began to dawn on her. "Oh, my . . ." she said weakly, her lip trembling and tears streaming down her face.

"That's right," said Elizabeth, seeming to guess her thoughts. "The girl you stabbed was Margo. Which means that it was Margo who kidnapped Jessica and brought her here."

"I killed my own sister," Nora whispered, as if waking from a nightmare. Suddenly she looked more like a lost child than a dangerous killer. "I killed her. . . ."

Jessica shivered, thinking how easily she could have been the one that Nora had stabbed to death that night. She looked at her sister, who was staring at the other girl with a mixture of loathing and pity, and she suddenly realized what Elizabeth had gone through in the last few days. "Oh, Lizzie!" she exclaimed. "I can't even imagine what it was like for you, thinking I was dead!"

322

Elizabeth nodded slowly as tears sprang to her eyes. She momentarily shifted her gaze toward Jessica while still keeping the gun on Nora. "I hope I never have another weekend like that," she said quietly. She smiled. "And Mom and Dad are sure going to be glad to see you!"

Footsteps pounded overhead as the police stormed the building. "I just have one question," Jessica said. "When you ran down the stairs and saw us on the floor, fighting for the knife—how did you know which one was me?"

Elizabeth smiled enigmatically. "What do you mean?" she asked. "You're my twin sister! How could I not have known?"

"But she and I look exactly alike!" she insisted. "How could you be sure you weren't pointing a loaded gun at *me*?"

Elizabeth lifted her eyebrow. "Well, besides my twin's intuition, I did have one teeny little hint," she admitted, smiling gleefully. "You don't have a tattoo!"

A half hour later Jessica and Elizabeth emerged from Sweet Valley High, their arms around each other's waists so that they moved as one. Elizabeth gladly supported her sister, who seemed weak from hunger and stress, but uninjured.

Red and blue lights flashed from three

police cars and an ambulance that were gathered in the parking lot. The strobe lights illuminated two men and a woman, running through the police line toward the twins. Jessica and Elizabeth stopped and grinned, recognizing their parents and Steven.

"It's the damnedest thing I've ever heard of," Detective Pappas exclaimed a few minutes later. The family stood near a police car, watching a paramedic bandage Jessica's wrists, which had been scraped by the ropes. "I owe you an apology, Elizabeth," the red-haired detective said. "I thought you were losing your mind when you insisted that Margo was climbing out your sister's window."

"And I owe *you* an apology," Elizabeth admitted. "I'm sorry I stole your gun," she said, gesturing toward the handgun and holster that were now draped around the shoulder of their rightful owner.

"To tell you the truth, I was ready to throw the book at you for it," the detective replied, raising her eyebrows, "if there was anything left of you to throw it at. You seemed so unstable. We were afraid you were planning to use the gun on yourself."

Her partner spoke up. "Your brother didn't think so," Detective Marsh added. "He said you had told him some far-fetched story about Jessica's being at school, lost in the dark, or some such nonsense. Whatever the case, we thought we ought to get over here and keep you from hurting yourself—or somebody else."

"I don't blame you," Elizabeth said. "And you weren't completely wrong. I guess I really did get a little crazy, taking the gun and all. But I knew Jessica was in danger, and I knew nobody would believe me when I said she was alive and here at school—"

"I sure didn't believe you," Steven said. "I guess I should take this psychic connection stuff more seriously, when it comes to you two clones."

Jessica laughed. "You could bring us into your psych class, for show-and-tell!"

"What about her?" Elizabeth asked, pointing to Nora, who was being led into the backseat of a police cruiser. "What's going to happen to her now?"

"She'll be charged with assaulting Jessica," Mr. Wakefield said, "and with the murder of Margo Black—if that really was Margo in Jessica's bed the other night."

"It had to have been," Elizabeth said, more certain than ever.

"I'm sure the district attorney will sort it all out in the next day or two," Steven said, putting his arm around Elizabeth.

Jessica looked at the officers. "What if you

can't get enough evidence to convict Nora?" she asked in a low, scared voice.

Detective Pappas smiled as she pulled something small and shining out from under her jacket. "That won't be a problem," she said. "We found this key in her pocket. It's from the Sweet Valley Inn. Also, a white Mazda Miata is parked on the other side of the school, with rental plates. Between the car and the hotel room, I suspect we'll find all the proof we need."

"It's time we got this family home," Mrs. Wakefield said. "Don't worry about the Jeep, girls. Let's all go together in your father's car."

Elizabeth looked at Jessica, and an unspoken sentiment passed between the twins. Elizabeth spoke for them both. "No, Mom," she said, shaking her head. "I'll drive Jessica and me in the Jeep. We have a lot of lost time to make up for."

Epilogue

Jessica stood on a chair by the pool at Fowler Crest two evenings later, waving her arms for attention. "OK, guys!" she called to a few dozen of her friends. "Everyone's had a chance to say nice things about me, so I guess it's my turn now."

"Speech! Speech! Speech!" Winston yelled through his cupped hands, just before Maria Santelli pushed him into the pool.

"First of all," Jessica said, raising her glass of punch as if it were a pom-pom. "I want to thank Lila and my sister and brother. This is the greatest 'Welcome Back from the Dead' party anyone ever had!"

Steven shook his finger at her, from an inflatable raft in the middle of the pool. "Now that you're back from the dead, sis, we'd like to keep you for a while," he called. "I'd sure feel a lot better if you'd get down from there!"

Todd reached up to help Jessica down, and she grinned, feeling nothing more than friendly affection as her fingers touched his. She noticed Elizabeth watching them—a warm, contented smile on her face.

"OK, OK," Jessica continued from the ground. "Are you satisfied? Now I have my feet firmly planted on the ground."

"That's a lot better than being planted six feet under!" Winston added in a Groucho Marx voice as he pulled himself, dripping, from the water. Lila groaned and pushed him back in.

"I don't know if you all realize this," Jessica continued, squeezing Ken's hand, "but I could hear everything that went on in the auditorium Monday morning, during my funeral."

"You're not going to let it go to your head, are you?" Lila asked. "We wouldn't want you to get stuck-up!"

Jessica raised her eyebrows. "I'll remember that," she promised. "Especially since it's coming from such an expert on the topic!"

Everybody laughed while Lila glowered. But Jessica flashed a sunny smile at her best friend, and Lila couldn't keep from grinning back. Jessica sighed deeply. It was great to be back from the dead and to know how much her friends had missed her. But there was one person who she knew had missed her more than anyone—the one person responsible for saving her life.

"I want you all to know how much I love every one of you," Jessica said. "Yes, even you, Winston!" she added as he climbed out of the pool again. He pretended to swoon, and Ken pushed him back in.

"But there's one person here who deserves special recognition," Jessica continued, linking her arm through her sister's. Elizabeth smiled and kissed her on the cheek.

"After more than three days in that basement, I was starting to kind of freak out, all alone in the dark," Jessica said, her voice quavering. "I made it through the first couple days by thinking about all of you, but by Monday morning, I wasn't sure I could hold on any longer. Then I heard Elizabeth read a beautiful poem she wrote just for me. Sure, it was a little sappy, but for the rest of that awful day, I repeated the words to myself over and over again: 'Reflection, soul mate, sister, friend, half of what I am is you.'"

Tears spilled from Jessica's eyes, but she made no attempt to wipe them away.

"I want my sister—and everyone here—to know that I feel exactly the same way about her," Jessica said. "If it weren't for my twin sister, I would be dead by now. I'm sorry we were too mad at each other to say it last week, but happy New Year, Elizabeth. I love you."

The crowd cheered as Jessica and Elizabeth embraced. "Welcome back, Jessica," Elizabeth whispered, her own cheeks wet with tears.

Jessica looked into her sister's face, so much like her own. And the twins made a silent vow that they would never go to bed angry again.

**Here's a sneak preview of the next exciting
Sweet Valley High miniseries.**

*Sweet Valley High is torn apart by gang
warfare. . . . When the smoke clears, will
Jessica and Elizabeth ever be forgiven?*

Ken violently slammed his locker shut. He was getting dressed with the rest of the guys from the team. Usually the locker room was like a zoo after a game, but today the atmosphere was quiet and subdued. The Gladiators' spirits were low.

Ken couldn't believe they had lost. And it was all his fault. He had totally blown the last pass. Ken replayed the moment in his head as he toweled off his hair and threw on a T-shirt. He could feel the rough leather of the ball in his hand, and he could hear the fans shouting. He saw his wide receiver, Danny Porter, in position near the end zone. The coast was clear. He lifted his arm for the winning throw . . . and suddenly a shooting pain stabbed him in the stomach. Someone had knocked the wind out of him. He gasped for air and fumbled the ball.

Ken gritted his teeth thinking about it. The Palisades Pumas' linebacker, Greg McMullen, had deliberately kneed him in the stomach. And then, to make matters worse, Greg had taunted him. "What's wrong, windbag?" Greg had snickered. "Ball too slippery for you?"

Ken could only wheeze in retort. Why hadn't he said something back? Ken threw his gym bag onto the bench in disgust.

Tim Nelson, the defensive linebacker, walked into the locker room, a towel wrapped around his waist. "Good game," he said, clapping Ken on the shoulder.

Ken grunted and sat down on the bench, fumbling under it for his shoes. He pulled them out by the shoestrings and pulled on a black high-top sneaker, a scowl spread across his face.

"Hey, don't worry about it, man," said Tad "Blubber" Johnson, his ample stomach creasing in rolls as he leaned over to put on his socks. "They were hitting below the belt."

"You can say that again," Danny said angrily, pulling on a pair of jeans. "They were out for blood."

Robbie Hendricks threw his clothes into his locker with a vengeance. "They took Bryce and Ricky out in the first half."

Zack Johnson, the linebacker, slammed his fist against the locker so hard that the entire row reverberated. "I'd like to take all of *them* out," he said, his eyes glinting angrily.

Ken sighed. Ricky's knee was damaged and Bryce had a concussion. Bryce would be OK, but he wasn't sure about Ricky. Knee damage was a serious problem for athletes. It was possible that Ricky would be out for the rest of the season. And Ricky was indispensable to the team. Ken clenched his jaw angrily. He'd seen teams play dirty before, but never as low as the Pumas had played that day.

"I don't think we should take this sitting down," Zack said, leaning against a row of lockers.

"Too bad we don't have another game coming up," Danny added, tossing his uniform into his gym bag. "Then we could give them a taste of their own medicine."

"Who says we need a game?" Zack asked.

Zack's right, Ken thought. He wasn't going to let the Pumas abuse his players and get away with it. The Gladiators could get their revenge off the football field. Ken opened his mouth to agree with Zack, but then he stopped himself. He was the captain of the football team. It was his job to set a high standard for the morale and ethics of the team.

Ken stood up and faced the rest of the guys on the bench. "Look, guys, we're all-star quality this year. We've got an exceptional team," he said. "Our record is clean. We don't want to stoop to their level. We don't need to engage in foul play to win."

"But they're going to sabotage our chance for the title this year," Robbie protested.

"We can't just let them get away with it," Danny added.

Ken held up a hand. "We played our best, and more important, we played fair. And that's what counts. Remember, the old saying is right: It's not winning or losing, but how you play the game." Ken slung his gym bag over his shoulder and turned to leave. "See you at practice on Monday."

"See you," the guys mumbled, sounding discouraged.

We played our best, Ken repeated to himself as he walked out of the locker room. *And that's what counts.* If only he could really believe his own words.

"Ken!" Jessica called excitedly as he exited the locker room. Ken turned to see Jessica running to him, her face glowing. She looked beautiful, as always. She was wearing white jeans and a light blue cotton button-down shirt, and her golden hair was falling in soft waves around her face. Her blue-green eyes sparkled and her smile shone brightly. Usually just the sight of Jessica raised Ken's spirits, but now he was too depressed even to manage a smile.

Jessica flung her arms around his neck. "How's my star quarterback?" she asked. She leaned her face back for a kiss.

"Hi, Jess," he said, giving her a perfunctory kiss on the lips and shrugging off her arms. He felt irritated by Jessica's high spirits. He wasn't in the mood for her perkiness.

"I can't believe we lost!" Jessica burst out. "It was so close."

"Yeah, and it was my fault," Ken mumbled.

Jessica wrapped an arm around his waist. "Of course it wasn't your fault, silly," she said. "You played a great game. You made two touchdowns."

Suddenly a car horn blared.

"Hey, lovebirds!" Amy yelled, waving out the window of Lila Fowler's lime green Triumph.

Lila rolled down her window. "You guys coming?" she asked. "The whole gang's going to the Dairi Burger." The Dairi Burger was the most popular teenage hangout in Sweet Valley.

"One sec," Jessica called, holding up an index finger. She hooked her arm into Ken's. "Let's go. They're waiting for us."

But Ken shook his head. "I don't think I'm up to it."

"C'mon," Jessica said in a cajoling tone, giving him a charming smile that caused the dimple in her left cheek to deepen. "It'll help get your mind off the game. You can have your favorite strawberry shake." Jessica lowered her voice to a whisper. "And then a late-night drive to Miller's Point—"

But Ken cut her off, shaking loose her arm. "Jessica, I said I didn't want to go," he said sharply— more sharply than he'd intended.

Jessica looked wounded for a minute, then shrugged. "Fine with me," she said curtly. "See you." She skipped off to Lila's car without a backward glance.

"Jess . . ." Ken called after her halfheartedly. But she was already hopping into the car. He stood and watched as Lila revved the engine and screeched out of the parking lot.

"Ah, the sweet taste of freedom," Todd said as he backed his black BMW out of his space in the parking lot at Sweet Valley High. He wiggled the toes of his left foot as he pressed down on the gas pedal. It was so good to be able to move both of his feet again. He felt as if he'd been in a cast forever.

Todd cruised the parking lot, looking for Ken or Elizabeth. He'd arrived at halftime, but the stands had been so crowded that he hadn't been able to find anyone. He'd ended up taking a seat on the highest tier of the bleachers and had been barely able to make out the action of the game. The Sweet Valley High fans had spent most of their time on their feet screaming, and some girls in front of him had been holding a huge banner.

Todd decided to take a quick spin down the highway while he was waiting. Elizabeth and Ken would probably be a while. It would take some time for the stands to empty out, and Ken had to change out of his football uniform—and probably had to boost the morale of his team, as well. From what Todd had gathered from the fans around him, the Palisades Pumas had played a brutal game.

Todd swung onto the main road and pushed hard on the accelerator, enjoying the sensation of the asphalt racing beneath the wheels of his BMW. He opened the window, letting the cool night air whip through his curly brown hair. He felt as if he'd been rejuvenated. He was itching to start working out again. He was going to train like a madman in order to get back into shape.

Todd took the ramp onto the highway and cut across the road to the left lane. He raced down the smooth road, his spirits high. *My life has been like a roller coaster lately,* he thought, shaking his head. Just last week he had felt as though his whole world were falling apart. He had damaged his ankle during the most important game of the season. All the college representatives had been there, and Todd had been determined to make a good impression. Instead, he had come down hard on his foot and had seriously hurt his ankle. The coach had thought he would be out for the season.

Then Elizabeth had taken a trip to SVU to visit her brother and had decided to stay there for good. When she had broken the news to him, Todd had been devastated. He had felt as if his whole life were falling apart. Everything that mattered to him was slipping out of his fingers—first basketball, then his girlfriend.

But now things are looking up, Todd thought happily, taking the exit ramp and swinging back onto the main road toward the high school. He'd be back on the court in no time, and Elizabeth had decided to stay in Sweet Valley. The doctor had been very pleased with his progress. He'd said Todd's ankle had healed perfectly and that he could start practicing in a week.

Todd slowed down and turned into the Sweet Valley High parking lot, which was now packed. Some kids were piling into cars and hopping onto motorcycles, and others were hanging around, talking in animated groups. Todd weaved his way carefully through the crowded lot, looking for familiar faces.

"Hey, Wilkins!" a voice yelled from behind him. Todd pulled the car to a stop and leaned out the window. Aaron Dallas jogged over.

"Need a lift?" Todd asked, leaning over to open the passenger door.

"Thanks, man," Aaron said. He climbed into the BMW. "My car's in the shop, and I lost the guys in the crowd on the way out."

"Have you seen Elizabeth around?" Todd asked.

Aaron shook his head. "I haven't seen any of the girls at all tonight."

"Well, maybe I'll catch her at the Dairi Burger," Todd said, revving the engine. "That's where you're headed, right?"

Aaron smiled. "Where else?"

Todd put his foot on the gas gently, slowly making his way through the parking lot.

"That was a close game, wasn't it?" he asked.

"I just made it in time for the second half."

"You missed quite a show," Aaron said. "The Pumas pulled just about every stunt in the book."

Todd shook his head. "Those guys give sports a bad name."

"Hey, there's Ken," Aaron said, pointing across the lot.

Todd looked in the direction he indicated. Ken was standing alone at the far end of the parking lot. He was walking in a small circle, mumbling to himself and kicking at the gravel.

"Uh-oh, looks like some male bonding is in order," Todd said.

Aaron nodded. "Big time," he agreed.

Ken kicked at a stone aggressively. The guys on the team were dissatisfied with his decision to turn the other cheek, and now Jessica was mad at him as well. He wasn't sure if he should have given the guys his pep talk. As captain of the football team, he was the one responsible for the well-being of the squad. It was his role to keep the ethical standards of the team high, but it was also his role to protect his players from foul play. How could he just let those Palisades punks take his players down one after another?

Suddenly Todd's BMW roared to a stop by his side.

"You coming to the Dairi Burger?" Todd asked, leaning out the window.

"Nah, I'm gonna just hang low tonight," Ken mumbled.

Todd cut the engine, pulled open the door, and sprang out of the car. "Look, man!" he exclaimed, jumping from one foot to the other.

Ken didn't know why Todd was doing a dance on the pavement, but it was irritating him. Everybody seemed to be in a good mood except for him. First Jessica. Now Todd. Didn't they realize the football team had just been slaughtered and that he had been personally humiliated?

"Notice anything different?" Todd asked.

Ken sniffed the air. "Are you wearing a new perfume?" he asked sarcastically.

Todd rolled his eyes and lifted a foot in the air.

"Oh, you got your cast off," Ken said in a lackluster voice. "That's great."

Todd looked at Aaron and shook his head. "It's worse than I thought." Aaron climbed out of the car and stood next to Ken.

"What's worse than you thought?" Ken asked.

"The postgame blues," Todd said. "I know it well."

Aaron clapped Ken on the shoulder. "Hey, don't take it so hard," he said encouragingly.

"From what I could see, you guys looked great out there," Todd said. "We should have won."

"That's just it," Ken said. "They took out my best players deliberately in the first half of the game."

"I heard about it," Todd said. "The ref should have done something about it."

"He couldn't," Ken said. "The Pumas were sneaky—and smart. Only the players could tell their hits were illegal. From the stands it looked like everything was in order."

Aaron shook his head. "Maybe the ref couldn't do anything, but it was clear to everybody what was going on. Players don't go down that hard in a normal football game."

"That's right," Ken said, clenching his jaw angrily. "And I don't like to see my players being abused that way."

"Let it go," Todd advised. "They may have won the game, but we're going to win the season."

Suddenly heavy footsteps sounded behind them on the gravel. "Well, if it isn't the little windbag!" a voice said behind Ken's back.

Ken wheeled around. It was Greg McMullen, the Palisades linebacker. Even without his football pads, he was a hulking guy. Two burly dark-haired friends flanked him.

"What did you call me?" Ken asked, his eyes flashing.

"I called you the little windbag," Greg said in a jeering tone. He turned to his friend and made wheezing noises, imitating the sounds Ken had made after he had got the wind knocked out of him. The guys snickered.

Ken could feel his blood boiling. His whole body tensed, and he clenched his fists into tight balls at his sides. He rocked on his feet, ready to lunge at Greg.

Todd blocked Ken's way with an arm. "Ignore them," he said in a low voice. "They're all talk and no action."

"What did you say?" Greg asked, his tone menacing.

"Nothing," Todd muttered, taking Ken's arm and trying to lead him away. Ken shrugged him off angrily.

"You want to say that to my face?" Greg taunted.

"Yeah," Ken said, taking a few steps forward and facing him squarely. He could feel the blood pounding through his veins, and he was itching for a fight. "He said you're all talk, McMullen."

Greg's eyes narrowed dangerously. "We'll see about that," he hissed. He jumped forward and punched Ken in the stomach, knocking the wind out of him again. Ken stumbled to the ground, gasping for air. The guys snorted, pretending to huff and puff. As the pain throbbed in his stomach, Ken was suffused with rage. He leaped to his feet and flew at Greg, his face contorted in pain. Todd jumped forward and grabbed Ken, locking him in a wrestler's hold.

"Let me at him!" Ken growled, struggling with Todd to break loose and lashing out with his fists. He felt like a caged animal struggling to get free.

"Aaron, help me out here!" Todd called. Aaron rushed over and pinned Ken's arms to his sides. Ken kicked at them both with his feet.

"C'mon, Ken," Todd said between clenched teeth. "Get in the car."

Aaron pulled open the door of the passenger seat, and the two of them finally managed to push Ken in.

Greg and his friends snorted with laughter.

"What's wrong?" Greg jeered. "Afraid Matthews will break a fingernail?"

"Good thing you've got your little friends to protect you," his friend sneered.

Todd started the engine and peeled out of the parking lot.

Ken slammed his fist into the dashboard as Todd swung the car onto the main road. Then he fell back against the seat, seething in frustration. He would find a way to get back at those Palisades jerks. This time they had gone too far.

Bantam Books in the Sweet Valley High series
Ask your bookseller for the books you have missed

SIGN UP FOR THE SWEET VALLEY HIGH® FAN CLUB!

Hey, girls! Get all the gossip on Sweet Valley High's® most popular teenagers when you join our fantastic Fan Club! As a member, you'll get all of this really cool stuff:

- Membership Card with your own personal Fan Club ID number
- A Sweet Valley High® Secret Treasure Box
- Sweet Valley High® Stationery
- Official Fan Club Pencil (for secret note writing!)
- Three Bookmarks
- A "Members Only" Door Hanger
- Two Skeins of J. & P. Coats® Embroidery Floss with flower barrette instruction leaflet
- Two editions of The Oracle newsletter
- Plus exclusive Sweet Valley High® product offers, special savings, contests, and much more!

Be the first to find out what Jessica & Elizabeth Wakefield are up to by joining the Sweet Valley High® Fan Club for the one-year membership fee of only $6.25 each for U.S. residents, $8.25 for Canadian residents (U.S. currency). Includes shipping & handling.

Send a check or money order (do not send cash) made payable to "Sweet Valley High® Fan Club" along with this form to:

SWEET VALLEY HIGH® FAN CLUB, BOX 3919-B, SCHAUMBURG, IL 60168-3919

NAME _____
(Please print clearly)

ADDRESS _____

CITY _____ STATE _____ ZIP _____
(Required)

AGE _____ BIRTHDAY _____ / _____ / _____

Offer good while supplies last. Allow 6-8 weeks after check clearance for delivery. Addresses without ZIP codes cannot be honored. Offer good in USA & Canada only. Void where prohibited by law.
©1993 by Francine Pascal   LCI-1383-193

Featuring:

"Rose Colored Glasses"

"Lotion"

"Sweet Valley High Theme"

Available on CD and Cassette Wherever Music is Sold.